Phoenix Tales: The Great Fire

R A CHARTRES

ISBN: 1540307484
ISBN-13: 978-1540307484

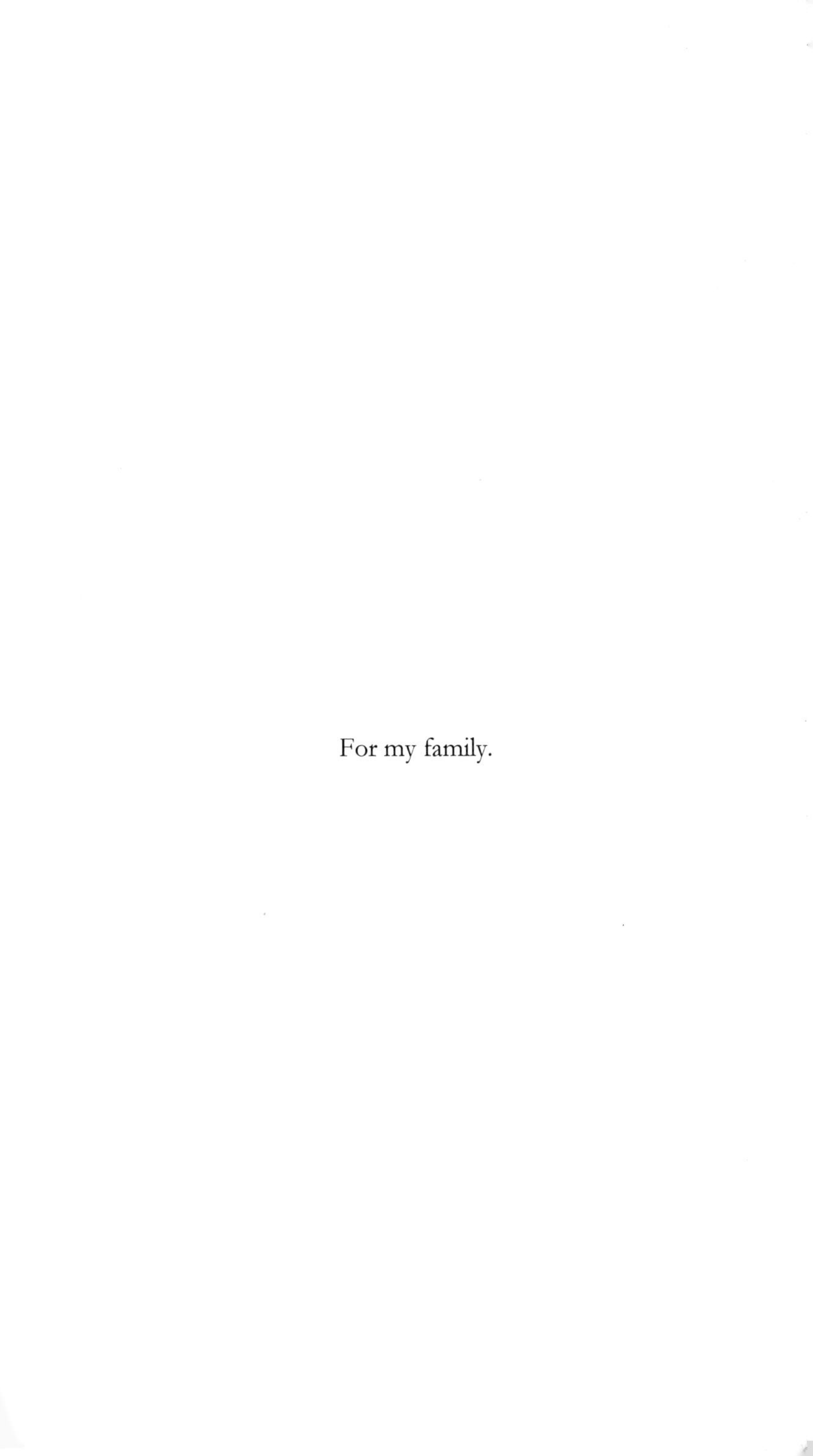

For my family.

ACKNOWLEDGMENTS

With grateful thanks to all those who have helped turn this story into a book, especially: my long-suffering mother for endless editing services; cousin Diddy for creating the marvellous cover and website; and my various proof readers for your invaluable comments and additions, most notably: Dad, Sophie, Clio, Georgie, Archie, Rosie, Emma & Amy.

Last but not least, special thanks to those who have made the past two decades so much fun.

St Paul's Cathedral & The Old Deanery in the City of London

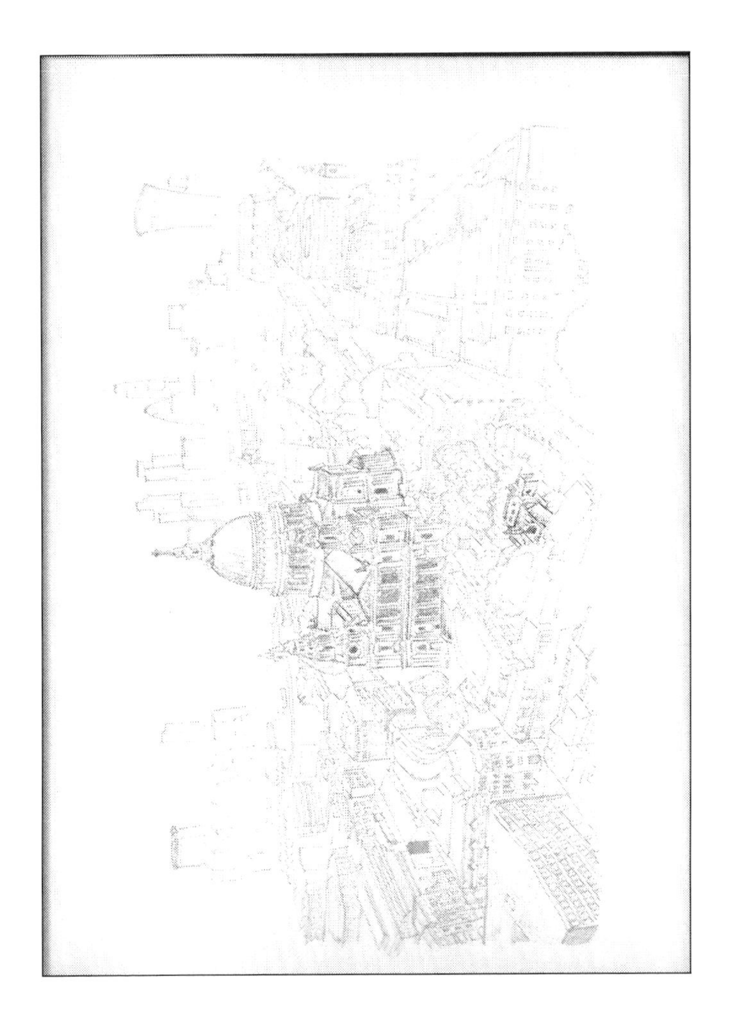

1 THE NIGHTMARE

Everywhere about him the wooden City crackled and burned, the voracious flames rising higher and higher, hungrily leaping from one building to another. The heat was unbearable. He was sweating intensely, but not only on account of the temperature: he was stuck in another world, another time, and could not get back to his own.

He breathed heavily as he pelted through the burning streets, a veritable vision of hell, desperately looking for a way back. Just a small opening – that was all he needed; anything not to be trapped here. He'd slipped his captors' shackles and fled – who were they, and why on earth were they after him? But it was no good: there was no way out without help.

The fact that there weren't any other people around – they all seemed to have retreated ahead of the fire – only increased the terrible sense of isolation and helplessness. He was running on a familiar street now: he knew in his bones that this was Ludgate Hill, the great road leading up to St Paul's Cathedral, and the highest point in the City of London. But the buildings of this other time and other world were totally alien to him, and he felt worn cobbles underfoot, rather than tarmac and pavement. The smoke and falling ash were blinding.

Halfway up the hill, he passed through the old Ludgate itself, the ancient gateway to the City, the beating heart of London. The heat was so intense that he could get no further; an impenetrable, pulsating wall of fire and pain. Ahead of him, just visible through the billowing smoke and flame, Old St Paul's stood, engulfed by the blaze.

I can't get back, he thought to himself desperately, over and over again. *I can't get back, I can't get back.*

Will awoke with a start, sitting up abruptly and grazing his head on the sloping beam above the bed in his attic room. Sticky from nervous sweat, he looked around him. In the half-light, he could make out his iPod and mobile phone on the bedside table; the laptop on the desk in the corner on one side of the solid brick fireplace and the stack of DVDs leaning precariously against the other; the mountains of books against the far wall. He was home, in his own room. Safe. He breathed a heavy sigh of relief, and allowed himself to flop back down against his pillow, exhaling slowly.

'Only little kids have recurring nightmares,' he said to himself angrily, biting his lip and rolling over in an attempt to get back to sleep.

It was perhaps the eighth or ninth time that year that the dream had come to him, and each time it was more intense, the heat more tangible. The first time he'd found himself in this strange fiery nightmare had been the previous term, at his boarding school in the Midlands. Although there he had his own study-bedroom, he had obviously shouted so loudly in his sleep that two friends in nearby rooms had burst in to see if he was OK. He'd not heard the end of the jokes ever since. He winced slightly, recalling the memory, and wriggled to get comfortable as the sweat cooled and became even less agreeable.

But school was out now, at least for the summer. Exams were a gloriously distant memory, and the new term still more than a month away. 'At least that's a happy thought,' he murmured to himself, slipping slowly back to sleep. The dream had never come twice in a night. Yet.

'It's completely bizarre, Tilly,' Will said to his younger sister the next morning over breakfast at the long refectory table in the family's kitchen/living room on the top floor of their house in the shadow of St Paul's. 'I dream that I'm running around in the City of London during the Great Fire of 1666, but I have no idea how I got there, or how I'm going to get back. It's getting stronger every time.'

'Sigmund Freud would have a field day, I'm sure,' said Tilly, real name Matilda, with a wry smile. 'What do you think it all means?'

'The funny thing is,' Will continued, 'it feels totally real. It feels much more like a memory than simply a bad dream.'

'Dreams do feel real though, don't they?' replied Tilly. 'I mean, none of us actually knows when we're dreaming that it's just a dream. Not usually, anyway.'

Her thoughts were interrupted by the arrival of Tom, the third sibling, two years younger than Tilly, who was herself two years younger than Will, the eldest. Where Will was tall and slim with straight brown hair cut short, and disproportionately wide, boxy shoulders that made it look as if there was a coat hanger stuck inside his clothing, Tom was shorter and more solid, with curly brown hair that was quite impossible to tame. Rather than looking as though he'd been pulled through a hedge backwards, Tom more often looked as though he was wearing one.

'Where's Katherine?' asked Will, enquiring after his brainy youngest sister.

'She's helping out at that charity bakery today,' said their mother, emerging from the hallway.

'She's only 10 years old!' said Will, through a mouthful of Marmitey toast.

'And very public-spirited,' replied their mother.

Will felt an unseen presence brush past his leg. 'Morning, Mufasa!' he said, looking under the table for the family's unruly hound. Will often thought Mufasa, a hyper-intelligent cross-breed terrier with a wild reddish coat of wiry hair, might be some kind of super-villain, and liked to imagine what adventures he might be having when not observed. He felt the dog's nose press against his knee, a well-established instruction for supplementary rations. Although not an especially large terrier, Mufasa was eternally ravenous. Will slipped him a corner of his toast, which the hound gulped down gratefully before nosing Will's knee again for seconds.

'Will!' said Tilly, reprovingly, 'you'll make him fat!'

'What?!' said Will, feigning innocence. His mother shot him a disapproving look. He knew he'd been rumbled. 'Right, well I'm off to see Cousin Diddy' he said, beating a hasty retreat from the breakfast table, as a frustrated Mufasa tried his emotional pressure tactics on Tom instead.

Walking out through the over-sized front door of his home some minutes later, Will wondered again what the vivid dreams meant. He walked down the dozen or so steps to the large cobbled courtyard in front of the house and turned around to face it. A substantial, red-brick-built seventeenth century London mansion house, it had stood on this site near St Paul's Cathedral since the 1670s, its medieval predecessor having been destroyed by the Great Fire in 1666.

'What are you trying to tell me?' he asked aloud, feeling slightly absurd for even wondering. He paused for a moment, contemplating his beloved home and speculating about what secrets it still had to yield, even after all these years. It wasn't a normal home at all, of course, but he'd always known that. Apart from being an unusually old and handsome building in the Square Mile, this house – The Old Deanery – was the official residence of Will's father, who was a bishop. That meant the house came with the job – rather like 10 Downing Street for the Prime Minister, or an embassy for an ambassador, albeit on a much more modest scale – and was, on a day-to-day basis, filled with people who helped his father do his work. The family had already lived there for nearly a decade: long enough to mean that 16-year old Will couldn't think of anywhere else as home. Tucked away in a side street just off the top of Ludgate Hill, the house was almost entirely hidden from view unless you stood right in front of it. Set back from the road, behind a twelve foot high wall, two vast London Plane trees and a cobbled courtyard, if you didn't know the house was there, you'd never guess. It was a secret kingdom; a miraculous survival.

Will turned on his heel and walked out through the imposing black gates into Deans Court, the little street in front of the house. He looked back over his shoulder: *You'll give me your secrets*, he thought.

The Old Deanery, as seen from Deans Court

2 THE SECRET COMPARTMENT

In the days that followed, Will spent a lot of time in The Old Deanery's large library, which was tucked away at the back of the house on one side of an internal courtyard. His father was a great collector of books of all ages, and the library's shelves teemed with works ranging across topics from philosophy and theology to cultures of all shades, but today Will wanted the history section.

What are you telling me? he repeated over and over to himself, feeling increasingly mad for believing that these dreams were a message. When his family had first moved to the house a decade previously, he and his excited siblings had immediately begun a comprehensive search for secret passages – as any self-respecting adventurer would have done. Will smiled as he recalled the obsessive tapping and listening on all the walls using the old stethoscope they had found in the dressing-up box. Yet, though they tried for months, they'd found nothing.

There were stories, of course, some of them spine-chillers. The house had a number of ghosts or, more accurately, things that went bump in the night with no plausible alternative explanation. Only the previous year, Will had heard for the first time the phantom on the first floor as he had walked down the old back stairs late at night. It was the only time in the last decade he could remember having been scared in the ancient building. And ethereal goings on were rumoured not to be the limit of the house's secrets. Their father's driver, Ted, who also kept the house in running repair and generally seemed to know what went where and why, had occasionally mentioned old tales about hidden tunnels, but always insisted that he didn't know anything else, and after a while Will and his siblings had stopped asking.

Will searched the shelves for a history of the house, thinking that perhaps it would record something about the medieval building which had previously occupied this hidden site and housed long-forgotten Deans of St Paul's Cathedral. Having exhausted the history section, he rifled through the cabinets underneath. Still nothing. 'Surely there's something here?' he mused aloud to himself.

On the wall between two of the tall sash windows which faced on to the courtyard, Will noticed an old print belonging to his father. He'd never really studied it before, but it depicted Old St Paul's Cathedral in 1666 being consumed by the flames of the Great Fire of London. That extraordinary conflagration had reduced most of the heart of the old City to nothing more than rubble and ash, destroying more than thirteen thousand houses, with eighty-six churches similarly consumed or beyond repair across nearly four hundred acres of incinerated city.

Remembering his dreams, he stepped forward with fresh interest to take a closer look. The black-and-white print was immensely detailed, almost as though the person drawing it had been close enough to have witnessed the great inferno themselves. In the foreground, in front of the cathedral, three small figures could be seen. A bit odd, thought Will, because they seemed to be moving up the hill and towards the fire, rather than down it and away from the blaze.

Frustrated by the extraordinary coincidence of the

picture but still without any sign of a useful book, he looked around again. The old chest under the far window caught his eye. 'Wasn't this always locked?' he muttered to himself as he approached it slowly, noticing that the ancient lid sat slightly ajar. He lifted it, and as the hinges squeaked their angry opposition Will wondered how it had suddenly sprung open. Perhaps the lock had simply rusted away, he mused, peering inside, expectantly. 'Nothing,' he said out loud, 'just great.' He reached into the dark interior of the chest and felt around – there could be something hiding in a corner, perhaps. There wasn't, but the central panel of the bottom of the chest was looser than the others and rattled slightly when pressed. Using a nearby ostrich-feather duster on a stick to wiggle the plank, Will looked underneath, trying to see if the underside of the chest wiggled, too. It didn't.

'Heelllooooo,' he said, suddenly excited, his heart rate beginning to climb. A few moments of slightly awkward fiddling later and the plank slid out to one side of the chest, revealing a long hidden space, perhaps only four inches deep. In it sat a solitary, leather-bound book. Will looked around, breathing more quickly now. This, he was sure, was what he was looking for. This was the beginning, the first piece in the jigsaw. 'Now we're making some progress,' he whispered, as much to the house as to himself, reaching gingerly into the secret compartment.

3 A MYSTERIOUS DISCOVERY

'I think a lot of it's in code,' Will said later that day, handing the book to Tilly, who grasped the battered leather-bound discovery in both hands.

'Where did you find it?' she asked, clearly wondering if this was another of her older brother's practical jokes. She never could be quite sure.

'Over there,' Will replied, gesturing towards the chest. 'The lid was just sitting ajar. Very odd. Almost as if it was goading me to find it or something.'

'That is strange,' his sister agreed. 'That chest has never been opened in our time – at least as far as I'm aware. What do you think this symbol embossed on the cover is?' she went on, running her fingers over the surface.

'It's a much worn hourglass and motto,' said Will, who'd already spent a good two hours studying the book, poring over its delicate pages and drinking in the history. 'Seems to be some sort of journal or log book – partly coded, as you see. Check out the dates. It starts in the 1660s, and runs, well, up to the early twentieth century by the look of things.

'Have you been able to read any of it?' she asked.

'Well, the un-coded bits seem to be in Latin, and maybe Aramaic, and I know I've just done my Latin exam but my Aramaic's non-existent. What I have found,' he continued, reaching forward and selecting a page for Tilly, 'is that.'

Tilly stared at the faint drawings, nonplussed. 'What do they mean?' she asked, looking up.

'I'm fairly certain that this bit here' – he pointed out a symbol at the top of the page – 'is *this* house.'

'So this is all *underneath* us?' asked Tilly, looking shocked.

'Exactly,' said Will. 'Don't you see? That old story Ted used to tell us about some hidden world under the house, the ancient crypt from the previous building on this site. . . It's true. This proves it.'

'It doesn't *prove* anything,' said Tilly firmly, handing the book back to Will. 'Nice idea, but how come *we've* never found anything.'

'Must be very well hidden,' Will replied, slightly crestfallen that Tilly was not more enthused about his find. 'I mean, look, this book has sat under a false bottom in a battered old chest for – how long? A century or something. We've got no idea who saw this last, or why they hid it. But they did hide it, and they must have done that for a reason. I don't think it's going to be someone's special recipes!'

'Fair point,' Tilly conceded, sounding more interested now.

Will glanced at his wristwatch and rose from his chair. 'I'm out tonight so let's make a plan tomorrow, and get the others involved. Many hands make light work and all that...?

'What are we going to do about it?' asked Tilly.

'Find the entrance to the underworld, obviously,' Will said, with a grin.

4 THE SECRET DOOR

In the small hours of the following morning, Will once again awoke with a start. Narrowly avoiding smashing his forehead on the beam once more, he made a mental note to move his bed. His dream had been particularly vivid, but this time there was no fire. Instead, he had dreamed the overwhelming smell of damp wood and stale air. The scent still lingered in his nostrils. He had been tiptoeing down an old spiral staircase and had arrived at a door guarded by two large stone statues. Thinking about them, he shuddered, and then, in a moment of pure clarity, he realised he had seen the way down to the old crypt referred to in the book. He racked his brains, trying hard to remember any clue which might indicate where the entrance actually lay. Several minutes passed and, try as he might, the images from the dream grew hazier. And yet the woody smell remained distinct.

Bingo! he thought, remembering where he had smelt the same scent before. He tapped his bedside clock which lit up. Squinting, he noted the hour: 2am. *No time like the present*, he thought to himself. Slipping silently out of bed and flicking on the bedside light, he hastily pulled on some clothes and, as quietly as he could, began to make his way down the back stairs towards the cellars, picking up his torch from the shelf by the mantelpiece on his way.

Switching on the lights for the former servants' stairs which led up to the family's personal accommodation on the top floor of the old house, he made his way down four levels and into the basement. If it was late, he always accelerated slightly past the first floor landing where he had had his extremely spooky run-in last year with the house phantom, and this time was no different.

After hopping down another short flight of steps in the heart of the house, he arrived at the ancient oak door to the archive, the deepest part of the building. Will felt a strange tug pulling him on, almost as though he were a bloodhound following a scent, drawing him inexorably closer to his goal. The door creaked noisily on its hinges as he pushed it open. He winced at the noise in the quiet of the night, worried that, even from fifty feet below, it might wake someone asleep far above. He remembered playing down here when he was younger. They'd even searched the archive room when they'd originally hunted for secret passages, but only half-heartedly, as the bookcases and old furniture lining the edges of the room had made it impossible to get close enough to the walls to search for hidden entrances, and they'd not been strong enough as young children to shift the obstructions.

Switching on the decrepit chandeliers overhead and the wall-mounted candelabra – in which only a handful of lightbulbs actually worked – he surveyed the long, narrow, windowless room in the bowels of the house. Not much had changed. Aside from the rather incongruent lights, the room appeared almost unaltered from the day the house had been built. For the first time, he appreciated that the floor was made of flag stones, not floorboards as in the rest of the building. Did this in fact hint that it was originally a part of a pre-Great Fire building, he wondered? Despite being clad in thick oak panelling, the room was cold, and he shivered slightly, wishing he'd put on a jumper. Now that he thought about it, this was obviously the place where any secret entrance might be. With no windows, you could come and go with total privacy. The room was lower than the rest of the house, so you were already well underground just being down here.

Will's heart rate was climbing now as the darkness and silence of the rest of the building pressed in on him. He paced up and down the room a few times, hoping for inspiration, or perhaps to hear the sound of a flagstone wobbling as he walked across it, which might suggest a trap door. Nothing.

Next, he turned his attention to the panelling on the walls. As he had remembered, various wooden chests, bookshelves and old gilded picture frames adorned the sides of the room, making close investigation challenging; he wondered now if this was deliberate. After all, why was the room still not used for anything? It was called the archive, but the only things being archived down here were dead woodlice, cobwebs and the odd mouse skeleton. Protective sheets shrouded many of the pieces of furniture, and a thick layer of dust lay over almost everything else.

'Come on, show yourself,' he muttered aloud, willing the house to give up its secrets. Somehow he felt the house watching him; considering him. Standing there in the silent night, he listed attentively. Yes, he was sure of it now. There was definitely a sound, almost as though the house itself was drawing a slow, deep, continuous breath.

Crouching down he placed his hand at the bottom of one of the cabinets which sat against the far wall. An almost imperceptible breeze flowed across the back of his hand. 'Gotcha!' he said under his breath, the excitement now building by the second.

Will heaved the chest away from the wall. It was incredibly heavy, and made a screeching sound like fingernails running down a school blackboard as he dragged it across the floor, leaving powdery trails in the dust as it moved. Some of the disturbed dust seemed to be slipping in between the wooden panels behind. Will's heart was in his throat now; but, if this was really the legendary entrance, how was he to open it? Doubts momentarily flooded his mind: might it just be a boarded-up old fireplace? That could explain the strange noises and the disappearing dust, which would be being sucked up into an old flue behind the panels. How embarrassing it would be, he thought, if he got all three of his siblings to come for the grand unveiling of the long-awaited entrance, only to discover that it wasn't the real thing after all. His gut told him he had finally found it, but he needed to be certain.

Will stepped back to consider the scene. The square pattern of the panelling could definitely be concealing the borders of some kind of door. He moved forward and began to press firmly at the edges of the central panel dead ahead. It didn't budge. Several minutes passed as he tried other neighbouring panels: still nothing. Knocking on this section of wall at head height, however, he could hear what sounded faintly like a hollow space behind. So probably not a fireplace if it's a void my size, he thought, encouraged. He looked around. In all the old films about haunted houses with secret passages, there was some kind of hidden lever which activated a door. He began tugging hopefully on nearby wall-lights without any bulbs illuminated – that could be a sign of an alternative, secret – use, or perhaps it was simply that the bulbs had blown. But there was only one way to find out . . .

'Damnit!' he cursed, as one of the light fittings came away in his hands, trailing rusty old wiring and quantities of crumbling masonry. Stuffing it guiltily under a nearby dustsheet, he hastily abandoned his probe of the fixtures and fittings and returned to the suspect panelling. Exploring the surface of the panels once again with his fingertips, Will was becoming increasingly frustrated. 'Just open, will you?' he hissed at the wall. He had no idea how long he had been down there now – perhaps an hour, maybe much longer. He had left his wristwatch upstairs but could feel the call of his bed as waves of sleep drifted over him. Walloping the wall in his irritation, he knocked a vertical wooden spine of the panelling out of place. It twisted down at a right angle and there was an audible click. Will staggered back, drawing a sharp breath, as the whole section of wall swung inward away from him, into the depths of the house.

The Great Door of Hades at the bottom of the secret staircase

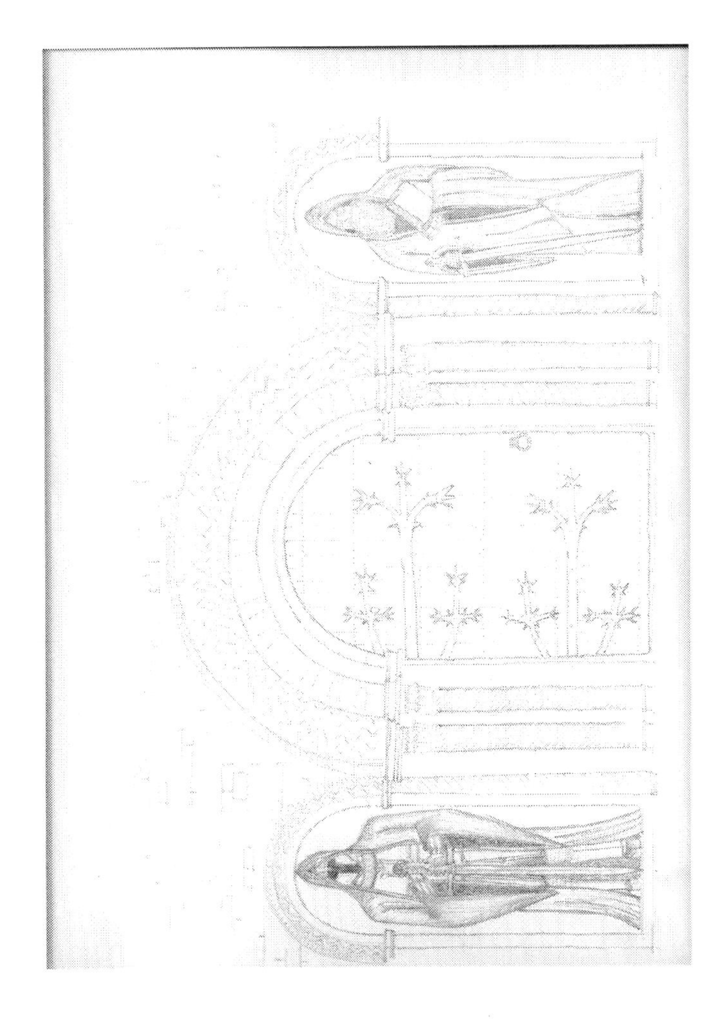

5 UNDERWORLD

With the entrance to the secret lair opened, The Old Deanery itself seemed to inhale deeply, sucking air into the void as though it had been holding its breath since this door was last opened. Will felt the suction of the air drawing him forward into the void, and he stumbled back clumsily resisting the pull, suddenly alive to the power of the house, and all thoughts of sleep banished. And then, all of a sudden, the rush stopped. Nothing. Just the faint sound of water dripping somewhere ahead of him, and the overpowering odour of dank darkness. 'That's a familiar smell,' he said with a confident smile. He was simultaneously excited and terrified.

Lifting his arm slowly, as though to avoid making himself jump, he clicked on his LED torch. Ahead of him lay a short passage of the same flagged stones on which he stood, ending abruptly with a broad spiral staircase which disappeared into the gloom below. He could see old torch brackets on the wall, but no sign of electric lighting. He took a tentative step forward, then another. His heart was racing. Why, he asked himself, was he not going upstairs to get the others? That would certainly be much less scary – and probably much less dangerous, too. After all, who knew what lay ahead of him? Perhaps the stairs had collapsed, and he would realise too late; perhaps the roof had caved in; or maybe the whole place was flooded.

Then another thought crossed his mind: what if the wall closed behind him and he became trapped – a fresh meal for the ancient hungry house, which clearly hadn't eaten properly in centuries. No one would know where he was. He might be stuck there for ever.

Looking around the archive, his gaze fell upon one of the packing-cases against the wall. With some effort - *what on earth was in these cases*? he wondered – he dragged it into position to prevent the wall from swinging shut behind him. Taking a deep breath of his own, he plunged into the bowels of the house.

'This must be like the journey to Hades,' murmured Will to himself, recalling the Greek god of the underworld whose name had become synonymous with his darkened subterranean realm. Will just hoped he wouldn't meet the three-headed dog, Cerberus, which guarded that realm, as he descended into the Stygian darkness. 'Now that would be unwelcome,' he muttered, as he inched cautiously down the spiral staircase, one foot at a time. Somehow talking to himself and breaking the silence made him feel that bit less alone and afraid. Aside from the strong smell of damp hanging in the air, it was very, very cold: had the hairs on his neck not been standing on end in fear, they would have been doing so on account of the plunging temperature.

Will's eyes darted furtively all over the place, taking in the stone steps, the smooth stone walls, the arched ceiling above him. Loops at intervals in the walls suggested there might once have been a rope to hold on to, but no longer. *Perhaps rotted away*, he mused. After what seemed hours, but in reality must have been only a few minutes, he reached what appeared to be the bottom, emerging into a rectangular, vaulted stone chamber. His torch beam cut through the darkness and picked up the remains of a wall-hanging suspended to his right. Was it a map? Hard to tell with the thin, greenish layer of mould on it. A table hewn straight from the rock with two candlesticks and a light covering of dust stood beneath the wall-hanging. Aside from the dust, the room might have been used only yesterday, as there were partially-burned candles in the candlesticks, waiting to be lit once more.

Will felt another shiver run down his spine, and flashed the torch around to see what else might be lurking in a darkened corner. The torch beam swung away from the table and fixed upon a huge, archaic wooden door dead ahead, with ornate iron mouldings cast like the branches of trees holding it resolutely in place on massive hinges under a solid semi-circular archway, itself carved with a multi-layered triangular pattern. Flanking the door like sentinels stood two carved and hooded figures, perhaps eight feet tall. 'Helloooo,' said Will, suddenly reassured. 'We've met before, I think,' he went on jovially, recalling his dream of only hours before.

The bearded statue to his right held a longsword and a Bible – the symbols, Will knew, of Saint Paul himself. But why was he hooded? The other figure appeared to be a heavily armoured knight, wearing the regalia of the late Crusading period and himself cloaked. The black void where his face should have been made Will shudder; but the question of who exactly it was would have to wait. The dinner-plate-sized round metal handle demanded further exploration, and Will was not going to stop now. This was it. He hoped very much that this was the door to the secret crypt, and not to the actual Greek underworld. He braced himself against the door: 'Here goes nothing.'

6 THE ROUND TABLE

Tom sat motionless in the dark. He had been awoken by Will's less-subtle-than-hoped trip down the back stairs in the small hours. The brothers' bedrooms up in the old servants' quarters were, after all, right next to each other, and the modern dividing walls were painfully thin.

When, after ten minutes, Will had not returned, Tom decided he must be up to something interesting. As quietly as he could, he slipped out of bed and into some shorts and a t-shirt – he was a creature of the cold and, to Tom, all weather was shorts weather. Picking up his own torch, he headed downstairs to find his older brother.

Not wanting Will to realise he was on his tail – partly because Tom intended to jump out at Will and terrify him, as his older brother himself loved to do to Tom and their sisters – he had been observing Will's actions through the large keyhole of the archive door. After a short while, sleep had washed over him and he'd sat down to snatch forty winks in a decrepit, spongey old armchair next to the door. Nothing much seemed to have been going on anyway. Will was just marching up and down and examining the walls, talking to himself. He wondered if his older brother was sleep-walking, as it looked totally mad. *But then, that would be par for the course*, thought Tom with a wry smile.

Now he had awoken with a start, hearing the huge gasp of air as the wall had swung inwards, as though a swimmer had just surfaced after too long submerged. Gluing his eye to the keyhole once more, Tom saw his brother dragging what looked like a crate to . . . '*Holy merde*!' he exclaimed. 'He's actually found it!'

Will paused, apparently steeling himself, before he turned on his torch and started moving slowly forward into the gap in the wall ahead of him. Quietly, and at a safe distance behind, Tom followed.

The wrought iron handle of the ancient door appeared to be stuck. Will re-doubled his efforts, holding the torch between his teeth as he applied both hands to the metal ring. He kept glancing nervously at the rather sinister statues on either side of him. They were particularly lifelike, especially in the shaky half-light provided by the unstable torch clenched in his jaws. He'd always hated waxworks, afraid that they might suddenly come alive. An absurd thought, he knew, but somehow it seemed much more likely down here with these flinty stone sentinels.

The light emanating from the torch illuminated puffs of his breath in the cold air, as though he were outside on a winter day, or smoking a large cigar. Putting his shoulder against the door again, Will jerked the handle forcefully once more. It moved suddenly upwards and around, and the door flew open, sending Will sprawling, his torch rolling into the inky darkness beyond, revealing the floor for a fleeting moment before coming to rest in the distance.

Momentarily stunned, he looked up from his temporary resting-place on the chilly ground. Some way ahead of him, the torchlight highlighted a thick, circular stone column which soared up into the velvety gloom. Regaining control of his limbs, Will scrambled forward several yards to recover the light. Directing the beam around him, he discovered that the pillar was one of eight, arranged in a large circle roughly twenty feet across. His whistle of admiration echoed around the unlit chamber for several seconds.

On a raised dais and up several steps in the middle of the space sat a huge round table with one, two, three, four. . . twelve high-backed chairs. Shivering slightly as he directed the torch beam upwards, he saw a canopy of vaulted arches overhead, perhaps also twenty feet to their highest point. *That must be immediately beneath the archive*, he thought to himself, calculating that he couldn't after all have gone more than thirty or forty feet down the spiral stairs.

Will shone the light at the walls. The beam barely picked out the far side, but the chamber appeared to be round, and expansive. It occurred to him that it bore a striking similarity to the layout of the twelfth century Temple Church where he had once been a chorister. The "round" of the Temple Church was itself based on the design of the Temple in Jerusalem, as the choirboys had been frequently reminded by their formidable choirmaster.

Between the pillars which punctuated the circular outer wall of the space were various alcoves and — 'Wait,' he said aloud, as he reached the first of these. What had appeared to be a darkened recess was actually another door. Will was increasingly spooked. Far from simply being a hidden chamber, this appeared to be far, far more. There was an entire underworld down here. He half expected to stumble into Charon himself, the ferryman of ancient Greek mythology, who transported souls across the River Styx to the underworld, Hades.

With this disturbing thought in mind, he decided to beat a tactical retreat and turned back towards the door to the spiral stairs. At that precise moment, to his utter horror his torchlight picked up a small figure darting from the bottom of the stairs into the little chamber adjoining the room in which he stood.

'Who's there?' shouted Will, trying to sound intimidating while simultaneously not wetting himself with fear. 'Show yourself! Now!' he added, with a slight wobble in his voice, and rooted firmly to the spot. Several tense moments passed and nothing moved, the tension building to near unbearable levels. Then someone sneezed, and Tom's rather sheepish face appeared in the doorway.

'Hullo, Will,' said Tom, trying to sound light-hearted.

'You little . . .,' shouted Will, as he lurched toward his younger brother to take revenge for the fright he had given him. A second later, he had thought better of it. 'Thank God it's you and not Charon,' he said, pausing to catch his breath. 'What on earth are you doing down here?'

'I might ask you the same thing,' replied Tom, wryly. 'Anyway, who's Charon and how on earth did you find this place? And, more to the point, what on earth is it?! We must have been through the basement a dozen times since we arrived here.'

'Never mind that' responded Will, testily. 'Check this out, over here.' He beckoned Tom proprietorially into the chamber. Now that he had company, he had forgotten his fear of ghostly mythological Greek characters and marched into the room with a renewed confidence. Will was always at his best when he had an audience.

'No one can have seen this in a couple of centuries,' he shouted speculatively, enjoying the echo and waving an ostentatiously relaxed hand towards the table and chairs on their dais.

Tom hurried after him urgently. 'Will, my torch is running out.'

'Then you'd better keep up!'

7 HOME SWEET HADES

By the time the boys were forced to beat a retreat from their newfound underground principality on account of Will's also dying batteries, it was getting light outside. They shoved the packing-case out from the tunnel entrance and pulled the wall shut behind them. It closed with a gentle click as the wooden spine moved back into the vertical position.

'Right,' said Will, turning to his brother. 'Do not tell a soul, Tom – you understand? As soon as Mum or Dad or any of the others find out about this, we've had it. No more fun exploration, no more adventures. We'll be stuffed.'

'Got it,' nodded Tom, grabbing a handy broom to start sweeping the dust off the floor. Will directed the operation, which he felt played to his managerial strengths.

'You've missed a bit,' he observed, gesturing towards a patch by the door. Tom glared back.

A short time later the boys wound their way up through the basement and began to climb the back stairs.

'And what are you two doing down here at this *astonishingly* early hour, might I ask?' enquired a deep, booming voice ahead of them. The boys froze at the sound of their father's question. Will always thought he sounded like God probably would – terrifying, and all-knowing. He also resembled the traditional stereotypical image of God: tall, solid, bald on top, but with plenty of white hair and a greyish-white beard.

'Um, just, er, looking for stuff,' said Tom, cringing at how unconvincing he sounded and fidgeting uncomfortably.

'Idiot,' hissed Will, elbowing his younger brother, 'let me do the talking.'

Standing at the top of the stairs to the basement, their father towered over them, looking down with an air of amused suspicion.

'Oh hullo, Father, didn't realise you were up already. Er, we're just trying to find the air rifle to deal with that rat that keeps appearing in the, um, garden. No luck though, so see you later – OK?' And with that the boys made good their escape up the stairs.

Later that morning, after catching up on a few hours' sleep, Will convened a sibling meeting in the library – their childhood conspiratorial hangout.

'Seriously, guys, what's this about? I'm meeting the girls for some shopping in less than an hour and I've got to go,' said Tilly, tapping her foot impatiently and looking pointedly at her wristwatch.

The boys exchanged a knowing look, much to the irritation of their sisters.

'Just spit it out, will you?' Katherine asked. Like Will, she was tall for her age, and slim, but with straight brown hair to her shoulders; like Tilly, she was very pretty. She also possessed a piercing glare when she chose to deploy it, as she did on this occasion.

'Follow me,' said Will, as he issued the girls with the battery-powered emergency lanterns he'd surreptitiously requisitioned from the car. 'No more meetings in here – I've found somewhere much better!' Swearing the girls to secrecy as he had done Tom, Will ran through the night's events as they headed into the archive.

'You're pulling my leg!' Tilly scoffed.

'Sssssshhhhhh, and barricade the door,' instructed Will, looking around to ensure that they hadn't been followed. The key was missing, so Tom and Kate pushed a chair under the door handle to prevent any unwanted disturbances.

'Really, I'm not,' he continued, as the secret door in the far wall swung inwards once more with its familiar swoosh. The intrepid four plunged into the darkness, and down the twisting stairs to the hidden world beneath.

'I just can't believe it,' Tilly exclaimed breathlessly. 'All this time! How has this remained hidden for so long? It's been here, under our feet, all these years.'

'Well we're at least thirty feet down,' said Will, 'probably more, and directly under the house, so it wouldn't have been disturbed by any other nearby building works over the years, and clearly The Old Deanery was purposely built right on top of it, because it all joins up. So no-one had any reason to discover it. 'In fact,' he continued, 'it looks like there was every reason not to discover it.'

With four bright lights between them, the layout of the chamber was clearer than it had been only hours earlier. So, too, were the colours: dark wall-hangings covered further hidden alcoves which had not been apparent before. Statues loomed out of the gloom from all sides, looking for all the world like real people frozen in time. Occasional tattered flags protruded at intervals around the chamber.

'Do you think these are tunnels, Will? Kate asked, nervously peering into a void on the far side of the room with rubble spilling out of its entrance.

'Looks like it, doesn't it?' he replied. 'We'll have to explore them, of course.'

'Of course,' repeated Tom matter-of-factly, nodding vigorously in agreement, and shining the lantern in Will's face for no particular reason other than to irritate him.

'What do you reckon, Tilly?' enquired Will. 'Up for a bit of Famous Five-style adventuring?'

'Don't you think it's a bit odd that the dust hasn't settled thickly in here?' she replied.

'What do you mean?' asked Kate, nervously.

'I mean that if no one had used this chamber for several centuries – perhaps longer – there would be a lot of dust everywhere, or at least a sort of damp covering to everything. But look at the table.' She walked into the centre of the chamber and up the steps to run her finger across its black and white segmented surface. 'Not so much as a speck here. And bone dry, too, despite the fact that the stairs are quite damp, and it's so cold down here. 'What's more,' she continued, 'that ante-room we passed through was filled with dust. But this room isn't.'

They stood in silence for a moment, digesting these observations. Then Tom said what everyone was by now thinking. 'So . . . you mean it has been used more recently?'

'Exactly. Perhaps until quite recently.'

Tom swallowed audibly. Their father had always said that his elder daughter was 'a talent lost to the Metropolitan police force' on account of her acute powers of observation; it seemed he was right.

'No doubt we shall discover all the answers in good time,' interjected Will, trying to regain the initiative. 'But we should sort out this place first. What about some less temporary lighting, for starters? It looks like the old candelabra were actually adapted for electric light, but aren't working anymore.'

'I know,' Tom suggested brightly, 'why don't we take the outdoor extension cable, run it down here from a socket in the archive, and borrow a couple of the old lamps from the store room.'

'Good idea, Tom,' said Tilly.

Over the course of the days following, the four siblings kitted out their new subterranean lair to make it a little more hospitable. Initially, they raided the wooden shed in the back garden, "borrowing" a long extension cable normally used by Ted for the leaf-blower. 'He won't miss it,' said Tom, guiltily, looking over his shoulder to make sure he wasn't going to be caught in the act, and knowing full well that it most certainly would be missed.

As Katherine stood guard at the top of the stairs to the basement, sitting on a step and pretending to read, the other three ran the cable from a socket in the archive, beneath the secret door and down the spiral stairs into the main chamber itself, attaching it to the walls with duct tape as they went. By rearranging the packing-cases and bits of unwanted furniture in the archive, they were able to do a pretty good job of disguising the fact that there was now a cable snaking its way under the secret door.

Next, they took the half-dozen rather decrepit-looking portable floodlights from a storeroom elsewhere in the cellars. Once these had been used to illuminate the barn at their grandparents' house in the countryside; now, the children stood them at intervals around the outside of the main chamber, directing light up and into it, all connected by a rather unstable-looking arrangement of extension cables, which made an angry fizzing sound, like an aggrieved wasp. One floodlight illuminated the rectangular ante-chamber at the foot of the stairs. A small fan-heater was strategically positioned in the middle of the room near the large, circular stone table, to provide a little warmth for anyone sitting there.

'What good is that going to be?' Will had scoffed when he had seen Tilly plugging it into the nearby bank of sockets and feeding the cable across the stony floor. She ignored the provocation and continued regardless.

Later, Tilly appeared bearing cushions and blankets lifted from the laundry room, which she also hoped wouldn't be missed. She arranged them over the chairs in the middle of the chamber, which were otherwise rather uncomfortable to sit on. Tom's very professional-looking walkie-talkie set – a handsome Christmas present from Aunt Poppy – sat beside the table on a packing crate, awaiting use. Coils of rope, taken from the piles of disused kit left behind by the scaffolders who had worked on the restoration of part of the house the previous year, also sat ready. It all looked terribly useful, although as yet no one knew exactly what for.

Will had also moved all his paintballing and army surplus kit down to the chamber from a chest in the entrance hall. Partly the legacy of his rather half-hearted time in the school's Combined Cadet Force, and partly acquired with the pocket money he had earned in earlier years as a chorister, it was quite a collection and included a substantial first aid kit, various heavy-duty tools, some climbing equipment, and assorted other pieces including military-grade webbing. Finally, several re-chargeable torches sat in a box by the door, specially acquired by Will for the pending derring-do.

'Make sure we keep those topped-up,' said Tilly, pointing Katherine towards the charger, which was sitting next to a foam fire extinguisher that they'd pillaged from the library. Their unstable cable network was still giving off a light humming sound, which they all concluded was unlikely to be a positive sign.

'So much better,' smiled Katherine admiringly, as they all stood back one evening to appreciate their handiwork.

'Certainly is,' said Will. 'Now look, you three, we need to have some ground rules about this place. First, no one comes down here on their own. It would be far too easy to get stuck – or worse,' he added, looking warily at the various doors and dark voids along the walls. 'Second, even if two of us are coming together, they must still tell the others, so someone always knows if there's anyone down here. Third, no one goes into the tunnels yet – at least, not until we've got a better idea of what we're dealing with. Several of them appear to have caved in, and heaven only knows what's behind the locked doors. Got it?'

'Yes, Will,' his siblings said in an unconvinced chorus, as though replying to the head teacher at a primary school assembly.

Tilly glanced at her watch. 'Guys, it's well past supper time. Mum will be wondering what we've all been up to – we'd better go upstairs sharpish. She's already getting suspicious about all the disappearing equipment,' and with that they trooped back up into the body of the house. Deeper exploration of the tunnels would have to wait for a new day.

8 DESTINATION: ST PAUL'S

'Have a look at this,' said Will, the following day, passing Tom the mysterious old book he'd found in the library. It was the tome which had originally confirmed to him the existence of the secret chamber – or Hades, as Will had now re-christened it in honour of the Greek underworld.

Tom grasped the fragile book carefully, for its pages were only loosely bound into the cracked leather spine.

'This is what I discovered that made me certain we were right . . . do you see it?'

'Yes I do. I admit it does look very like the layout of Hades. What do you think it means that it's all mapped out in the book?' asked Tom.

'It means, of course, that the person who drew it must have been down there. Or, at the very least, must have known someone else who had.'

'Or,' ventured Tom, 'found a plan of it somewhere else.'

'I suppose that's possible,' Will agreed grudgingly, but unconvinced.

They sat in thoughtful silence for a while longer. Both the girls were out being social, apparently less gripped by the historic discoveries of the past few days. By contrast, the boys had become consumed with the idea of further exploration, and had returned to the library to see if the book would yield any more clues about the chamber and its various secrets.

Now that they looked more closely, however, the book appeared rather different from Will's first impressions of it. For a start, it appeared that the chronology of contents jumped around – like some sort of jumbled-up history book, with some passages written in Latin, others in Greek. There were even a couple of sections in Aramaic, and yet more scrawled in what appeared to be English short-hand – or was it encoded?

'How do you know that's Aramaic?' asked Tom, sceptically. Will had a habit of conjuring out of the ether plausible-sounding answers which, on closer interrogation, proved to lack foundation in verifiable facts.

'Dad's got a few books on it that I've seen – it's the language that Jesus spoke, after all,' Will replied, straining his schoolboy Latin and Greek to try to make sense of at least part of the text.

'There's a lot of stuff about time in here,' he said eventually. 'Like, really a lot.'

'What do you think this means?' Tom asked, looking at the inside cover. Someone had inscribed a passage by hand, obviously much more recently. 'It's Tolkien, isn't it?' he added, recognising the line from a book he himself had just devoured, *The Lord of the Rings*, and reading it aloud:

'"I wish it need not have happened in my time," said Frodo. "So do I," said Gandalf, "and so do all who live to see such times. But that is not for them to decide. All we have to decide is what to do with the time that is given us."'

'You see – more about time,' said Will. 'And, given that *The Lord of the Rings* was only written in – what? – the 1950s, we can be confident that someone's seen this book within living memory. Anyway,' he continued, 'this is going to require some serious de-coding, not least because I think this is probably one of a series of books. For now, I feel like a quest. Shall we try that sizeable Georgian-looking door downstairs in the meantime – the one with the crossed swords over it?'

'Yes, let's,' said Tom enthusiastically. 'But first I'm going to get Dad's tool box – we might need it.'

Back in the underworld, the boys stood in front of the imposing door in question. They reckoned it was at least seven feet high.

'Judging by the shape and style, it looks as if this was all updated at the same time as The Old Deanery was rebuilt,' observed Tom, thoughtfully.

'Indeed,' replied his older brother, shining his torch through the large keyhole. 'It's difficult to see what's on the other side,' he added, standing back to try to get a better view but to no avail. He took out a small pocket compass and held it steady. 'We're pointing roughly east.' The boys studied the details around the stone door frame.

'Hmm, well I think I know where this leads!' Will announced aloud after a short while.

'St Paul's?' replied Tom, hopefully.

'Exactly. It's in roughly the right direction, and that' – he gestured to the top of the door-frame – 'is a rather finely-carved phoenix set against the flames, above a crown of thorns and those crossed swords of St Paul. The phoenix has long been the symbol of the cathedral. Logical enough, I suppose, after the fires which destroyed two earlier St Paul's on the same site – the cathedral rose from the ashes again and again, reborn like the phoenix from the flames.'

Tom was well used to the history lessons to which Will periodically treated them all, whether or not anyone seemed particularly interested. But then, Will did quite like the sound of his own voice. This was the first occasion he could remember for a while, however, when it seemed actually to be informative. 'What do you mean two St Paul's got burned down?' he asked, surprised. 'I thought it was just Old St Paul's that was levelled in the Great Fire.'

'Yes, there was that one,' explained Will, delighted that Tom had asked for more detail. 'But there was also the one before it, which was built by the Normans when they arrived in the eleventh century. And in fact there was at least one earlier cathedral on the site even before that; and probably some kind of Roman structure earlier still. Did you know, in fact, that the mythological founder of Britain, Brutus of Troy – who was supposed to have been King Arthur's father – reputedly erected a temple to the Roman Goddess Diana on the site of St Paul's? Apparently that's because medieval references to the Dean's Chamber became bastardised to "Diana's chamber", which, now I think about it, might have something to do with this place . . .'

'Right, so, um, how are we going to open it?' asked Tom, returning to the topic at hand and already regretting having unleashed his older brother's historical enthusiasms.

'Ah, yes, sorry. Erm . . .,' Will turned the large handle. This was optimistic, given that he already knew it was locked, but of late things did seem to have a habit of revealing themselves at the crucial hour. Apparently, however, this was not one of those moments. 'I bet the key is in here somewhere,' he said, casting his eyes around the area near the door. 'Better not to have to destroy the lock. Have a look around, Tom – start with the alcoves on that side.'

'Roger that,' replied Tom, moving off to grope around in the darkened recesses.

It took only a couple of minutes of reaching nervously into any and every cavity in the walls immediately adjacent to the door before Will heard an excited 'Look what I've got!' coming from a swathe of shadow, a few yards away. Tom emerged triumphantly, bearing a large key. 'It weighs a ton. Here!'

'Crikey, yes it does,' Will acknowledged, taking the

key from Tom.

The key itself was dark and discoloured, but now that it was in better light the boys could see that it gleamed in places. 'I bet it's brass,' speculated Will. Sure enough, after a little light buffing on his jumper the key glowed brighter still. The crossed swords of St Paul and the familiar phoenix adorned the two faces of its oval base.

'I think we have a winner!' he added jubilantly. With a minimum of wiggling, the key drove home smoothly in the lock with a satisfying click. 'Stand back,' Will warned, glancing excitedly at his brother.

The immense black door swung open easily, with virtually no creaking of the industrial hinges. 'That's a little odd don't you think? The hinges must have been oiled.' Will moved closer to inspect them and saw traces of oil glinting in the light. His thoughts were immediately distracted, however, by what lay ahead. A long passage stretched away from them, paved in fine alternating black and white stone slabs. Wide at first, but narrowing, the walls were made of a distinguished red brick, as was the arched ceiling, which was approximately the same height as the door. Iron brackets on the walls stood ready to hold candles, lanterns, or perhaps torches. Once again, although the passage certainly looked more modern than the chamber in which they stood, there was no evidence of working electric lights.

'No sign of a cave-in,' noted Tom, hopefully.
'Nor any cobwebs,' agreed Will, again suspicious. 'Hmmm, get the big Maglite will you -- the small ones won't be enough. It's like a black hole in here, the tunnel's swallowing all the light!'

Tom returned a few moments later bearing the requested large torch, and dragging a rope. 'We should attach this to something at this end, just in case we lose the lights and need to find our way back,' he suggested.

'Good idea – just like Perseus and the Minotaur,' said Will, privately wishing he'd thought of it.

Placing a stone Civil War cannonball which Tom had "borrowed" from the drawing room in front of the door to prevent it from closing, the boys fastened the end of the long rope to the leg of a statue of a knight standing near the door, and attached another rope to the free end of that one, extending it yet further.

'Let's see how far this gets us,' Will said, tugging the rope experimentally. And with that they swaggered off into the tunnel, imagining themselves as two budding Indiana Joneses.

The tunnel was in amazingly good condition for a structure that must have been at least three hundred years old. The passage sloped gently downwards for about fifty yards, sinking perhaps another seven or eight feet and bending subtly to the right – southwards – before climbing abruptly as the passage swept more sharply to the left, back towards the north. 'We're certainly heading in the right direction for the cathedral,' Will muttered as he consulted his compass, more to himself than to his brother, who was following a few yards back, whistling the Thunderbirds theme tune. They had been moving roughly east but now tracked directly north. Abruptly, the rope ran out.

'Damnit. We'll have to go on without,' said Tom, untying the rope from around his midriff and allowing it to drop to the floor.

As the boys pressed on, the passage floor turned into steps which rose gradually at first, and then more steeply, alternating between black and white like piano keys. They paused, looking up the winding flight of stairs. Exchanging excited glances, they quickened their pace. As they went, the boys noticed that the brickwork became patchy as the tunnel passed through different layers of thick stone. Some was recognisable as the Portland stone which made up the modern cathedral.

'These walls must be twenty feet thick,' wheezed Tom, by now out of breath and running his hand along the side of the passage. But the off-white Portland stone clearly stood on top of a much deeper layer of darker stone – and perhaps rubble – beneath, indicating that they were passing through the ancient foundations of the older St Paul's cathedral which had been lost in the Great Fire of London of 1666.

'Did you know,' Will gasped, 'that after the Fire they just dumped a lot of the rubble from Old St Paul's at the bottom of Fleet Street?'

'Erm, no I didn't,' said Tom, trying and failing to give this new information the welcome such a bombshell obviously expected.

Arriving, slightly breathless, at the top of the long flight of stairs, they emerged into a compact stone room with a curiously-shaped roof. The air up here smelled relatively fresh. They paused, trying to stifle their gulps of air to listen attentively for any indication of where they might be.

'Presumably we're in the crypt of the cathedral?' Will suggested quietly.

'Guess so,' Tom concurred. That this was a hidden entrance to St Paul's they were by now sure, but they didn't want to burst into a crowd of tourists and have their cover blown instantly.

'I hear something,' said Tom, grabbing Will's arm to stop him from rustling.

'Sshhh,' said Will, noisily, getting in on the action. The sounds of talking, though muffled, were clearly nearby. Was that Italian being spoken? 'I reckon we're in a tomb,' said Will, finally. 'Perhaps a sarcophagus or something, or behind one of those substantial wall memorials.'

'What's a sarcophamus?' asked Tom.

'Sarcophagus,' corrected Will, irritably. 'Oh, you know, it's basically a big stone coffin – just like what the pharaoh mummies of ancient Egypt were buried in. You remember the ones in the British Museum, right?'

'But there aren't any pharaohs in St Paul's, are there?'

said Tom, sounding very surprised indeed.

Will slapped his hand theatrically to his forehead. 'No, dum dum. But there are plenty of large tombs, and not very surprisingly most of them are in the crypt. Clearly, if this is one, it's actually a fake, designed to hide the tunnel we've just emerged from. 'Quite brilliant, really,' he added admiringly. 'Look here' – he pointed to the wall at the far end – 'I bet this is the door. Above the steps. Must be, see the scrape-marks on the ceiling? The wall swings inwards, and that's how we're going to get out.'

'It pains me to say it, Will, but sometimes you are actually quite smart,' Tom said begrudgingly, knowing that the backhanded compliment would feed his brother's already over-inflated ego. 'We'd better wait until after everyone's left the cathedral before we try and open it,' he added. 'Don't want to give the game away after all this.'

'Very wise,' agreed his older brother, and the boys beat a retreat back down the narrow stairs cut through the foundations to the by now familiar surroundings of Hades. 'We'll come back after tourist sightseeing is done and evensong is over,' said Will, with a gleam in his eye. 'Then we'll have the place to ourselves. Mwah ha ha haaa,' he added, theatrically.

'Mwah ha ha haaa ha,' echoed Tom, laughing.

Looking up at the West Front of St Paul's Cathedral

9 THE PLAN

It would be an understatement to say that the girls had been more than a little irritated that their brothers had broken Will's own guidelines and headed off to explore tunnels without telling anyone where they were going. Their irritation had dissipated somewhat, however, when the boys had revealed the afternoon's thrilling discovery.

'So can we get in there this evening?' asked Tilly.

'Absolutely,' replied her older brother. 'In fact, it's perfect. Mum and Dad will be at some kind of diplomatic reception, so we'll be home alone and should have several clear hours to do some proper exploring.'

'Sounds marvellous,' said Tom, rubbing his hands together expectantly and looking around. Katherine looked more worried than anything else.

'Look it'll be fine, Kate,' Will comforted, spotting her expression. 'I know the cathedral like the back of my hand. We'll just have a bit of a poke around after hours, you know – maybe go up and have a look at the old library or something. Nothing too adventurous.'

'Library?' Tom asked, his head cocked inquisitively to one side.

'Do you never listen?' replied Will, exasperatedly.

'Yes, library. One of the great libraries of London, if not the country. It contains about sixteen thousand volumes, including one of the original William Tyndale bibles dated 1526.' As usual, Will sounded as if he'd swallowed the guide book and then gone back for an extra helping.

'OK, I get it, it's a bloody good library,' said Tom. 'Geeeeez, Louise.'

Tilly ignored the bickering. 'I bet there'll be loads of amazing stuff up there. Whenever I've been there before we've been supervised so I couldn't really hang around, but Horace – '

'Amazing chap,' Will interjected, and they all nodded in agreement. Horace was a remarkable, kindly man, a former head teacher, now more than a hundred years old, who had been a loyal volunteer at St Paul's for decades, showing people around and generally keeping the place going. 'Did you know his first memory of London was, as a child, seeing a German Zeppelin flying menacingly overhead on a bombing mission during the First World War?'

'Anyhoo . . . ,' Tilly continued, 'you know how Horace remembers all the old stories about the cathedral? Lots of them are about things that were kept in the library at one point or another – it used to be where the Church kept a lot of its secrets for safekeeping, apparently. Basically, the view seems to have been that it's kind of a fortress in its own right, and pretty much anything is safe up there.'

'I bet they said that about the last one, too, and look how that worked out,' said Will, referring to the destruction of Old St Paul's on 4 September 1666 during the Great Fire. 'In fact, just imagine what must have been lost in Old St Paul's – although, having said that, if I remember correctly, a clerk actually managed to save a huge number of important documents by taking them upriver to Fulham Palace.'

'What kind of stuff, Tilly?' asked Kate, hanging on

her every word.

'Well, most recently he was telling me about the Grail story.'

'You mean, as in Dan Brown Da-Vinci-Code-style grail?' asked Tom.

'Not exactly,' Tilly replied. 'The Da Vinci Code alleges that the Holy Grail is not actually the cup that Jesus drank from at the Last Supper. Brown claims there's some secret bloodline of Jesus' descendants which is protected by a stealthy brotherhood, or something like that.'

'Ridiculous,' scoffed Will, although he had secretly enjoyed the book very much.

'But,' Tilly went on, 'there is an ancient legend in these islands that, after Jesus' crucifixion, the Holy Grail was brought to England for safekeeping by followers of St Joseph of Arimathea – the man who gave up his tomb for Jesus's body.'

'Why to England of all places?' asked Tom. 'Bit of a trek from the Holy Land, don't you think?! It's got to be well over a thousand miles.'

'You might well ask. Apparently it was at the outer limit of the Roman Empire, and so the disciples thought that the Grail would be out of reach of the Roman Emperor here. And it was the Romans after all, who had Jesus killed.'

'Right. So, er, is it true?' Katherine asked.

'Unlikely, but that's the legend,' Will replied. 'Horace said that at one point St Paul's library held a secret book – or was it a parchment? – which contained clues to the whereabouts of the Grail. Unfortunately, it was also understood to be in code.'

'If this clue trail existed, why has no-one found it?' Katherine queried.

'Well, Kate, I guess we're going to have to find out,' said Will, that maniacal expression returning to his face.

10 CLOSE CALL

Later that evening, after their parents' departure, the siblings headed down to the archive once more, through Hades, and into the tunnel which led to St Paul's. The small chamber at the top of the stairs seemed a lot more crowded with all four of them in it.

'OK, who farted?' said Tilly. 'That's really disgusting. The air is stale enough in here. Just try and control yourselves, boys.'

'Must be Tom,' said Will quickly, covering his nose in protest at the smell. 'What? Lies!' replied Tom. 'She who smelt it dealt it,' he added, pointing accusingly at Tilly, 'but I think we all know it was almost certainly Will. It usually is.'

Will had gone ahead with Tilly to work out how to open the secret door to the crypt. A sprung lever concealed on a ledge provided the answer. When it was yanked firmly – it didn't seem to have had quite the same oil treatment as the door at the entrance to the passage – the stone panel swung inwards and they had to duck quickly to avoid being squashed against the side wall. There were three large, broad steps leading up to the sizeable doorway which had just opened up. It was dark, although not pitch black. The cathedral crypt had large windows, and the moon that night was nearly full.

As beams of moonlight cut through the gloom, Will levered himself awkwardly out of the hole, and crouched down beside what did indeed transpire to be a large memorial. 'To the sacred memory of Thomas Bennett. . .' he began to read. He looked about, trying not to make a sound as the heads of his siblings appeared out of the wall behind him, like the undead emerging from the grave. Had he not just emerged from the same space himself, it would have been a truly terrifying sight.

Will knew immediately where they were. This was one of the alcoves near the Chapel of the Order of the British Empire, at the eastern end of St Paul's crypt. Beyond the entrance to the chapel, in that part of the undercroft which housed the tombs of the greatest British military heroes of the Napoleonic era, the first Duke of Wellington and Admiral the Lord Nelson, he noticed that a couple of lights were on, and listened intently for signs of life. After a few tense moments he dismissed them as, in all probability, just nightlights. The place certainly seemed to be deserted. It was well after choir- or organ- rehearsals would normally have finished, and there were no big services coming up, so they could be reasonably confident that the works team wouldn't be rearranging the seating or staging on the cathedral floor, as they often were, late into the night.

'Come on then – quietly does it.'

One by one, Will's siblings slid out of the tomb entrance. Tom gently pulled the memorial to behind them, to leave no trace of their stealthy entry.

'Don't let it shut completely or we're totally stuffed!' Will hissed, just in the nick of time, and Katherine wedged her scarf into the join to prevent them from getting locked out.

They set off in single file towards the principal stairs up to the main floor of the cathedral, hugging the shadows of the walls as they went. Out of an abundance of caution, they had all worn dark clothes, and trainers to avoid unnecessary noise, but somehow Tom's squeaked all the same.

Only the gentle jangle of their father's master-key set – a privilege of office, it was his cathedral after all – in Tilly's bag gave them away. Tom had "borrowed" the keys from their father's massive desk shortly after his parents had left for their evening engagement, hoping he'd be able to put them back without their father noticing. He didn't think the bishop even knew that they had discovered the hidden panel under which the keys lay. Many of the keys were original, and some looked as if they dated from well before the seventeenth century.

Up on the main floor of the cathedral, barely half a dozen of the main chandeliers were on. Suspended twenty feet or so above the ground, they cast a warm, yellowish glow over the thousands of empty seats, memorial statues of all shapes and sizes, and battle standards carried by long-lost regiments in long-forgotten wars. Dark shadows crept like spindly fingers across the black and white patterned stone floor.

'Just like a giant version of the passage floor,' Katherine observed, as quietly as she could.

They slipped from one vast column to another as they skirted the space which rose several hundred feet above them: St Paul's enormous dome, inspired by the dome designed by Michelangelo for St Peter's Basilica in Rome.

The interior of the dome was decorated with Sir James Thornhill's splendid three-dimensional classical depictions of the life of St Paul. When the cathedral was empty, the scene was particularly awe-inspiring. The fact that, despite the bright moon outside, the upper recesses of the dome were shrouded in darkness gave the impression that the building was open to the night sky, connecting it directly with the heavens.

The children made their way towards the south stairs, which would lead them to the cathedral's upper levels.

'Locked, predictably,' said Will, as he tried the door.

'Got it,' said Tilly, pulling the vast key-ring out of her bag. Tom stood guard several yards behind, looking up and down the nave to give them more notice lest an as yet unspotted member of staff should suddenly appear.

After a few moments of rather tense and jangly trial and error with the various keys, they were through the door and climbing the wide, winding wooden stairs up towards the Whispering Gallery, so-called because a whisper on one side could be heard with crystal clarity on the other, a hundred-and-twelve feet away.

'Oooh, let's go to the gallery tonight, Will,' suggested Katherine. 'It'll be even better with no tourists there.'

'At some point, we definitely can, but not tonight – don't want to get busted on the first outing, hey!?'

After a few minutes of modest clattering on the stairs and heavy breathing, they arrived at one of the half-dozen nondescript black painted doors which pockmarked the stone walls of the broad spiral stairway up to the galleries. A small square sign, no more than three inches across, carried a simple letter-number identifier.

'S/W B2,' read Katherine aloud. The thousands of tourists who passed it daily on their way to St Pauls' various viewing levels would never know what treasures lay behind it.

'Keys,' commanded Will, holding out his hand imperiously without looking round.

After further trial and error, the door opened with a prolonged creak and the four conspirators slipped through, stepping down the short flight of wooden steps which lay behind it. They were careful to close and lock the door behind them, again in case anyone was doing the rounds – any delay would buy them precious extra seconds to escape or hide. To their left, the huge gallery spread out with its vaulted ceiling and intricate parquet wooden flooring.

'It's not actually that dark,' hissed Tom, as light from the almost-full moon streamed in through the large gallery windows. He flicked on his torch anyway, and the others followed suit.

'Right, team, this is the triforium,' said Will. 'The library is dead ahead of us on the left.'

'What's a triformium?' Katherine asked Tilly, not wanting Will to hear as she knew he'd scoff.

'Triforium,' corrected Tilly, sympathetically. 'It's basically just the name for a gallery within the wall of a church.'

Will continued his breathless history lecture: 'On the right you will see shelves filled with fragments of masonry from Old St Paul's . . .' he gestured to the large section of wall where parts of the heads and limbs of old statues lay mingled with other, less obviously interesting bits of rock.

On either side of the shelves stood small doors with portholes just like a ship. These gave access to another gallery running right the way round the interior of the cathedral. Tiptoeing swiftly along the expansive passageway, it took them less than a minute to arrive at the pair of sturdy oak doors to their left. Glass-fronted bookcases lined the walls on either side, stuffed with centuries of cathedral records.

'This is it,' whispered Tilly, selecting an especially large key from the giant ring and unlocking the door. The others stood either side of her in their dark clothes and torches, looking for all the world like some American SWAT team about to storm the room to rescue kidnap victims.

Mercifully, the door opened noiselessly this time and the children filed in as quickly as possible, once more taking care to lock themselves in. Though no lights were on, the room, like the triforium outside, was lit by moonlight which poured through the huge, high windows, and danced across a scene almost unchanged since Wren's master joiner, the legendary Grinling Gibbons, had created the chamber three centuries before. Fine carved oak shelves lined the walls on all sides, rising almost to the zenith of the double-height ceiling, from which dangled a lonely chandelier. A wooden gallery, carved in the same style as the shelves, ran around the room at first floor level. Below it, reading tables stood piled high with manuscripts, books, and busts of famous figures.

'We can only hope these aren't the finer elements of the collection,' said Will, disapprovingly flicking the edge of a pile of papers. Katherine moved over to the fireplace which stood on one side of the room beneath a large portrait.

'Who's that, Will?' she asked.

'Er,' said Will, stalling for time, 'it's um, ah – look over here,' he said, hoping they wouldn't notice the crude diversionary tactic. He didn't like admitting he didn't know the answer to something he thought he should. The trouble with all these pre-Victorian bishops is that they just looked so, well, interchangeably bishopy.

'OK, team,' said Tilly, enthusiastically, 'have a look around. I think that we should look at the shelves first, and we'll move onto the tables if we don't turn up trumps.'

'Let's do it systematically,' interjected Will. 'Tom, why don't you start up in the gallery? Katherine and Tilly, you two begin over there and just work your way along. I'll start over here.'

'Even with the moon, it's quite difficult to do this just by torchlight,' Tom said in hushed tones after a while. 'Anyway, remind me what we're looking for. I've forgotten the title.'

Will groaned. 'Haven't we been over this about five thousand times? We want the book Horace told Tilly about. You know, the one we think might reveal where the Grail is hidden.'

'Right – but why couldn't Horace have just lent it to us?' Tom asked.

'Because no-one knows where it is and we can hardly go around saying "Oh hey, we're just looking for the map which leads to the Holy Grail, does anyone know where it is?" Apart from anything else, if people knew where the map was presumably they'd have gone looking for the cup themselves! We don't even know what it's called, or even if it exists for sure. It's an old story.'

Suddenly, the room was illuminated as the lone chandelier blazed into life. They all froze, wheeling round to focus on the light-switch near the door. Katherine smiled back, hopefully. 'I bet no one will even notice,' she said, slightly bashful.

'Turn-it-*off*!!' the other three replied in unison.

'This will rather advertise our presence here, don't you think?' hissed Will in an exaggeratedly sarcastic whisper, moving swiftly across the room toward his youngest sister who recoiled slightly as he flicked the switch upward. 'Let's just hope no one saw.'

Their search continued for some time with very limited success. Periodically a hopeful 'Aha!' would emanate from some corner of the library, to be shortly and inevitably followed by, 'Ah, no, sorry – my mistake.'

'Guys, it's getting on for 11 o'clock,' said Tilly, checking her phone. 'Probably time to pack up and head back. We don't want mum and dad to have a heart attack when they find all of us gone with no explanation. That would require rather a tricky bit of explaining.'

'Good point, let's make tracks ASAP,' Tom concurred.

But at that moment they heard the distinct sound of the door at the end of the triforium outside the library slamming shut, and two animated adult voices drawing nearer at speed.

'Well, if some lady reports seein' the lights on up 'ere we 'ave to check it out – you know, insurance and whatnot,' one unfamiliar muffled voice said to the other. The four children exchanged terrified glances.

'Oh sugar. Quick –' said Will to the girls, 'over here…'

'Tom, you'll have to make do. Lie as flat as you can and as far away from the edge of the gallery as possible. Don't make a sound or we're all toast.'

'What are we going to do?' asked Katherine, panicking and stamping her feet quietly in desperation.

'The flue above the fireplace is big, and there's a ledge inside it. Climb up, right now. Don't think about it, just do it,' Will directed.

Tilly gave Katherine a boost up into the chimneypiece above the fireplace, as Tom went to ground in the gallery like a hunted fox. Will boosted Tilly up after Katherine; then, with his sisters' help, levered himself awkwardly into the cavity just as a key was inserted into the lock of the library door.

'Don't even breathe,' mumbled Tilly, pressed uncomfortably against her two siblings as Katherine accidentally knocked some rubble and soot from the chimney out into the fireplace. 'Ooops,' she said guiltily.

'Dammit – my bag,' Tilly added. 'It's on one of the tables.'

'Too late,' muttered Will, 'just pray that they don't spot it.'

They heard the sound of the lock turning and the library door opening. The light went on again. Even in the chimney the increase in light made the three siblings squint a little.

'You see, nothin' to worry about,' said the man with the thick accent.

'Hang on, we should be thorough – seems unlikely the light will have come on by itself,' replied the other, as the sound of a booted foot clanged on the lowest rung of the iron spiral stair up to the gallery, followed by another, and then another.

The other man spoke again. 'Maybe, or maybe the woman didn't see anything at all – maybe it was a reflection, or her imagination, or a hoax. Look, there's clearly no one here. All the doors were locked on the way up 'ere, weren't they?'

'Yeah, you're right,' replied his companion, going into reverse on the gallery steps. 'My shift's up anyway, and I want to head home.'

A few moments later, the light was out, and the key was turning in the lock once more.

'Don't move – give them a few minutes to get clear,' said Will, struggling to maintain his footing amongst the loose stone chips in the chimney. At that second, the great clock of the cathedral located in the south west tower adjoining the library boomed 11pm.

'No time to spare – quick!' squeaked Tilly, 'Mum and Dad are due back imminently.' Katherine jumped down and doubled over to exit their hiding place. The others followed suit.

Tom was sitting on the gallery floor, looking a little shaken but smiling. 'Thought I was a goner,' he said, almost excited by the near-miss.

'Fortunately, they missed this,' said Tilly, putting on her backpack.

'I tell you what,' suggested Will, 'going back the way we came is probably quite risky. Who knows where on earth those chaps have got to. We might run straight into them.'

'Let's use the Geometric Stair instead,' interjected Tilly, pre-empting Will.

'Precisely, although one of us will have to go via home and back through Hades to rescue the scarf in the secret door.'

They lined up silently behind the other pair of doors on the west side of the library, listening closely. Nothing. Exiting the room and locking the door behind them, they found themselves at the very top of Christopher Wren's legendary geometric stair, an architectural and artistic masterpiece. This spiral staircase turned two full rotations, right the way down the length of the south west tower. Its cantilevered steps extended from the walls, each seemingly unsupported by anything other than the step below.

'This looks like something from Hogwarts,' Katherine marvelled.

'That would be because it appears in one of the Potter films,' replied Will, looking around to check that the coast was clear.

The team moved down the staircase as quickly and quietly as they could, passing the great metal gate which led to the main floor of the cathedral, and down again to a huge pair of wooden double doors embedded with iron nails, which led straight to the outside world.

'The old Dean's door,' explained Will. 'It always was meant for people coming to our house. . . '

They drew back the huge bolt which secured the inside of the door before the master key set worked its magic again on the nineteenth century lock; and then they were out and over the churchyard railings in a matter of seconds, stopping only to avoid being squashed by the number 11 bus which hurtled past, hooting anti-socially. It was five past eleven.

'Please God, say the parents are delayed,' said Tilly as they sneaked into The Old Deanery via the side door.

Sir Christopher Wren's magisterial Geometric Staircase, looking up from the floor of the South West Tower.

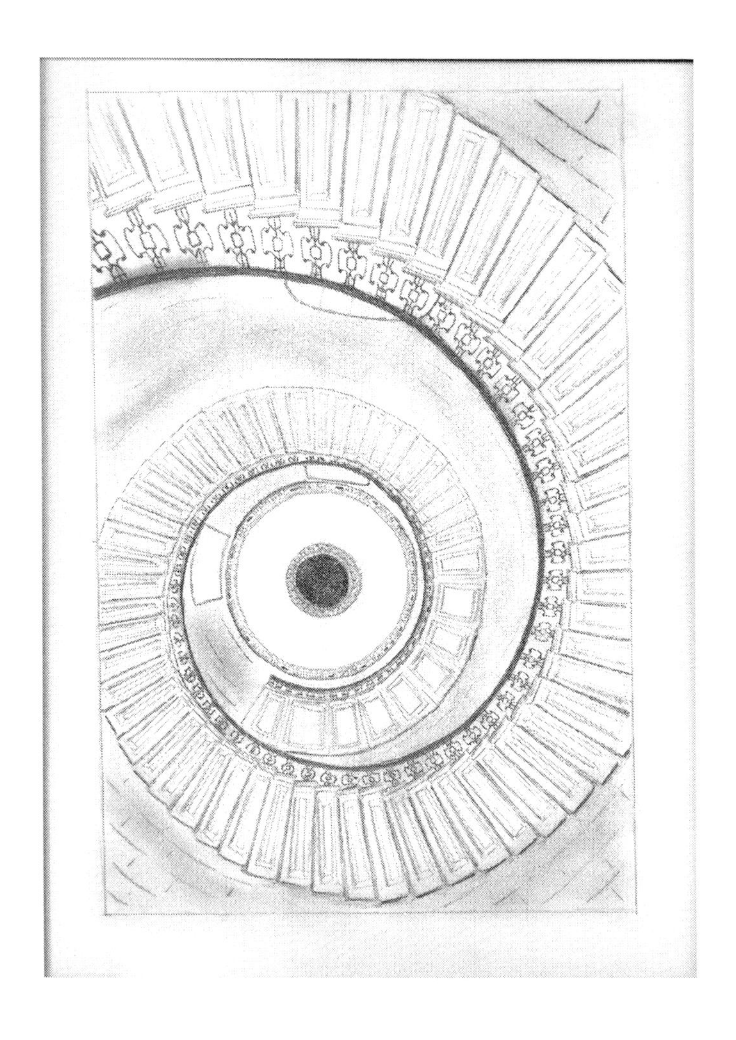

11 HUNTING IN THE SHADOWS

Over the following weeks, the children made repeated night-time forays to the cathedral at opportune moments to continue their hunt. Sometimes they went *en masse*, sometimes just two of them, but always to the same end: hunting for the whereabouts of the manuscript or book which reputedly revealed the resting-place of the most important relic in all Christendom: the Holy Grail.

Inevitably, there had been further close calls with members of the cathedral community. On one occasion, Tilly and Katherine had very nearly walked straight into a crocodile of two dozen choristers who were heading down to the crypt after a late filming session for a TV documentary in which they were featuring. They had only avoided discovery by concealing themselves behind Field Marshal Wellington's enormous Luxulyanite sarcophagus (which had originally been intended for Cardinal Wolsey before he fell out with Henry VIII), after one of the choristers shouted that he had seen something move in the shadows. A schoolmaster had marched off to investigate, amidst roars of derision from the other choristers who obviously thought the whole episode was a hilarious wind-up. 'No, I'm serious – there's something in the shadows,' said the hapless probationer, backing away nervously.

After yet another near-miss, Will convened a sibling council. 'I've called this meeting to suggest that we tell someone else about Hades.' The others looked sceptically at him.

'Isn't that exactly what you've been telling us not to do?' said Katherine.

'Look, we all know there are risks in telling anyone else, but we need some help,' Will continued, ignoring her. 'The risk of discovery is currently excessively high. At the present rate of progress, we're going to get caught soon. Then the game might be up for good. The local planning authority, snoring-boring museum specialists and archaeologists will be all over this place like a nasty tropical rash, and we'll never get a chance to investigate properly – to discover what the secret complex was originally intended for, and perhaps even to use it that way.'

By now, Will was in full Churchillian mode, pacing around the library at the back of The Old Deanery. He went on, 'What we need is a way of monitoring what's going on in and around Hades more effectively. In the CIA, they call it "situational awareness". And I know just the person who can help us achieve that, and, crucially, someone who can be trusted.'

'And who's that?' asked Tilly, dubiously.

'Boffin!' said Tom, brightly, following his brother's line of thought, 'of course. Great idea.'

Tall for his age and tousle-haired with a mousey-coloured mop, Boffin was their youngest aunt's eldest son, and a year younger than Tilly. Needless to say, his real name wasn't Boffin at all – that was Walter. Prodigiously good with technology from a young age and a bit of a brainbox, Boffin had been building circuits and remote-control vehicles for as long as any of them could remember and, inevitably, had picked up his nickname at school. Given the alternative, he was happy to embrace it, and had even recently started wearing geek-chic glasses which made him look a little like Harry Potter.

"Boffin, look, I can't speak on the phone, but can you come to us ASAP?' Will asked. 'Need to show you something – something big. But you have to swear you won't tell a soul. Not even Aunt JJ. In fact, especially not Aunt JJ. OK?'

'Er, OK. Sure, coz. What about Saturday morning?' Boffin replied, sounding a bit taken aback. 'What's this all about anyway? This isn't another of your practical jokes is it, Will?' he added, suddenly suspicious. 'Because you remember what happened when you put that Royal Python in mum's handbag, don't you?'

'No, no. I promise, no jokes this time,' replied Will, roaring with laughter as he remembered his aunt's terror as she withdrew her hand from the bag to find the chubby but non-venomous snake had attached itself to her thumb before furiously windmilling her arm in a desperate attempt to detach it. He still hadn't been fully forgiven. 'Super, just tell your mum you're coming over to study with Tom or something – no, wait, say Tilly, that's more believable! See you Saturday then.'

Saturday morning duly arrived. Being a history anorak like his older cousin Will, Boffin was instantly seized by the importance of the discovery of Hades and the secret tunnels, and immediately swore on the nearest available bible – never in short supply in a bishop's house – that he would take the secret to his grave, although he did add somewhat nervously that he 'really hoped that wouldn't be necessary'. Tom stood nearby in his hunting outfit, looking as if he was entirely ready to enforce the oath. Boffin eyed him anxiously for a brief moment, before setting down his holdall full of bits and piece of techy-looking things. The boys then showed Boffin around their underworld kingdom.

'Thing is, Boffin,' Will began as they paced around the edge of Hades, 'we've been doing some extracurricular exploring and, um, we need to make sure no one finds out about any of this. We need some kind of early warning system to tell us if anyone's sniffing around, or equally if the coast is clear. Plus we're getting suspicious that perhaps persons unknown have been using the chamber more recently, and we want something to keep an eye on the place.'

'Yeah, what about a laser grid??' asked Tom, optimistically. 'Like in *Mission Impossible* or something.'

'Erm, Earth to Tom, everyone would see the lasers for a start, so it would actually give away your little secret,' Boffin replied. 'Also it would be nearly impossible for us to rig up. You'd need quite a lot of power and wiring to pull that off,' he added, thinking the idea through from a typically practical perspective.

'But what, realistically, *can* we do?' asked Will, impatient for answers.

'We'll start with some cameras,' Boffin suggested. 'I've actually got a handful of pencil cams I built last summer – wireless, size of a small, well, pencil, I guess; but they offer a great field of view. The only thing is, we would need a power source for them.'

'Easy in here,' said Will gesturing to the growing ball of furiously buzzing cabling near the door, where the siblings' various efforts at extending their power and lighting arrangements had become rather entangled and were now, Will suspected, an accident waiting to happen. 'But not so easy in the cathedral.'

'Maybe we could feed off an emergency lighting circuit?' mused Boffin, more to himself than the boys. 'I'd need to have a proper look myself.'

After a couple more 'reconnoitre' visits, Boffin had helped the four of them establish a remarkably sophisticated wireless camera network within Hades, The Old Deanery and the cathedral itself. One camera covered the entrance to Hades from their house; another covered the area immediately around the secret entrance into the crypt of St Paul's, with, lest they should be disturbed, a wide enough field of view to see most angles of approach to the memorial. Two other cameras covered approaches to the crypt and stairs, while a fifth, concealed above the statue of the eighteenth century prison reformer John Howard on the cathedral floor, covered the main staircase to St Paul's library and a large section of the cathedral floor itself. The final pencil cams were hidden in the triforium, outside the library and on the door-frame at the top of the Geometric Stair, covering that approach.

Another innovation involved installing small, discreet, remote movement-sensors at either end of the triforium outside the library. These wirelessly alerted a pocket key-fob, which vibrated when the sensors were triggered, warning the carrier that someone was coming and, hopefully, buying them precious seconds to conceal themselves or escape.

'Boffin, you're an absolute legend, thank you so much,' said Will. 'We'll need you back soon to help us explore some of these other doors and tunnels, but we've got some unfinished business in the cathedral before we embark on that.'

'Copy that,' replied Boffin, 'although Mum's getting a bit suspicious that we're doing so much revision *after* exams!'

'Well then it's lucky we all know you're a keen bean getting ahead for next term, Boffin!' Will responded, patting him on the back.

Yet days of further investigation still yielded no sign of the mysterious manuscript for which they searched, and the children were growing frustrated, despite one useful additional discovery. Climbing up inside the chamber which housed the secret entrance to the cathedral, Tom had discovered that it was possible to clamber into one of the rainwater shafts which honeycombed the walls of St Paul's all the way around the cathedral. The two-foot square shafts had iron bars set conveniently into the walls at intervals like ladders, enabling the siblings to climb unnoticed to various higher levels of the building. This included the surveyor's office which was hidden above the south transept. By emerging through a door with a large red warning sign which read 'DANGER – RAINWATER SHAFT – KEEP OUT,' they could move with increased freedom without risking running into people in the more public areas of the building. Conveniently, the surveyor's office led straight on to the triforium in front of the library; they just had to be careful not to use that route on a Monday or a Wednesday, when the surveyors were actually working there, as Tom had nearly found out to his cost.

'You know, we've spent so much time exploring the cathedral that it almost feels like we've given up on the rest of the tunnels,' said Katherine one morning after breakfast as she and Will took the mischievous family dog, Mufasa, out for a walk along the riverside.

'Agreed,' replied Will, yanking hard on the lead to restrain the ravenous terrier from wolfing down a discarded baguette on the pavement. Mufasa's appetite was the stuff of legend, and the fact that the baguette was fully half his size and probably very mouldy didn't for a moment deter him – if anything, it seemed to encourage him.

'The thing is, though, two of the other tunnels look caved-in, and it would probably be suicidal to try and get down them, at least without serious planning and preparation. There is that other very narrow one behind the tapestry – you know, the one where you can feel that draught – there might be something down there. Plus the two we can't get into yet, of course. Or else either of those brick ones. . . I'm pretty sure the left-hand tunnel leads to the Fleet River and the sewers, and both doors are operable.'

'Oh, the one with the funny smell?' replied Katherine. 'That makes sense. Gosh, I don't fancy that at all.'

'Quite,' agreed Will, 'which brings us back to. . .'

'. . . what about trying the other large jammed door again?' finished Katherine.

'I'm not sure it is jammed, you know. I think it's just immensely solid, and almost certainly locked. The issue is that there's no obvious keyhole. Very mysterious – but yes, let's have another look. If it's so hard to get through, stands to reason that there must be something worth the wait behind it. Only one way to find out!'

12 THE ARROW OF TIME

Descending once more into the underbelly of the house, Will and Katherine made their way through the secret door from the archive and down the spiral staircase, which was by now cast in the warm glow of light from their various *ad hoc* installations of recent weeks. Passing the sentinel figures of St Paul and the cloaked crusader (whose identity still eluded them), they entered Hades, the distinctive smell of history filling their nostrils as they walked and talked. On that late summer's day, the cool of the chamber was for once a welcome escape from the broiling heat above ground.

Crossing the chamber, they approached the door opposite the tunnel to the cathedral. On the far side of the room, the door itself appeared to be of similar dimensions to its hefty seventeenth century opposite number, except that somehow this one appeared even more formidable. Perhaps it was the strange carvings adorning the frame, or the fact that the door was painted matt black rather than being varnished. Viewed from across the chamber, it appeared as though there were simply an endless abyssal void within the marbled white of the surrounding stone.

Katherine was running her hand over the carvings on

the left hand side of the surround when she stopped and stood back, squinting up.

'Will, have you ever looked closely at these carvings? There's an inscription at the top – it doesn't look quite as old as the rest of the frame though.'

'*In the universe, there are things that are known, and things that are unknown, and in between, there are doors*,' she read out loud. 'Do you think it's a clue to what lies behind the door?'

'Maybe,' Will said pensively, also taking a step back to get a better view. 'I think it's a quote by the poet William Blake – you know, one of Dad's favourites. I'm sure I've heard him read that aloud before. And that would explain why it looks more recent: Blake lived from the eighteenth to the nineteenth centuries I think, so obviously no one could have added that until Blake had actually said it.'

'So that means we know that people were making changes to Hades until at least the early nineteenth century . . .' Katherine concluded.

'Looks that way. In fact, the wiring for the chandeliers suggests even more recently than that – perhaps late nineteenth century. And,' Will continued, looking around, 'judging by the surprisingly shipshape state we found it in, I guess that, at the very least, someone's been keeping an eye on this place more recently still.' He exchanged a slightly nervous look with his youngest sister, before laughing it off.

'Right,' he added, regaining his composure, and only allowing himself a small glance over his shoulder to check that they weren't being watched by some unknown observer, perhaps hiding in one of the shadowy recesses of the wall. 'So how do we open the door? – that's the real question.'

They looked again for a keyhole, running their fingers over the surface of the door in case they had missed anything.

'Hang on, I'll get a torch – the lighting's not good

enough to see all the details on this side.' Moments later, Katherine returned with a flashlight, and began probing the surface of the door with it. 'Nothing I can see here,' she offered after a while. 'Hang on, what's this?'

Her beam of light had found some signs of wear on the section of the frame beside Will, at about his shoulder height. Now that they peered more closely, they saw a three-dimensional carved hourglass, around six inches high, set in a sunken circle the size of a small side plate. But the most interesting discovery was the grooves in the circular surround.

'It looks as if this moves,' observed Katherine, prodding it gently.

'Great spot, clever clogs,' complimented Will, smiling. 'I think we've got it.' He reached out and grasped the hourglass with his right hand as Katherine held the torch steady on the target.

'It's stuck,' he grunted, adding his left hand to the effort. The hourglass budged a little; then a little bit more. 'One more push . . .' he said through clenched teeth, Katherine noticing a small vein pulsing in his forehead with the effort as he pushed up and away at the bottom half of the hourglass. Suddenly, it rotated through 180 degrees, then jarred to a halt with a faint click. The siblings held their breath, but nothing happened.

'Uuumm, do you think it's broken?' whispered Katherine after a couple of seconds, as though trying not to scare the door out of responding to the stimulus.

Her remark was greeted by the sound of a chain and pulleys moving on the other side of the door in front of them, and a dull thud. Then, with a dramatic screeching of hinges, the huge door swung away from them into the dark void beyond. They were in.

13 THE BEEHIVE

'Call the others, quick, they're going to want to see this,' Will instructed Katherine, who scampered off up the stairs to establish some phone signal and summon the absent siblings back to the house.

'Don't do anything without me,' she shouted over her shoulder at her older brother.

'Fair enough!' he replied disingenuously, his fingers crossed in his pockets.

As Katherine disappeared back to the surface world, Will stood at the threshold of their latest discovery. Light from Hades slanted through the doorframe, illuminating fragments of what lay beyond, and casting a stark and slightly creepy silhouette of Will on the floor in front of where he stood.

Marching swiftly to the entrance at the foot of the stairs up to the house, he picked up one of the large Maglites from the battered old shelving from the archive which was now enjoying a new lease of life as racks for their exploration equipment. No-one would miss them from under those old dust-sheets anyway, although it had been an immense challenge to dis-assemble the shelves and transport everything down the winding staircase.

His hand hesitated over an orange builder's hard hat. *Might be a good idea*, he thought to himself, before deciding that he'd rather not look too nerdy when the others arrived and retracing the fifteen or so paces to the open void.

Flicking on the torch, he whistled at the scene which unfolded before him. The wide beam of the Maglite revealed another circular chamber, albeit one considerably smaller than that in which he stood. In place of stone and tapestries, the walls were wood-lined with a panelling similar to that used in the cathedral library; they rose perhaps twelve feet before converging in a vaulted ceiling of exposed, ribbed brickwork high above.

As the beam tracked along the walls a shiver ran down Will's spine and he let out a gasp – who were those hooded figures, propped against the walls?

'Oh my good Go. . . – phew!' he muttered to himself after a few seconds, realising that, in fact, the ominous shadows were a large collection of coats and cloaks of different colours, shapes and sizes, hanging on elongated iron hooks which ran right the way around the chamber.

Advancing into the room, he looked down at the distinctive design of the inlaid marble floor and recognised the famous Labyrinth of Chartres Cathedral, the greatest of Europe's medieval gothic masterpieces. In the middle of the labyrinth sat a solitary round table, rising to waist height. Around the edge of its inlaid marble surface he could make out an inscription. '*To be no part of any body, is to be nothing*,' read Will aloud. 'Hmmm,' he pondered, nonplussed.

But then something very curious indeed caught Will's eye. Dead ahead, opposite the entrance, stood a pair of metal gates, just like those used in the earliest elevators he had seen. Yes. It was absolutely unmistakeable. It appeared to be some kind of lift.

'What on earth . . . ?' he exclaimed, walking a little closer. No doubt about it. He could even smell the greased machinery which presumably operated it. Thoroughly perplexed, he jumped at the clatter of feet behind him, as Katherine re-appeared with Tom in train, slightly out of breath.

'Came as quickly as I could.' Tom wheezed. 'Oh wow. . .'

'Quite. . .'

'Is that a lift?' exclaimed Katherine in surprise.

'It does appear to be.'

'Where do you think it goes?' asked Tom, wide-eyed, looking from Will to the lift and back again. 'And what are all these robes and stuff on the walls? This place is the most bizarre yet. Hang on, we haven't wandered into your private dressing room, have we, Will?'

'Very amusing, as always. Have you looked at the floor?' Will enquired of the other two.

'It's the Maze of Chartres,' said Tom, 'but what's so special about it?'

'Well, the maze itself is an ancient symbol of Christian spiritual pilgrimage, but the particularly strange thing from our point of view is that it's one of the symbols which I would say Dad is most associated with.'

'This place just gets stranger and stranger,' said Katherine, walking over to stand by the lift with Will. Tom joined them, their three torches managing to illuminate much of the space.

'Do you think it works?'

'Not sure, but there's only one way to find out.'

'I'm really not convinced that this is a great idea,' said Katherine. 'I mean, it looks pretty old doesn't it? Who knows what it's going to do – or even where it goes.'

'Come on, Kate, don't be a killjoy. Let's a least get some proper lighting in here and have a nose around. Fair enough?'

'Fair enough, Will, but on your head be it,' said Katherine.

Several minutes passed as the three rootled around in the new chamber.

'Gosh, boys, look up!' Katherine exclaimed after a short while. 'The chandelier is electric in here, too! Look at that wire – and those old bulbs. That means there must be a switch somewhere.'

'I hardly think late-Victorian bulbs will be working,' Will responded dourly. 'But the lift presumably works off electricity, so perhaps there is a current, or at least was. Let's call Boffin. It's too dangerous to be mucking about in here with the lift without proper lighting anyway.'

Boffin duly arrived later that Saturday afternoon, equipped as usual with a highly suspicious bag of wires and tools.

'Boffin, um, doesn't anyone ever stop you,' asked Tilly, who had by now joined the party. 'I mean, in the nicest possible way, you might look as if you're about to embark on some extensive terrorist activity.'

'Shall we get to work?' interjected Will.

'Yes let's,' seconded Tom.

'As you'll see,' Will went on, 'there appears to be some kind of electrical power in that room – or at least there was. We need to know if we can fix up the lighting. Frankly, we'd also love it if you could fix the lighting here in Hades, Boffin, whilst you're at it, as I'm pretty sure that the angry ball of fizzing wiring by the door is well past its sell-by date!'

'Hey look, the switch is on the wall over there next to the door,' Tom observed, wandering into the Beehive and gesturing to an ancient-looking brass panel set into the wood with a solitary flick-switch in it. The others followed him in.

'Shouldn't be a problem,' Boffin replied breezily, shinning up the ladder they had borrowed from Ted's maintenance equipment in the boiler house.

'Yup, got a current,' he said after a few moments, detaching from the chandelier a small yellow voltage tester which he'd bought with him. The whole operation looked extremely dangerous, thought Tilly, praying that Boffin wouldn't electrocute himself or, indeed, fall off the ladder onto the unforgiving black and white marble floor below.

'Hand me that storm lamp, will you?' asked Boffin with a pair of pliers between his teeth, and Tom dutifully passed up the large lamp as Will held the ladder steady. A few anxious minutes of cutting and twisting of wires passed.

'Voila! We have light,' said Boffin proudly, as the room filled with the warm glow of the camping light. He descended the ladder steps and all eyes turned to the lift gates. 'So what's all this about d'you reckon?' he asked, intrigued.

'I've been wondering that myself,' answered Will. 'If you think about it, there are a lot of glaringly unsubtle hints surrounding us. For a start, you see that painting hanging above the lift gates? Above the cornice . . .' he pointed towards it. 'Do you know who that is?'

'Er, nope, don't think so,' said Boffin, moving closer to study the picture of the figure with a pair of wings, a flowing beard and a scythe. 'Maybe the Grim Reaper? That's a bit sinister though, isn't it?'

'How about some kind of angel?' ventured Tom.

'Not bad guesses. And Boffin, you're right that he does look a bit like the Reaper, but actually it's Cronos, the Greek god of Time.'

'Right, so what does that mean?' asked Tilly, none the wiser.

'Well, if you look at the carvings on the door frame, they include the Greek goddess Ananke – she's the Goddess of Inevitability,' he added, looking at the blank faces staring back at him. 'Add to that the fact that the door release to get in here is a carved hourglass, and I think it's fair to conclude we're being given a fairly strong message that this beehive-shaped chamber is all about time.'

'But what *is* that message?' asked Tom, frustrated at the lack of straight answers, and jigging lightly on the spot with excitement.

'Well I guess we'll just have to call the lift,' replied Will, a mischievous glint in his eye once again.

He stepped towards the gates, and pulled the foot-long brass lever which was to one side of them. An adjacent plaque read *Down for travel – Up for return.* 'Here goes nothing,' he said, as the whirring of ancient motors filled the room.

14 THE ELEVATOR

The five adventurers stood quietly in a semi-circle, facing the lift gates. The whine of an old electric engine seemingly straining to lift the elevator car elicited some nervous glances between them. Several moments passed as they stood in silence before Katherine voiced what the others were thinking. 'Er, guys, I know this is really exciting and everything but, um, don't you think it's a bit different getting into an ancient lift which no one's probably serviced in God only knows how long? I mean, it just seems a bit of a risk.'

The group digested the reality of the situation. Exploring Hades and the rest of the structurally sound-looking tunnels and spaces was one thing. Plunging further into the earth to who-knew-where in a rickety old machine was a different proposition altogether. They might as well be heading blind into an old Cornish tin mine on a wing and a prayer.

Tom was watching the curiously designed floor level indicator – assuming that's what it was, of course – above the pediment but below the portrait of Cronos. A mechanical arm was moving smoothly around the circular metal plate on the wall, which had numbers – presumably floor numbers, thought Tom – engraved on it. He had originally assumed it must be a clock, but on closer inspection the numbers ran from zero to one hundred. The hand had been at, or rather near, 12 when it started; now it ran through 17, 18, 19. . .

Then the arm stopped, just slightly to the 21 side of number 20 and an inviting 'ping' greeted the arrival of the lift car, as though they were in a department store. The solid doors behind the gate slid open, revealing a surprisingly large oak-panelled space, roughly eight feet square.

'They really do love their panelling,' Tilly observed.

A solitary light – working, improbably – illuminated the square lift car from its position in the dead-centre of the 8-ft high ceiling. On one side of the elevator, four discs were embedded in the wall: a bit like a combination lock, but each disc was the size of a CD, and about an inch thick. Below, another wheel with shapes carved at intervals was horizontally embedded in the wall.

'What on earth are they?' Tilly asked, spotting the discs, her eyes also taking in the short brass lever which was near them.

But no one else moved or spoke, as though the lift were exerting some kind of mystical, hypnotic force upon them all. Eventually, Will stepped forward, leaning in further to inspect the car, though making a point of leaving the Victorian mesh gate in place. 'Just to be safe,' he said with a nervous smile at the others while gripping the cross-bars of the frame. The lift doors stayed open, beckoning them in.

'I think you're right, Katherine,' he said, finally. 'It actually looks OK to me, but, as you say, it's a massive gamble. Boffin, anything we can do to take a closer look at the integrity of the shaft and running gear of the lift? That might give us an idea whether it's worth taking a punt on it or not.'

'I reckon if we put a camera on a bit of rope with a

light and drop it through that space there' – Boffin pointed to the gap, around three inches wide, between the floor on which they were standing and that of the lift car – 'we'll get a pretty good idea of what's underneath, and what the condition of the lift shaft is. We can use a camera on a stick to look at the running gear overhead – same idea, really. The only thing is, it'll take a bit of time to put the kit together, and I don't have everything I need here.'

'No problem,' responded Will. 'Probably best we take it slowly, anyway.'

'Ohhhhh noooooooo!' moaned Tom, frustrated and surging forward to rattle the cage doors and take a closer look himself. 'Look, it still works doesn't it? I know it sounds a bit creepy and like a motorised tin can and everything, but I'm sure it's absolutely fine. Everything else here still works doesn't it? It's like it's all been waiting for us. Anyway, we need to know where it goes. Especially as the floor indicator suggests that we're on the 20th floor, but we know the lift doesn't go up through the house. That clock-like thing has numbers up to a hundred, and naturally we know there are definitively *not* eighty further floors above us!'

'He's right, Will – look,' Tilly chimed in, pointing out the engraved numbering on the clock-like indicator.

'Obviously we're going to investigate more,' said Will, somewhat impatiently. 'But it's too dangerous to do it now. Boffin, get to work on those other bits will you?'

'Anyway,' Katherine pointed out, 'it's supper time, and Mum will have our guts for garters if we're late again.'

'Cripes, you're right,' Will replied. 'And Mum has already been getting a bit suspicious about where we've all been hanging out. Quick. . .'

And with that, the five of them beat a hasty retreat from the beehive, back up into the house, leaving the lift doors wide open, and waiting.

15 DOWN THE RABBIT HOLE

No one talked much over supper that evening, despite their parents' best efforts to provoke conversation. Katherine responded politely as always, but the other three seemed lost in thought, though not too lost not to wolf down the delicious meal.

'So good, Mum,' said Tom through a mouthful, as usual by-passing the ritual of cutting the food up into manageable pieces before tucking in. Before pudding, Tilly made an excuse about going to see some friend or other, and disappeared off.

'It's the geniality which kills you,' their father said, narrating another long day, and settling down with their mother to watch yet another gruesome murder mystery. As far as the children could see, their parents enjoyed nothing better than murder plots, the higher the body count, the better!

Katherine then muttered about needing to do some homework which she'd been putting off all holiday. Tom also slipped away, and Will retired to his room to regroup. He knew what they were all thinking; it was just that no one wanted to say it aloud for fear of being laughed at – it would sound too insane. Yet the clues were plain for all to see. Whoever had been responsible for constructing the secret underground complex, perhaps over many, many generations, had concealed it well – very well indeed – and they'd been able to do so consistently for perhaps a thousand years, or maybe even longer. They were hiding something incredibly important. And not just the secret tunnels leading to St Paul's, and who knows where else.

Then there was the mocking figure of Cronos, the Greek god of Time, hanging over the entrance to the lift: was it some kind of joke? An ironic comment on the age of the organisation which built it, perhaps? The various passages of text in the history of the house also alluded to time, however, and the hour-glasses dotted around the Beehive, as Will had decided it must be called, provided additional evidence of a connection. And surely there couldn't be twenty floors below them, not to mention eighty above. But this was the 21st century, and the lift had stopped just beyond the number 20. It all made a sort of sense – unless of course this was some bizarre extended dream, from which he would shortly wake. He just had to know for certain, one way or the other.

Will sat on the battered old sofa in his room, wondering whether he should ask Tom to join him. He wouldn't ask the girls – instinct said it was too dangerous, and he was over-protective of them at the best of times. Anyway, Tilly was out; but it might be better if at least one other person knew his whereabouts. If it was indeed a time-warp, it would be a bit of a shame to discover he was right, only to get stuck, well, back in time. But he decided against asking Tom, not wanting to be responsible for him in such a risky situation either; besides, he'd already gone to bed.

He sat up, reading his latest Clive Cussler half-heartedly for an hour after he thought everyone else had retired, waiting for them to drift off to sleep. Then, as quietly as he could, he opened his bedroom door and moved the short distance toward the back stairs to head down to Hades. He was resolved to settle the matter for himself. He wouldn't be able to sleep anyway with so many thoughts racing around in his over-active imagination.

'Oi! Where do you think you're going, sneaky?' someone hissed quietly but indignantly behind him.

He spun around to see Tom, torch in hand and dressed for action, standing slightly alarmingly in the darkened corner of the upper hall. As he stepped forward, his untameable curly hair made it look as though he were a giant floating mushroom emerging from the gloom.

'I might well ask you the same question,' Will retorted, trying to conceal his surprise, and relief.

'I knew you were up to something,' continued Tom, accusingly. 'Always plotting, aren't you Will?!'

'Be quiet and hurry up if you're coming,' his older brother replied, setting off down the back stairs. Silently, the boys slipped down into the archive, through the secret door, and down the spiral stairs into Hades, flicking on the lights of their hidden kingdom as they went. Will checked his watch. It was just before midnight.

'So, what are you thinking?' Tom asked, as they walked down the steps into the Beehive chamber which contained the elevator.

Will didn't reply for a moment. 'I think we both know,' he said finally, 'that this is not a normal lift at all. In fact, I believe that this might be one of the great secrets of all time – quite literally,' he added, as mysteriously as he could. His sense of historical drama sometimes got the better of him.

'I knew it!' said Tom excitedly, practically hopping on the spot, his enthusiasm building by the step.

'OK here's the plan. I'm going to go down one floor or level or whatever it is, to number 19,' said Will definitively, inviting no challenge. 'I will then return and let you know what the form is. If it's safe, then we can go back down together. If I am gone for more than fifteen minutes, call the lift back up please. I might not be able to bring it back if there's a technical problem or something. If you call the lift and I'm not in it, well then I'm not sure what you'll have to do. Get the girls, and call Boffin. Anyway, whatever happens, don't just leave me down there, OK?!'

'Fine,' said Tom, trying not to sound too disappointed, but impressed by his elder brother's confidence.

Inside, however, Will was feeling very far from confident. He passed Tom a walkie-talkie. 'Channel three, OK? I've got a camera so I can take a few snaps if there's anything of interest. Don't wander off!'

'Roger that,' said Tom, suddenly excited again.

'Synchronise watches on my mark, little brother. It will be 11.57pm in five, four, three, two, one . . . mark!'

'Got it.'

The lift door was still sitting open, as they'd left it. Tom helped Will to pull back the metal gate, which moved surprisingly easily. Like the doors around the central chamber, this too seemed to have been oiled in the not–too–distant past.

'No time to worry about that now,' said Will, 'just keep your eyes peeled,' and he pulled the gate shut behind him. The car felt steady under his feet. 'Seems OK,' he said to Tom through the open ironwork, doing a small experimental hop and trying to sound reassuring. He looked about him for buttons to select his destination. The only interruptions in the panelling were those strange wheels.

'How odd.'

'What is it?' asked Tom.

'No buttons for the level, just these wheels. . . They've got numbers all over them. Plus this brass handle of course.'

'What's on the wheels then?'

'The larger first wheel looks like it's the floor number – yes, it's on 20 right now, so this must be it. 19 is right below, so if I just rotate this wheel. . .' He pushed the wheel up very slightly so that the number 19 clicked into place. Nothing happened. Will looked at Tom, slightly nonplussed.

'Maybe push it in or something,' Tom suggested.

'No luck,' replied Will. 'I'm going to try the brass lever instead.' He did so, and the doors began to slide shut.

'Once more unto the breach, dear friends, once more,' said Will grinning weakly and reciting the only bit of Shakespeare's *Henry V* he could remember, as he disappeared from Tom's view with an apprehensive wave. *Let's just hope we don't have to close up the lift shaft with our English dead, i.e. me*, he thought, completing the quote with a self-indulgent twist as he plunged into the bowels of the earth.

16 INTO THE BREACH

Will stood alone in the middle of the elevator as the two sets of double doors closed, one set attached to the lift itself, and the other directly behind the metal gates set into the lift shaft walls. His younger brother waved back through the narrowing gap between them. The single bulb above Will's head flickered eerily as the lift car jolted on its way. Curiously enough, it felt to him less as though the lift were moving downwards, as he thought it ought to be, and more as though he was being pulled backwards, and at some very considerable speed. It was as if someone had hooked his stomach with a fishing-line and was reeling him in, as a huge salmon might be played by an angler.

The hairs on the back of his neck stood on end, and the rumbling continued for what seemed like minutes; *perhaps that's what's causing my vision to blur a little*, he hoped, as the images around him became slightly less distinct. Will was starting to feel a bit stupid for having embarked on this without waiting for Boffin's scheduled inspection of the lift shaft.

Then, quite suddenly, the vibrations stopped, and the light shone steadily once again. The musty smell of the oak panels and flooring mixed with old oil and dirt assailed him as the doors began to open. Will held his breath, his stomach now in his throat. What new underworld had he discovered, and what new secrets might it yield, he wondered. He felt as he imagined Howard Carter and Lord Carnarvon might have done, back in 1922, when they opened the tomb of the 18th Dynasty Egyptian Pharaoh Tutankhamun for the first time in thousands of years. 'Let's hope there's no equivalent mummy curse,' he said aloud, steeling himself.

Looking out of the open doors, however, he thought there had been some mistake. The lift didn't appear to have moved at all; in fact, he was still looking out at the Beehive. Irritated that he had needlessly suffered the terror of the rumbling lift, and feeling slightly stupid about how excited he had been, he stepped forward purposefully, and pulled back the familiar Victorian metal gate, drawing it closed again behind him. He looked around. Already cheesed off that his adventure had come to a premature end, he was even more annoyed that Tom appeared to have done an immediate runner, and hadn't even hung around as instructed to check Will was OK. 'You little bas . . .' he began.

'Tom!' he shouted over and over again, 'where the hell are you? Not funny. OK, the lift didn't work. We're going to have to wait for Boffin after all. . . Tom, Tom! Seriously not funny, come out from wherever you're hiding or there will be consequences . . . '

He stood in the chamber, waiting for his brother to jump out and startle him. That's probably what I'd have done, he admitted to himself. Yet still nothing stirred. And then the doubts started to creep in, slowly at first, then more quickly. It was disconcerting. The last time he'd felt like this had been rather embarrassing. He'd turned up for supper with his friend Georgie at the allotted restaurant a week early, and it had taken him three-quarters of an hour to realise he'd got the day wrong, by which time the girls at the desk obviously thought he'd been stood-up on a date.

That was pretty cringing, he recollected, flushing slightly pink at the memory.

He looked around the chamber once more. The floor was the same, ditto the ceiling, and there were robes and cloaks and all sorts of other paraphernalia around the sides of the room. Now he thought about it, however, the table was missing. 'He can't have moved that on his own,' Will muttered under his breath, stepping into the centre where it had stood. The table was made of solid marble, after all. He looked up to inspect the lighting.

'Oh cripes,' Will continued quietly, suddenly noticing that the light filling the chamber wasn't from Boffin's bodged camping-light arrangement dangled from the old chandelier. The chandelier itself was actually illuminated, with a complete set of very antiquated-looking bulbs. He wheeled around to look at the floor indicator above the lift door. It had settled just past the number 19.

'Holy smoke,' he said, under his breath. 'No wonder Tom's not here – he hasn't even been born yet.'

It took some moments for the surreal situation to sink in. A few minutes in a rickety old elevator – if indeed that's what it was – and Will seemed to have been transported back in time. Yes, he had entertained the idea that the elevator might be an intertemporal portal of some kind, given all the mocking clues he and his siblings had found pointing to the extraordinary nature of the lift, but he'd never *actually* believed it. That kind of thing only happened in the Chronicles of Narnia.

'I must have gone back exactly a hundred years,' he mused, wishing very much that one of his siblings was with him. 'Surely I must be dreaming.'

He pinched his arm hard and, failing to wake up, felt his pocket for the camera he had bought with him to take a few shots as evidence for the others. Would the camera even work? Perhaps technology wouldn't function if it was transported back to the time before it had been invented. He pressed the 'on' switch. A quiet electronic chime announced that the digital camera was indeed ready for action, and he snapped a couple of shots of the Beehive, just to make sure.

Suddenly remembering that he'd asked Tom to send a rescue mission after fifteen minutes, he checked his watch. He'd already had perhaps five minutes just standing and gawping. He took a few paces forward, towards the door into the main chamber of Hades. I really hope there's no one here, he thought to himself, placing his head against the door to listen for a while. Not a sound. You could have heard a pin drop or a mouse fart. Then again, the door was extremely solid, so there could be a party in full swing on the other side and he might well not hear a peep. Opening the door just wide enough to slip through, he took a peek out into Hades. The chandeliers were brightly lit, the wall-brackets apparently illuminated with some kind of electric lighting, too. No sign of life at that moment, but certainly signs that the chamber was in regular use.

Stepping back into the Beehive and rummaging around in the legion of cloaks and capes which hung from the pegs, he picked one about his size, and what he imagined was a hat which might have been worn about a hundred years ago – a sort of Sherlock Holmes-style deer-stalker. 'I must look absurd,' he thought, taking a quick selfie.

Silently exiting the Beehive, he tiptoed over to the spiral stairs up into The Old Deanery. The coast appeared to be clear, and he ran as quickly and quietly as he could up the staircase to the secret entrance from the archive. It was shut.

'Probably a good thing,' he muttered, opening it with the catch from the inside after listening once again for signs of life and moving up to look through the keyhole of the archive door. The outer hall was brightly lit. Nearby, he heard the clattering of pots, and shouting.

'Mildred!' shrieked a woman's voice, 'Mildred! I thought I told you to do these pans earlier. . . But they're still–not–washed! It's late and I want to go to bed!' The owner of the voice smashed the pans together with a deafening crash after each word. Several seconds later a short girl with dark hair pushed up under her white linen hat charged past the door towards the old kitchen looking very flustered.

'I'm so sorry Mrs Keen,' she gasped, 'I was just helping Mistress Tiggles with the washing. I'm coming right now. . .'

Will looked at his watch again. Bother, only five minutes left. He doubled back to the Beehive in record time, replacing his outfit on the pegs and dashing back into the lift. Rotating the wheel back to 20, he pushed the brass lever into the upright position, and watched the doors close.

'Please, please, please take me back to the present,' he thought, willing it with all his might, as though that might sway any alternative plans that the mysterious, inter-dimensional elevator might have. Once again, the shuddering stopped after a few short minutes, and the doors opened.

'Crikey, that was quick!' said Tom, looming into view once more.

Relief washed over Will, his old confidence reasserting itself. 'You are *not* going to *believe* this,' he said, unable to contain his excitement. Then, 'Hang on, what do you mean that was quick?' he asked. 'I took nearly the whole fifteen minutes.'

'Erm, no you didn't,' retorted Tom, in a 'how-stupid-actually-are-you' sort of voice, looking at Will as though he were pulling his leg. 'The lift doors closed, and there was some rumbling. Then more rumbling, then the doors opened again and you reappeared. You can't have been gone more than maybe a minute or something. Hold up, did you actually go anywhere or is this a lame prank?!'

'You're just about to find out,' said Will, grabbing his brother's arm and pulling him into the lift and, before

Tom had much time to protest, he'd made a small adjustment to one of the control wheels and the doors were closing once more.

17 1916

'You're right: I can't bally well believe it,' Tom agreed, as the by now familiar wrenching feeling seized Will's stomach, and the overhead light spluttered weakly.

'It's some kind of time-warp, we're actually in a time-warp. This is the discovery of the century, no, wait, the millennium! No wait, all time!'

'Or maybe this is just a dream,' pondered Tom aloud, somewhat crushingly. 'That's probably more realistic, wouldn't you say?'

'This is not a dream, Tom! Everything adds up, as you're just about to see. Look, I'll hit you to prove it.'

'Ouch! Hey, stop that.'

'You see.'

'OK fine, I get it, it's not a dream,' snapped Tom, rubbing his upper arm.

The jolting stopped, and the doors opened once more in the familiar–yet–not–so–familiar Beehive.

'Oh heavens, you really are right,' said Tom, trembling slightly and forgetting the pain in his arm.

'Shhh, we don't know who might be down here. All the lights were on when I left a moment ago and there were some people up in the old kitchen having a bust-up over some pots and pans. You'll be glad to know, therefore, that I shifted the hour control in the lift backwards by several hours, so it should be late afternoon outside rather than just gone midnight.

'Look, grab a disguise from the pegs and let's try and get upstairs and see what we can find out. If I was back in no time when you saw me off earlier, time must run super slowly if we're in the past.'

'Or maybe not at all, given this time has already passed – maybe we're just sort of observers.'

'Interesting thought, but let's crack on,' commanded Will, already rummaging amongst the various costumes. Donning slightly ridiculous cloaks and hats once more, the boys made their way through the still unoccupied Hades and up the stairs into the archive, fortuitously meeting no one *en route*. The archive was rather different from that which they had left in the present day, Tom noticed, with not a dust-sheet in sight. Instead, the room was well ordered, if rather over-filled with old books and mahogany furniture. Its smell, however, remained unmistakeable.

The boys moved silently towards the door up into the main basement once more. Tom opened it cautiously, and peered round the corner. There was no evidence of the melee in the kitchen nor the flustered maid Mildred – evidently that had yet to start, as Will had intended. 'Coast is clear,' he hissed, and they rushed over to the side-door out of the house, and slipped out into the alleyway between The Old Deanery and what in the twenty-first century was to become the youth hostel next door.

'Do you think we could sneak out the back, through the hostel?' Tom suggested.

'No,' replied Will, 'not least because it won't be the Youth Hostel for at least another fifty years – it's still the choir school of the cathedral!'

'Your Sherlock Holmes hat looks completely stupid, by the way,' remarked Tom, grinning impishly. 'You look like a real plonker. Correction – even more of a plonker than usual. . .'

'Oh, thanks for the sartorial advice,' Will retorted sarcastically, but nevertheless removing the hat and stuffing it roughly into his pocket. 'Just try not to look massively out of place,' he added, walking along the alley towards the front courtyard of the house. Peering around the iron gates, the quiet courtyard seemed empty, except for a fine vintage Hispano-Suiza car with running boards parked adjacent to the far wall. The two large sets of gates of the house were rather different from their twenty-first century counterparts – all wooden, for a start – but both were standing open. The most remarkable difference, however, was that the front of the house itself was rendered, which gave it a radically different look.

'I prefer the brick,' Will offered, to no one in particular. 'OK, let's just go for a bit of a wander. Don't attract attention. Stroll quickly but calmly. Try not to interact with anyone – we don't want to get back to the future and discover that, because we inadvertently did something minor to change the course of history, Germany won World War One! If anyone asks us who we are, say we're the Lord Mayor's children – no one will ask any more questions after that. Got it?'

'Got it,' seconded Tom, as the two cloaked figures hurried out across the cobblestones they recognised so well, past the rustling London plane trees, which were rather less large than they remembered, and out into Deans Court, their beloved street.

The first thing they noticed was the grime. Absolutely everything was filthy. The walls, windows and paper posters everywhere were covered in a layer of dark, sticky dust, and the stink of it hung thickly in the air and clung to their faces.

'Smells pretty ripe,' whispered Tom, as the boys turned left at the top of Deans Court and headed down Ludgate Hill.

'I think we can agree that the cloaks were a bit of a

mistake,' Will groaned, already sweating under the woollen garment as the hot late afternoon summer sun beat down upon them. They were attracting some strange looks for wearing winter cloaks in the humid high summer, but it was too late to turn back now. Better to plough on.

'Gosh, there's a bridge over the hill,' observed Tom, pointing ahead to the green-painted wrought-iron structure sitting on stone buttresses. The City's familiar dragons held up the coats of arms of the Corporation of London, two on each side.

The boys ambled down the hill and under the railway bridge, noticing that all the familiar shops and twenty-first century chain restaurants were gone. In their place stood unfamiliar names such as Hope Brothers – 'whatever they sell,' muttered Tom, peering through the plate glass window inquisitively. Firms advertised their wares with large, bold posters, mostly black and white; not a photograph or graphic anywhere in sight. Old London buses with their open-air drivers' stations and staircases at the back up to the exposed top deck trundled past noisily as inspectors in smart dark uniforms barked their demands for tickets. Amidst the hustle and bustle of summer 1916, the boys noticed a number of uniformed men walking about.

'Oh cripes,' said Will, 'of course, it's right in the middle of the First World War, and we must have arrived in the thick of the Battle of the Somme, the bloodiest battle in the history of the British Army!'

'Let's hope no one tries to sign us up,' said Tom, looking around furtively and quickening his pace somewhat, secretly hoping that a wandering recruiting sergeant might target his older brother, who could just look old enough to be eligible if squinted at in the right way. Sure enough, the Evening News paper-sellers who were stationed at the bottom of the hill holding clutches of papers were yelling at the tops of their voices about 'news from the front! The Bosch on the back foot!'

Huge lettering adorned the sides of the Victorian and Edwardian office buildings around them, promoting the biggest brands of their day.

'I've had Bovril,' said Tom, reading one of them. 'Disgusting now, and disgusting then or, er, should I say now?! I'm confused.'

'I'd take Marmite any day,' agreed Will.

'I can't believe how many horse-drawn vehicles there still are in central London,' he added, watching a flatbed cart transporting a teetering tower of beer barrels across the junction, as one of the horses relieved itself on the already filthy street.

'That explains some of the smell, anyway,' commented Tom, sagely. 'It's rather hot isn't it,' he added, tugging theatrically at the cloak–tie around his neck. 'Shall we pop into the pub for a drink?' and he looked thirstily at the King Lud pub opposite them. 'Just a juice or something?'

'Go for a drink? Just a juice!' exclaimed Will, as a man in a top hat bashed roughly past him, nose deep in a newspaper.

'Look where you're going!' the man snapped at him.

'And I'm delighted to meet you too!' Tom shouted sarcastically at the retreating man, gesturing rather rudely after him.

Will smiled. 'And erm, what exactly will you be paying with, little brother?' he asked, condescendingly.

Tom patted the pocket with his wallet in it; then got the point. 'Oh yeah, right. Different century, different coins and stuff.'

'Let's head back in the other direction,' Will suggested, changing the subject and keen to steer his younger brother away from the shady-looking public house with its grimy windows and apparently equally grimy clientele. 'We'll cut round the other side of the cathedral maybe. We don't want to linger too much. The less time we spend here, the better – less can go wrong!'

Pacing back up Ludgate Hill they approached the cathedral, its lower half almost totally blackened with soot and grime, the upper half not much cleaner.

'It's filthy,' remarked Tom in disgust.

'Remember that there are still power stations belching pollution into the air only a few hundred yards away,' Will offered by way of explanation.

Skirting the cathedral churchyard to the north they walked past unfamiliar office buildings and then past the Chapter House, which was completely unchanged, if a little grubbier, towards the junction of St Martin-le-Grand and Cheapside, the old market street at the heart of the City. The boys emerged from the side of one of the drab buildings which stood adjacent to the cathedral to find themselves looking down Cheapside, toward the famous Wren church of St Mary-le-Bow. Awnings protruded from almost every building on the long street, flapping every so often in the gentle summer breeze.

'Obviously they haven't invented road markings yet,' Tom observed, as a rather harried-looking police officer with a gigantic moustache tried to resolved a dispute between two horse-drawn carriages which had got locked together. A queue of petrol-driven vehicles was building up behind the disturbance, their irritated drivers honking aggressively.

'Come on,' said Will, and they walked smartly past the disagreement which was getting ugly, and on down towards the junction at the bottom of Poultry, overlooked by the Royal Exchange, the Bank of England and the Mansion House.

'I've always wondered why this is called Poultry,' Tom said quizzically.

'Like so many streets in the City, it's named after the goods or services that were sold there – in this case, chickens and geese,' replied Will. 'That explains why other streets are called things like Bread Street, Garlick Hill, Wood Street or Skinners Lane. . .'

'It's so busy,' cut in Tom, to prevent Will inevitably listing all the relevant City streets he could think of.

'The funny thing is that it looks far more congested than the modern City. Next time you hear someone complaining about the traffic in 21st century London, just remember this image!' said Will, surveying the chaotic scene in front of them. Six major roads converged at a single junction without any apparent traffic lights or road markings. Hatted pedestrians wandered around, mingling with petrol-driven buses and trucks galore, plus dozens upon dozens of horse-drawn carriages and traps. Various moustachioed police officers tried to maintain some semblance of order, much to the boys' amusement. 'OK, no damage done. Let's head back before we touch something we shouldn't. Perhaps just a quick detour via the river to see the old wharves?' Will suggested, the surreal nature of the experience still sinking in, but his enjoyment growing by the second.

Turning their backs on the Bank of England and leaving the Mansion House – the Lord Mayor of London's vast eighteenth century Palladian official residence – on their left, they dived into the warren of old alleys and passageways which still comprised so much of the ancient heart of the City. Down Walbrook they went – 'named after the stream that passes underneath here, dontchaknow?' said Will, as Tom rolled his eyes and kept going. Across West Cannon Street and onto Dowgate Hill, which ran steeply down towards the river as Will ploughed on with his history lecture, apparently largely for his own benefit: 'The City is, of course, built on two hills, St Paul's is on Ludgate Hill, which is the higher, obviously, and. . .'

But Tom's mind was elsewhere, drinking in the tightly-packed warehouses and old offices, and the smart clothes of the passers-by, many of whom seemed to be wearing tailcoats. As London had not yet suffered the German Blitz bombing of World War II, huge swathes of buildings which in future years would be lost to the bombs and flames still stood proudly, unaware of their date with destiny rather more than two decades ahead.

Tom was also becoming aware that he was attracting the odd strange look, and not just for his magician-style cape with its colourful lining.

'Why are people looking at you oddly?' hissed Will, noticing the same thing and clearly irritated that not everyone was gripped by his monologue.

'I think my trainers might have been a bad call,' Tom replied, glancing at his feet.

Will looked down. 'Oh, you think?!' he said, sharply. 'I simply cannot believe that you wore those lurid shoes, you moron! How did I not spot them in the Beehive? Move your trousers down a bit or something. No, better yet, scuff up the shoes in the gutter.'

'But they're almost new!' protested Tom.

'I don't care, just do it now!' Will replied, directing his younger brother forcefully toward the nearest available – and abundant – source of London grime.

With the lurid orange and green trainers disguised after their close encounter with a particularly foul gutter, Will walked faster, with Tom in a major sulk and jogging slightly to keep up. They were now moving down Upper Thames Street – much narrower and even darker than it was in the modern era – past St James' church, then St Michael's, and on past St Mary's. Will's rambling history lecture continued, seemingly untroubled by the apparent lack of interest from his companion. 'An astonishing reminder that Wren alone built fifty-one churches in the City after the Great Fire of 1666 . . .' he explained, gesturing to the churches.

To their left, vistas to the River Thames would open suddenly between the tall dark brick wharves, before disappearing again just as quickly. Most of the lanes teemed with people, loading and unloading vessels of all shapes and sizes, though others seemed eerily deserted, the small warehouse cranes that sprouted from the buildings' roofs sitting idle, awaiting employment.

'This is extraordinary,' said Tom, moving off down one such avenue. 'Paul's Wharf' the sign proclaimed in large, white peeling letters. The riverscape which unfurled before the boys was both familiar and yet strange at the same time. Thousands of boats and ships of all descriptions lined the banks of the Thames on both sides, though there were more on the boys' side of the water – the north bank. Immediately in front of them, a wooden pier jutted into the river, with a 'T-section' at the far end. The distinctive Thames barges moved slowly from left to right, and right to left. Across the river, huge brick chimney-stacks belched out their putrid black breath only a couple of hundred feet above the busy streets below. Tall wooden stakes the size of tree trunks rose up from the swirling brown waters at intervals along the river, providing mooring points for gaggles of smaller barges and vessels.

'No Thames Walk then,' said Tom, noticing that, unlike in present-day London, there was no walkway permitting access to most of the water's edge. Instead, the wharves jutted out directly into the surging water, allowing boats to pull up beneath their fixed cranes and unload goods directly. A substantial vessel named the *Preston Rhonda* emerged from beneath Blackfriars railway-bridge and steamed at a stately pace toward Southwark Bridge. The name of its proprietor was clear from the large writing daubed on the side: *The Gas Light and Coke Company*.

The boys stood by the quayside for a few minutes, absorbing the hypnotic scene, and the ghastly smell, although the cool breeze provided gentle relief. Will got out his camera and took a few surreptitious photographs, taking care to conceal the electronic device under his long cloak. 'I can't believe how many sailing ships there still are,' he observed.

And then they were marching back to The Old Deanery at top speed, as the late afternoon light shimmering across the brown turbid surface of Old Father Thames receded from view behind them. Five minutes later they arrived back at home – or at least what would become their home in about seven decades' time.

'The gates are shut!' said Will, a note of panic in his voice, as they rounded the corner into Deans Court from Carter Lane. 'We'll have to get around the back.'

'Let's slip through the choir school,' Tom suggested.

'My thoughts exactly.'

The boys waited outside the choir school in the safety of a shaded doorway for their opportunity. After about an hour, as the evening light settled across the City and the shadows of the buildings around them grew longer, a party of choristers, chaperoned by a very formally dressed schoolmaster emerged from the building, and the slow-closing door gave them their chance.

'They must be off to evensong,' said Will, in relief. Slipping stealthily inside, they made their way through the building and out into the back courtyard behind 'their' house. From there, they were able to access the side door of The Old Deanery – which, Will reminded himself, was actually still just The Deanery -- and down to the Beehive. Mercifully, they met no one *en route*, although the echo of excited voices from somewhere higher up in the choir school as they raced through the building made their hearts beat that much faster.

'What an adventure!' beamed Tom, panting.

'Let's just hope we end up back where we began,' said Will, gritting his teeth, as he closed the lift gate behind them, adjusted the control wheels and operated the lever. 'Fingers crossed,' and he held up his hands to Tom, demonstrating two sets of crossed fingers on each.

'How do you do that?' Tom asked, seemingly unconcerned that they were about to embark on a hazardous journey between dimensions.

18 A FATEFUL MISTAKE?

'This will blow your minds!' said Will, practically hopping as the boys led their sisters down to the drawing room the next day to recount the tale, out of earshot of their parents. The girls sat in silence, suspecting a wind-up.

Tilly looked unamused. 'OK guys, very funny. You've had your fun now. Did you actually go down in the lift at all, or are you completely wasting our time?'

'I'll bet on the latter,' said Katherine sceptically, getting up to leave.

'I can prove it all!' said Will, triumphantly pulling his camera out of his pocket with a flourish and brandishing it in front of his sisters.

'They're photo-shopped,' said Katherine finally, after Will had taken them through his half-dozen snaps of riverside London in 1916. 'Though I'll give it to you on this occasion – this is one of your better practical jokes.'

'They are not fakes,' said Tom, firmly.

'If you are telling the truth – and I'm not saying I believe you,' Tilly added cautiously, 'but if you are telling the truth, you've been very stupid indeed.'

'What do you mean?' the boys demanded in defensive unison.

'You've got no idea what you might have done by changing something in the past which has then rippled through time to the present. Haven't you ever heard of the Butterfly Effect? Perhaps you'd better check that we still won both World Wars!' she said, only half-joking.

Looking slightly panicked, Tom got out his iPhone and went straight for Wikipedia to make sure it was still 2-0 to the Allies.

'Yeah, we still did!' he said defiantly after a few moments, brandishing the results for all to see.

'Nevertheless,' Tilly went on ceremoniously, 'I don't think we should be meddling with the past, if indeed that is what you've been doing.'

'We made it back OK, didn't we?' demanded Will, 'and everything seems the same. I'm not even sure that we could influence things. I mean, suppose that we were always meant to go back in time, so that our being there merely fulfilled actions which we'd already taken, but we just didn't know it yet. In fact,' he continued, 'what if by not going back in time we'd changed things? In other words, we needed to fulfil our fate, or something . . .' he tailed off slightly. He had always been good at thinking on his feet and talking his way out of any situation, but this time he was feeling slightly foolish for getting carried away.

'You've lost me,' said Katherine.

'Me too,' said Tom.

'A bit too clever by half, as usual, William,' interjected Tilly. Her use of his full name was a sure sign of trouble. 'Regardless, it was not very wise. I'm surprised at you, actually. It may be fine to use the elevator – after all, it clearly exists for a reason, though one far beyond our current understanding – but let's hold off until we know more to avoid any, er, unintended consequences.'

Will flushed a deep shade of beetroot. 'You're not Mum, Matilda!' he said angrily, but knowing she was right all the same. 'Anyway, look. I've had another idea, if you'd care to listen, that is?' He glowered at Tilly.

No-one said anything for a while. Tom hummed and whistled an indecipherable tune, deliberately awkwardly, tapping his foot to the beat. Finally, Will recovered himself.

'That Grail map we were looking for in St Paul' s. . .' he began, leaving the idea hanging in the air and looking around for support, his maniacal grin reasserting itself once more.

19 THE INVISIBLE HAND

Having planted the seed of his scheme in the fertile soil of his siblings' minds, Will went looking for his father. He wanted guidance, and he knew that the bishop would have something wise to say; he always did.

Will found him working in his study, which was situated on the ground floor at the back of the house, overlooking the courtyard garden and facing the library. It was a generously-proportioned room, with one wall covered to ceiling height by bookshelves filled with tomes on every topic imaginable. Beneath the shelves were low, lockable cupboards, the repositories of many secrets and early family photographs, some of which Will very much hoped would never see the light of day since they featured him in infancy with an appalling bowl haircut. A fourteenth-century, white teak statue of Jesus Christ stood guard near one of the two doors into the study, and at either end of the room was a desk. The one overlooking the garden from between the two tall sash windows hosted the computer, printer, telephone and other accoutrements of a typical modern office. But the Bishop preferred the gigantic eighteenth–century desk at the back of the room, with its expanding cabinets and secret drawers. The walls of the room were painted a dignified shade of green, befitting the age and style of the house.

That afternoon, Will knocked tentatively on the study door, which was ajar.

'Come,' said his father's voice, almost a growl. The Bishop didn't especially enjoy being disturbed whilst working.

'Hullo, father,' opened Will, trying to keep it light as he walked into the room.

'Hello, William, and what are you up to?' his father asked, leaning back in his chair and lowering his reading spectacles to get a better view of his elder son. Will had always believed his father was something of a mind-reader, and on this occasion he felt particularly sure his thoughts were being probed. He sat down in the old high-backed armchair on one side of the desk.

'Oh, er, not much,' said Will unconvincingly. 'Just been doing a bit of preparatory reading before I head back to school on Monday.'

'I see.'

Was that a note of scepticism in his voice, wondered Will, or was he just being a bit paranoid. Probably paranoid, he decided. Or maybe that was what his father wanted him to think.

'And what have you been reading about?' continued the Bishop, deliberately.

'Um,' Will began, 'I've actually been reading up more about the Grail story you told us about.' He gulped, guiltily. His brow began to sweat slightly, and the effort of thinking about not sweating seemed to make it considerably worse.

'Ah yes.' His father put down the chunky Russian fountain pen he was writing with and closed the lid of the ink well in front of him. 'And what exactly have you discovered?'

'Well, not that much really. It's hard to find original sources. Mostly it's just conjecture and stuff, you know.'

'Indeed.' His father was watching him closely.

Will fidgeted with his phone. 'So, um, you said it was last seen on the night of the Great Fire – the map that is?'

'So the story goes,' said his father. 'Three hundred and fifty years ago this year, of course,' he added, a discernible twinkle in his eye.

'Of course, historians tell us that the fire began by accident in the small hours of Sunday 2 September 1666, in the bakery of one Mr Thomas Farrinor on Pudding Lane – only a short walk from here, as you know. He was a baker to the King's Navy and, at the time of the Fire, rumours spread that enemy agents, probably of France, our most ancient and devious adversary, and against whom we were then waging war – that's been something of a national past-time for the last millennium – had started the fire to destroy the capital of this Protestant country. We were also fighting the Dutch, of course, and Sir Robert Holmes had just burned one of their cities to the ground: West-Terschelling. So people feared London's fire might be revenge.'

'Right, and what's the truth of that?' enquired Will, sitting back in his chair and relaxing into the conversation a little.

'No one today can be sure, of course, but accident is entirely probable. Fires used to happen all the time – the houses were made of wood and other readily flammable materials, and buildings were packed together like sardines. Brick was very unusual. Metropolises teemed with industry; people lived above their shops and forges and bakeries. The summer of 1666 was widely reckoned to have been especially hot and dry, so the City was really a huge tinder–box waiting to burn. And of course then there was the wind.

'Er, the wind?'

'Yes, a strong easterly wind blew across London for the duration of the fire, the aftermath of a storm in the English Channel. It spread burning embers far and wide, making the blaze particularly difficult to control.

'Have you read Mr Pepys' diaries in the course of your research?' he asked rhetorically, continuing without waiting for an answer. 'I do remember, however, in my youth, coming across another remarkable story which is very little known today.'

'Go on,' said Will, leaning forward once more and realising that he was gripping the arms of the chair a little too tightly.

'It was once said that a colourful character by the name of Jules Mazarin was questing for the Holy Grail, and was sighted in London shortly before the Great Fire.'

'Mazarin?' asked Will, confused. 'I've never heard of him…'

'Yes, Mazarin,' the Bishop affirmed. 'His Grand Eminence Jules Raymond, Cardinal Mazarin. An Italian by birth – his name was actually Giulio Raimondo Mazzarino – he succeeded the greatest of the Chief Ministers of the Kings of France, Cardinal Richelieu . . .'

'Richelieu, from the Three Musketeers?' interjected Will from the edge of his seat.

'Precisely. Mazarin succeeded as Chief Minister on the death of Richelieu in 1642, and himself died, officially, at least, in March 1661. He was impressive, though not as great as our old favourite, Richelieu . . .'

'Er, right, I'm not following. What do you mean, 'officially'? How does a man who died five years before the Great Fire come to be hunting the Grail in London that night?'

His father ignored the comment and continued his train of thought. 'Cardinal Mazarin's obsession with precious stones, famous artworks and other treasures was very well known during his own lifetime. He memorably gifted the "Mazarin diamonds" to King Louis XIV in 1661 – the year of his own death – and they subsequently became a small but significant part of the magnificent French Crown Jewels.

'His enthusiasm for treasure extended far beyond mere trinkets such as diamonds and jewels, however. He prized most those things which, he believed, were imbued with special powers – sacred objects, for example, or legendary weapons which had belonged to great warriors of ancient times. He sent agents all over the world to find and recover such objects by force, or guile, or both. Much as Napoleon did a century and a half later; and Hitler after him.'

'But I still don't see how, if he was dead in 1661, he can have been in London just before the Great Fire,' Will objected.

His father looked at him patiently.

'He faked his own death,' said Will, eventually, his eyes widening.

His father said nothing, but smiled slightly.

'So he faked his death to hunt for the Grail?' asked Will.

'Now let me see if I remember. Ah yes, the story was that, with the permission of King Louis, Mazarin would spend the final years of his life hunting down the greatest such treasures the world could offer. And of course the greatest of all these treasures was the cup that Christ used at the Last Supper, the Holy Grail. It was this trail which led Mazarin to London in summer 1666. So the legend went, anyway.'

'How do you know all this?' asked Will, suspiciously. 'And why isn't it more widely known?'

'Oh, I don't know,' said the Bishop, 'probably just a tall story. No identifiable witnesses to the escapade that I remember.' He smiled again, turning carefully back to his writing, straightening in his chair and popping open the ink well once more.

Will persisted, however, ignoring the signal that the conversation was at an end. 'So, um, do you think that he got hold of the Grail map that we've been looking for – er, I mean that Horace was telling us about?'

'Ah, you're talking about St Joseph's Scroll? The directions to the Grail's final resting place in England, according to the legend. I don't know why Horace would have told you it was kept in Old St Paul's. It is conceivable that there was a copy hidden there, of course, as so many other documents were – and, indeed, still are.'

'So where was the original – if it existed, of course?' Will asked, trying not to sound too enthused but feeling the excitement inside him building with every passing moment.

The Bishop stretched out a solid arm, the purple amethyst in his episcopal ring catching the light from the desk lamp. He pointed to a framed drawing hanging on the wall beside the desk. 'Where else, but the ancient fortress of this mighty city? The Tower,' he said, with a dramatic flourish.

Will thought it was one of those moments where he might have expected a distant roll of thunder and a sudden flash of lightning, but the weather today seemed disinclined to oblige. Following the line of his father's arm, Will's eyes settled upon the large and detailed nineteenth–century print of the Tower of London, the sprawling citadel begun by the Normans in the eleventh century to control their new capital, and gradually expanded in succeeding years.

For generations the home of the Crown Jewels, the royal palace had also housed the monarch's menagerie – the repository of exotic animals, from bears to giraffes, gifted to the sovereign from all over the world. The first lions had arrived there in the thirteenth century.

It was also where Churchill had decreed Adolf Hitler should be incarcerated if he were ever captured by the British. Will had actually once seen the loo installed especially for the Fuhrer, hidden in one of the castle's many round towers.

'The Tower?' said Will, looking slightly bemused. 'So King Charles II knew of the existence of the map, if it was housed in one of his royal fortresses?'

'Not necessarily – in fact, very unlikely,' his father replied. 'The scroll's exact location was known to very few people. Amongst them was my predecessor, the former Bishop of London who, by the time of the Great Fire had become Archbishop of Canterbury, Gilbert Sheldon.'

'So, um, the freemasons aren't involved at all are they?' said Will, jokingly.

'Don't believe everything Dan Brown tells you!' said the Bishop, concealing a smile.

'Three Watchmen – including Sheldon – kept the secret of the scroll's existence, protecting the whereabouts of the cup in case it were ever needed again.'

'What do you mean, needed again?'

'I'll leave that to your imagination. Legend has it that, at some point in the seventeenth century, the Watchmen had hidden the map for safekeeping in the Conqueror's chapel in the White Tower, since the Tower was believed to be the safest place in all England. The country had after all been racked by Civil War in the 1640s and early 1650s, and then Oliver Cromwell seized power with a military dictatorship under what was known as the Commonwealth until the return of the rightful King, Charles II, with the Restoration of the Monarchy in 1660.

'Given that Parliament's forces had no idea that the map was in the Tower during their period in charge, it was safe there. But, during the Great Fire, the Tower seemed suddenly vulnerable in a way it had not before. As the flames spread, and efforts to create firebreaks to stop its relentless advance stalled, there were fears that even the Tower itself might not be a safe resting place for the map, lest the burning embers jump the protective moat and catch any of the many wooden rooves of the castle, toasting the contents – not least the vast stock of highly explosive gunpowder.'

'So what happened?' asked Will, consciously closing his mouth which had been hanging open in a slightly gormless fashion. 'In the end, the Tower didn't burn at all, did it?'

'No it did not. But the Watchmen couldn't risk that, of course, and after a hurried meeting they dispatched a troop of loyal soldiers from the Archbishop's private army to recover the case containing the scroll. The soldiers were not, of course, told of the case's unique contents, but instructed to bring it to Sheldon on pain of death.'

'And where was it taken?'

'The case was loaded into a boat at the Tower's Traitors' Gate entrance and rowed out onto the Thames to be taken up the river to Lambeth Palace, the Archbishop's London residence and itself something of a fortress, but crucially at a safe distance from the fire and on the other side of the river.'

'Right, so what happened next?'

'No one alive today knows for certain. Somewhere between the Tower and Lambeth Palace the boat was sunk and some of the escorting soldiers killed, and the scroll's case vanished into thin air – assuming that the legend is true, of course.'

'Or possibly vanished into deep water,' said Will, attempting humour and moving on quickly as it fell flat. 'Seriously, how do you know all this?'

'Oh, it's just an old story William, lost in the impenetrable mists of time, inaccessible to us mere mortal creatures bound by space and time.'

But his father's pointed gaze directly at him and slightly rhetorical tone suggested to Will that perhaps he thought there was something to be done.

Yet Will felt unable to ask the obvious question. *Is he really saying what I think he's saying?* he asked himself. From somewhere deep at the back of his mind he found the answer. He looked again at the picture of the Tower, and then back at his father. 'Anyway, gripping stuff,' he concluded, bracing himself to rise from the chair and leave.

'Of course,' his father continued, allowing himself a wry smile, 'sometimes history does not play out in quite the way it was intended. Or indeed, the way it actually happened,' and he turned slowly back to his writing, the lamplight catching his eyes and momentarily making his eyeballs seem to glow.

'Erm,' said Will, pondering the final riddle, 'OK then – well, see you at supper.'

'Until supper then,' the Bishop replied without looking up, his fountain pen gliding effortlessly once more over the surface of the paper.

20 PLANTING THE SEED

I know what we've got to do, Will repeated to himself as he lay awake that night, replaying the conversation with his father over and over in his head.

Strolling along the bank of the River Thames the following morning with Tilly and Mufasa, the headstrong hound, Will rehearsed his conversation with their father the previous day. As they talked, they meandered their way past the Customs House, heading east along the riverside walk towards the Tower of London.

'I know what he was telling me, Tilly. Somehow he knows. I think he knows about it all, though he's not letting on how. Dad said '*sometimes history does not play out the way it was intended. . . Or indeed the way it actually happened.*' He's telling us to go back and get that scroll, I'm sure of it. Or at least to stop it from disappearing.'

'It does sound very odd,' mused Tilly, as they chewed over the facts. 'And as you say, almost as interesting is the question of how would he know that story anyway if, as he says, there are no records or eyewitnesses, and he's not revealing his sources. I've certainly never heard it. It's very dramatic – surely it would be famous if it was widely known but – well, clearly it's not.'

She paused, thinking, as Mufasa strained to get close to the remains of a chocolate bar lying by the wall between them and the water. 'No, Mufasa!' said Will, yanking him backwards.

Tilly continued. 'Perhaps Hades was used by people to correctly remember history – in other words, to make what happened actually happen? To sort of guard it against manipulation.'

'Come again?' said Will.

'Well, let's suppose for a moment that Hades isn't the only tear in space-time on earth, or indeed off it. There's no reason to suppose this will be the only one, after all. If there is one sitting under The Old Deanery, there could be one somewhere else – or maybe many of them.'

'Logical enough, I suppose,' agreed Will, one cautionary eye on Mufasa who sat sulking at his feet and eyeballing the chocolate bar intently, biding his time to have another shot at it as the two of them paused to look out over the Thames where the scroll was said to have vanished.

'So, if that's the case, and assuming it's possible to influence future events by going back and doing something differently, don't you think it would be a huge temptation to travel back in time and start trying to change things at critical moments?' Tilly suggested. They began to walk on again.

'Or to steal items of historical significance when they are vulnerable, using the benefit of hindsight to work out exactly when that was,' said Will, picking up the thread. 'I suppose Hades could have been used by people who were either trying to change history themselves, or perhaps trying to keep it in order by preventing anyone else with access to the past from – well, mucking it up. So when Dad says sometimes history isn't as it is meant to be, you think he was saying that there are people who have gone back and done things differently?' concluded Will.

Exactly right – or tried to, at least,' replied his sister.

'Tilly, you're a genius!'

'I know.' But she looked pleased.

'Not quite as much of a genius as me, of course,' said Will, as he puffed himself up like a robin.

'Sure,' Tilly teased, jabbing him hard in the stomach so that he had to double over. 'So I think we agree what we've got to do, then. 1666, here we come,' she said, grinning broadly, as Mufasa, clearly still smarting from the loss of the chocolate bar, strained at the leash to catch another overfed City squirrel legging it up the nearest tree.

'There is another possibility of course,' added Will. 'What if the world as it is today is a result of people going back in time to "fix" history? In other words, if we – or anyone else for that matter – failed to go back in time and do something which we were "meant" to,' Will put the word in exaggerated speech marks, 'then things today might be different.'

'So you're saying that, in some circumstances, *not* going back in time might be what changes things today,' said Tilly.

'That's right,' said Will. 'As I suggested the other afternoon, you may remember.'

'Gosh, we are geniuses aren't we?' said Tilly, only half-joking. 'Let's assemble the troops. We've got the whole family descending for Gran's 75th birthday party this weekend, haven't we? That means there will be loads of people around and plenty of distractions.'

'Agreed,' said Will, 'plus that rogue Angus will be in town.'

'He'll probably be very useful,' Tilly agreed, as she glanced up at the mighty walls of the Tower now revealed directly ahead. In front of them lay the wide dry moat, which would once have been fed by water straight from the Thames.

'I might ask him to bring a few bits and pieces from the country then,' suggested Will rhetorically. 'They've got loads of useful outdoorsy-type stuff. Oh cripes, since it's already Thursday, I'd better speak to him tonight. This is going to be epic!'

21 THE CALM BEFORE THE (FIRE)STORM

A very wet, windy and autumnal Friday duly dawned, and with the rain came the deluge of extended family for the end-of-summer-holiday get-together in honour of their grandmother's 75th birthday. Board games would be played, spoof rap–battles joined, and terrible pun-related jokes made aplenty, while the agglomerated adults struggled with the family history of mild narcolepsy. Fun through these gatherings always were, the children had something else on their minds: the mission.

Having performed the obligatory meet-and-greet in the main entrance hall, Will, Tilly, Tom and Katherine sloped off to the basement, taking with them Boffin, and Cousin Angus. About the same age as Katherine, Angus was the son of their mother's brother Charles, and his two sisters were locked in conversation with Boffin's own sisters and various aunts.

'They don't need to come,' said Will, 'not yet anyway,' and he beckoned Angus to follow them all down the back stairs as the grown-ups settled down in the first floor drawing room. Outside, the howl of wind racing down the gaps between the house and adjacent buildings, and the hissing as it passed through the trees, grew steadily louder. Cranberry–sized drops of rain continued to pound the large seventeenth century sash windows as the downpour grew even heavier.

'What's going on?' asked Angus suspiciously, hopping down the stairs two steps at a time, realising that something strange was afoot, and anticipating one of Will's wind-ups.

'You'll see,' said Tom, in a confidential sort of way, tapping his nose with an exaggerated wink and clearly enjoying being in the know.

'We're going to show you something, Angus,' said Will, finally, as they arrived at the entrance to the basement archive. 'But from now on, you are sworn to secrecy. What you are about to see really is worth more than your life, and you will tell no one at all.'

'Is this for real?' asked Angus, looking around nervously. Impassive faces stared back at him.

'Deadly serious,' Tilly replied, uncharacteristically coldly.

'OK, I swear,' said Angus.

'What do you swear?' Katherine enquired.

'I swear that I will not tell a soul what you are about to show me, and I will take the secret to my grave.'

'Damn right you will,' said Tom, stepping forward rather menacingly.

Then after a moment everyone smiled, and Angus relaxed a little. 'Come on then, what on earth requires this secrecy?'

'This way,' directed Will, leading the party into the archive and down into Hades through the secret door, taking care to close it behind them.

It had taken Angus several minutes of near hyper-ventilation to recover from being shown the hidden underground kingdom – not through any fear, mind you, but due rather to over-excitement. A mischievous Just-

William type who enjoyed catapults, cricket and, like Will, practical jokes, Angus gawped at his new surroundings. Repeatedly pinching himself, he walked around Hades, and into the Beehive. A quick trip in the elevator with Tilly and Boffin to see a previous incarnation of the room a full hundred years earlier was enough to convince him of the truth of the tale the others had told him.

Will, Tom and Katherine waited in the main chamber, and the three travellers returned in barely a minute, having reportedly spent far longer in the past. Retreating to the rather warmer confines of the library – not least so that the adults wouldn't get too suspicious about their immediate disappearance – Will concluded the story, and what they had discovered so far. He included an account of his conversation with his father two days previously; and the discovery, by means of various other exploratory time-hops, that the additional control wheels in the elevator allowed you to select the hour of an individual day as your destination, in any month of any year. Or at least, any year back to 1066 AD, the year of the Norman invasion of Britain. They hadn't yet dared go further back, though there didn't seem to be any reason this would not be possible.

A fifth wheel replete with strange symbols on it, which the children had originally spotted embedded horizontally below the four others, had not yet been deciphered, so for the time being they had decided not to meddle with it on a better–safe–than–sorry basis.

'So there you have it,' Will finished, sitting back in his chair.

Tilly picked up the thread. 'So really what we're saying is that we think that we have a unique opportunity to rescue the lost scroll and, potentially, discover the location of the Holy Grail ourselves. Clearly, it's massively risky, as we've got practically no idea what we're doing – and we're running out of time to do it,' she added, noting that everyone would be back to school in only a few days, and that they could not be sure that the portal was always open, although it currently appeared to be so.

Will went on, 'It's not only that we think we *could* do this – it's that we think we *should* do it. The trail of breadcrumbs has led us here for a reason. We've arrived at the gingerbread house at the end of the path. . .' He tailed off, realising the feebleness of the metaphor.

Excited glances were exchanged by all nonetheless.

'Everyone will be back to school next week, and we'll need Boffin, and probably Angus, if we're going to pull it off – assuming you're both up for it, of course?' Will added.

'I'm game,' said Angus immediately, pulling a catapult out of his pocket as a gesture of commitment. Boffin nodded, too.

'You're right,' agreed Tom. 'We need to crack on as soon as possible. What's the plan, Will?'

'I think we're going to have to go tomorrow night,' Will replied. 'The legend suggests that the scroll was moved from the Tower up the river by boat towards Lambeth. We have a couple of options. First, we can try and sneak into the Tower, get to the Conqueror's chapel ourselves, and grab the case . . .'

'We don't actually know where it's hidden though, do we?' put in Katherine.

'No, we don't, Will agreed. 'And obviously there are risks in being caught sneaking around in a Royal fortress which houses the crown jewels!'

Tom winced, imagining being subjected to the rack or the scavenger's daughter any of the other ghastly punishments which he had learned about in History at school.

'Plus it would be very hard to get into the Tower in the first place,' Will added, 'what with it being a heavily defended castle and everything. Apart from anything else, in the seventeenth century the Tower still had its huge moat, which was filled with water from the Thames.'

'So what's the second option?' asked Angus from the edge of his seat, apparently itching to get going.

'Well, the other obvious option is that we keep the Tower under observation and wait for the boat carrying the scroll–case to leave. Then we keep that under surveillance and wait for our opportunity to recover it. It's not a problem if it gets to Lambeth Palace, because then we'll know that the story was wrong and it made it to its destination after all; and anyway I know the Palace well, and we could probably get in and recover it from there if we needed to.'

'And what if it's stolen *en route?*' asked Tilly, voicing the question everyone was thinking, 'or the boat sinks . . .'

'Well then, we'll have to be close by on the river, ready to intervene,' replied Will, optimistically.

'Right, and we're taking our own motor boat back with us, are we? What about a couple of jet-skis?' asked Tom, sarcastically, 'or perhaps you'll be asking Boffin to construct a makeshift submarine, crucially of a size that can fit in a lift?!'

'There were two thousand Thames ferrymen at the beginning of the seventeenth century, Tom, so there'll still be some in 1666 and we'll be able to requisition one of them,' Will replied testily, having already thought it through, though hoping that the Great Plague of 1665 hadn't wiped out all the ferrymen.

'What, when the whole city's burning and people are fleeing for their lives, and we're going to form an orderly queue at the river–taxi rank?' asked Tilly, sceptically. 'I hardly think so.'

'Look, we'll just rent one early, before the whole thing kicks off,' Will answered, thinking quickly on his feet.

'And what money will we be using for that, precisely?' asked Tom, turning Will's earlier sarcastic enquiry outside the King Lud pub in 1916 back on him.

'Already thought about that as well,' shot back Will, smugly. 'Tom, you remember the tunnel that we explored a few weeks ago, which took us into the sewer network and down to the old Fleet river?'

'Yup,' replied Tom warily, remembering the unpleasant experience and already thinking he knew what was coming.

'And the right fork up toward the Barbican?' continued Will.

'Yup . . .' Tom did now know exactly where this was heading. 'Oh, I see where you're going with this – and no, before you ask, I don't want to.'

'What are you planning now?' asked Katherine. 'And when have you been in the other tunnels without me and Tilly?' she added, indignantly.

'Oh, we were just checking them out, for security and stuff, you know,' said Tom, nonchanlantly, picking offhandedly at something under his fingernail.

'Aaaannyway,' said Will bringing the conversation back to the point, 'that sewer passes right underneath the Museum of London, and – of particular interest for us – its historic City Collections vault, basically a huge storeroom of all the stuff they don't have on display. And guess what they've got a lot of . . . ?'

Silence greeted his dramatic question. Will appeared frustrated that his audience wasn't playing along. 'Coins, obviously! I know, because I've seen them; and a lot of them are in pretty good nick. So that's our seventeenth century holiday spending money sorted.'

'Sorry, boys, but I am simply not going down the sewers,' said Tilly, looking revolted and playing unconsciously with her long blonde hair. 'Just totes not my scene at all. I mean, what if people knew I'd been in a *sewer? Ewww* . . . And think of all the enormous rats down there. *Definitely not for me.*'

'That's OK.' said Will, 'because Boffin's going with Tom, aren't you Boffin?'

'I, er, well, OK. I mean I'd probably rather no . . .'

'Grreeeeeeaaaaatt,' Will cut in, 'just great. You'll be

fine, Boffin. Thanks a lot for volunteering. Really decent of you.'

'But I said. . .' began Tom.

Will cut in quickly again: 'OK, guys – you need to make sure you get the correct coinage. And get plenty of it. That access ladder goes right up to the drainage grate on the floor of the vault. A decent pair of bolt-cutters will see you through.'

'Oh, brilliant – *"a decent pair of bolt cutters will see us through"*,' mimicked Boffin, looking flustered and glancing worriedly at Tom.

Suddenly flushed with responsibility and realising he'd be able to order Boffin around, however, Tom quickly dropped his hostility. 'Roger that,' he said, saluting smartly.

'I feel sick,' murmured Boffin queasily, imaging what ghastly horrors awaited them in the gloom of Joseph Bazalgette's Victorian sewer system.

Will ignored him. 'Take a couple of sturdy bags, don't linger in the vault, and for God's sake don't get seen or, worse, caught. Being arrested for burglary wouldn't be a marvellous start to the mission. We'd have to start by going back in time to prevent you from cocking it all up in the first place – assuming we can, of course.'

Angus and the girls chuckled, and even Boffin managed a weak smile as he scratched his tousled mop of hair nervously and straightened his glasses.

'I'll dig out a couple of contemporary maps,' suggested Tilly. 'Dad's collection of old London maps is right . . . here,' she said with a little effort, pulling out a large drawer in the chest behind Will.

'Great,' he said, jumping out of the way. 'I'll start putting together a plan, and some of the kit.'

'Can we be ready to go tomorrow night after supper, do you think?' he asked looking around. 'Oh, yeah – what about costumes?' he added.

'Costumes?' asked Tom suspiciously, and then, remembering suddenly that his regular shorts and t-shirt combo might look a bit odd in Restoration London, 'oh right, yeah.'

'Boffin, let's have a separate discussion about the equipment and support requirements,' suggested Will. 'I reckon we keep the team going to grab the case small – I don't want to draw too much attention if at all possible. But we've got an ace up our sleeve, haven't we?' he added, his maniacal grin reappearing.

'Tech,' said Boffin, finally.

'*Précisement, mes amis*,' Will agreed, in a dire, mock-French accent.

'We can use our walkie-talkies, night vision scope, cameras, torches, blah blah blah. It'll be a huge advantage.'

'Where did you get the night-vision scope from?' Tilly asked, accusingly.

'Oh, I brought that', piped up Angus, cheerily. 'Dad won't notice it's gone for ages – he only takes it out to the Western Isles with him, and that's all over for the summer now anyway.'

'The other thing we could do,' suggested Tilly, thinking aloud and turning to look at Boffin, 'is to use drones.'

'Brill idea,' said Tom. 'Then we can keep track of what's going on from overhead.'

'Excellent!' Will agreed. 'That's more like it, team.'

'Boffin, have you got anything which could be a sort of "eye in the sky" overhead so you can play overwatch? Could be jolly useful if we get lost, plus you can let us know if we're missing anything, watch out for the Cardinal's minions and just generally keep an eye on us.'

'Should have just the thing,' said Boffin, confidently. 'Also, I might have a little one you could fly down chimneys or through open windows to, you know, check stuff out. See if anyone's hanging around, *etcetera*,' he added, accentuating the last word.

Tom's eyes were practically popping out of his head in anticipation of the great adventure. 'This is a bit like the

Famous Five crossed with Mission Impossible,' he said breathlessly, 'except with . . .' he paused to look around and double-check his maths '. . . with six of us.'

'Sounds like we've got our work cut out then,' said Will with a smile. 'OK, Tom, you're in charge of drones from our side as you and I will be the snatch team. Make sure you can use the micro-bug thing Boffin was talking about. No doubt it will come in handy.'

'Boffin, you help Tom, and sort the eye-in-the-sky, please. And do remember there'll be a decent wind blowing so it will need to be able to cope with that. You and Tilly will be our base team; we'll have to identify a good hiding place for you whilst we go in for the smash and grab.'

'Katherine, can you try and put some costumes together with Tilly; make sure we look the part?'

'Ha,' replied his sister, 'No gender-stereotyping in the roles we're all playing then, Will?! I'm going to make you look particularly silly.

'Correction,' she added sweetly, 'even sillier than you already look in that t-shirt.'

Will looked down at his favourite t-shirt, which was emblazoned with a large toucan and advertised Froot Loops cereal. 'Thanks a lot,' he said in a resigned voice, as Katherine and Tilly headed off to the basement storeroom where old clothes, costumes and bedding could be found, and would shortly be chopped up and stitched back together.

'Use that book on seventeenth century historical costume, will you?' Will shouted after them, suddenly appreciative of their father's somewhat niche interest in historical dress.

'We don't need that to make you a peacock costume, Will!' Tilly retorted, disappearing through the library door.
'I'd better help you find the right coins,' Will continued, leading Tom and Boffin over to the reference book section for a briefing using one of the library's encyclopaedias of

historic British coins.

'Let's reconvene here tomorrow, after family lunch,' said Will. 'Right, now try not to look too guilty,' and with only 24 hours to go, the rest of them filed out on their various errands. The game was afoot.

22 GEARING-UP

At just past three o'clock the following afternoon, the six conspirators were to be found assembled once more in the library. A slight pong hung in the air.

'Stop looking at me like that,' said Tom, testily, noticing the girls' pointed glances and quiet sniggers. 'I've already had two baths. The sewers were quite full. It was sodding raining when we went down there, wasn't it?! All sorts of foul things came floating past us and a lot of it got in over the top of my boots.'

'That's as many baths as you had all last year, isn't it?' Will enquired, in mock surprise.

'Thanks a lot, Will,' Tom replied sulkily. Boffin looked equally unimpressed, though he had somehow managed to disperse the smell rather more successfully.

Will allowed himself a crocodilian grin. 'Well, you did a fine job, team, and the good news is, Tom, that you'll fit right in with the smells of Restoration London. What a haul!' he added, looking at the large cloth bags of crowns, half-crowns, pennies and halfpennies which the boys had retrieved from the Museum's storage vault.

'We're only really borrowing them,' he said, looking slightly embarrassed to have lifted coins from the neighbourhood museum. 'We're not *really* stealing. We'll give most of them right back,' he reassured everyone. 'Great, so we've got the money,' he continued, idly rotating a well-worn half-crown in his fingers and examining the faded detail. Tom patted the heavy bag of historic cash with the satisfaction of a man who'd just eaten a large meal and was admiring a rather full stomach afterwards. The sack made a deeply satisfying metallic rustle every time Tom moved it.

'Maps covered,' said Tilly, clutching a tightly-rolled bundle of photocopies.

'Costumes downstairs,' said Katherine, somewhat flatly, resigned to the fact that she would not be embarking on this adventure herself. Not at first, at any rate.

'Ditto drones and tech,' said Boffin.

'Super. Then let's go and do a dry run,' said Will, leading them all off to Hades.

The team spent the next couple of hours checking and re-checking all their equipment and plans, and trying on their historic costumes. The girls had done a remarkable job in fashioning fairly authentic-looking late seventeenth century outfits from what was available in the dressing-up room. Predictably, however, not everyone was happy.

'Why do *I* have to be dressed as a *peasant*?' Tom sulked, clearly deeply aggrieved.

'So that no one will want to talk to you, *obviously*,' said Katherine. 'Not that anyone would want to anyway,' she added, laughing. Tom shot daggers at her.

'But why does *Will's* costume look so much better?' he asked angrily, eyeing the smart arrangement of waistcoat, trousers ending below the knees with boots, and a decent-sized lace ruff-like collar, all composed of fine materials, which the girls had produced for his brother. Topping it all off was a Captain Hook wig and moustache and a wide-brimmed hat with a theatrical feather emerging from it. By contrast, Tom was wearing similar trousers, although made out of what appeared to be an old mail-sack, a baggy off-white shirt and crude, ill-fitting waistcoat of his own and a particularly ridiculous hat, like a sort of cloth swimming-cap with a bit that came down on each side of his head, covering the ears. The girls could barely conceal their silent laughter and tears rolled down their cheeks. Boffin, too, was openly weeping with laughter at the spectacle, doubling over and holding his sides.

'Because in the seventeenth century he's your *master*,' Tilly explained, gleefully.

'And *you're* the servant,' continued Katherine, revelling in the mental torture that this inflicted on Tom, who groaned again, knowing his older brother's ego had just expanded yet further to unimaginable proportions.

'Suits the natural order of things anyway,' Will said, cackling enthusiastically, and secretly loving his outfit, which he thought made him look a bit like a gentleman pirate.

Beneath their slightly billowing seventeenth century disguises, the boys wore their own clothes – dark cargo trousers rolled up to the knees and T-shirts – and various harnesses and pouches which concealed equipment, including their walkie-talkies, binoculars, maps and various other bits and pieces.

A few yards away, Boffin and Tilly were checking through their own equipment, from which they would remotely direct the boys, and use the drones to keep an eye on them and the scroll case. The girls had obviously skimped on Tilly's and Boffin's costumes; given that, ideally, neither would be revealing themselves at all, this didn't seem to matter too much. Boffin's merchant outfit was just about passable, indeed it rather suited him, but Tilly was essentially dressed in a series of sack cloths, and looked decidedly less glamorous than usual.

'You look like you're modelling something from the *Derelicte* collection,' said Tom, snapping at her vengefully.
'The *what* collection?' asked Tilly, pretending to be

unbothered.

'It's a reference from Zoolander,' Will laughed, marching across to the shelves and removing his outfit. 'It's the villain Mugatu's fashion collection, made out of bits of rubbish.'

Tilly rolled her eyes. 'What*ever*,' she said, dismissively, holding up the palm of her hand.

Their pre-game checks complete, the six conspirators trooped off to the evening's festivities – their grandmother's seventy-fifth birthday party – after which the mission would begin.

23 INTO THE UNKNOWN

After a typically delicious birthday supper cooked by their mother and three intense rounds of the board game Articulate later, the family curse of mild narcolepsy was taking its toll. As adult members of the family gradually began to snooze loudly in their seats, most sounding not unlike dozing walruses, Will indicated that it was time to move.

'Have you got an idea of where we're going to hide you?' Tom asked Tilly and Boffin as they slipped out of the drawing room, through the haunted main corridor, and trooped down the back stairs.

'Yep, we're going to hide out in the tower of Old St Paul's to start with,' said Tilly.

'Are you completely insane?!' asked Will. 'You do know that the cathedral gets burned to a crisp in the fire, don't you?'

'Yeah, yeah, we know, but not until the third day; and it's the tallest point in the City by far, so we'll have a jolly good view of what's going on. Plus we'll be able to launch and recover the drones easily from there – people below will just think they're birds probably,' Tilly added.

'And what are you going to do when the fire catches

the scaffolding and you're sitting in the middle of an inferno?' asked Will, dubiously.

'Take a look at this,' Tilly said, holding out one of the maps she'd extracted from the chest earlier, depicting details of the immediate vicinity of Old St Paul's and the medieval Deanery. A web of faint lines was superimposed over the top of the map.

'What is it?' asked Tom, leaning in.

'Well, we're pretty sure this shows where the tunnels run to. Or at least ran to in 1665, the year the map was made,' said Tilly, pointing to the tattered bottom corner of the paper where the date was inscribed in faded ink. 'If you didn't know the tunnels were there you'd probably think it was just how the paper was folded or something. But it matches up for sure. And this tells us that the St Paul's tunnel existed even for *Old* St Paul's. So we'll have direct access back here from the cathedral. And we know this place survives the fire unscathed, don't we, so it's a fool-proof plan!'

'I'm very impressed,' commended Will, sounding for once as though he genuinely meant it. 'Right, well let's hope we don't need the full three days anyway, but everyone make sure you've got your allocated food and drink rations, as well as water purification tablets. There aren't going to be any fast food shops if we get hungry. And, crucially, remember that London experienced the Great Plague in 1665, and it's still infected in 1666. Much of the food stock is riddled with rats and fleas.'

'Check,' replied Tom, patting his bulging haversack which was filled with chocolate bars, biscuits and bottled water, as well as various other pieces of equipment.

'Do you have anything for self-defence?' asked Angus.

'Well, I've got my sword,' said Will, clasping his hand around the handle of the entirely blunt weapon which they had lifted from above the fireplace in the drawing room. 'But you're right, Angus, we probably should take something else.

'Grab some of those Chinese firecrackers, Tom,' he suggested, secreting a couple of packs himself in the hidden bandolier he wore which already contained a dozen Enola Gaye Burst paintballing smoke grenades.

'They're not exactly lethal,' he went on, handing Tom several more firecracker packs, 'but if we find ourselves in a sticky spot or need a diversion, my bet is they'll be a bit of a shock to seventeenth-century Londoners.'

'Excellent idea,' Tom said, gladly taking the palm-sized blocks of fire crackers and stuffing his available cargo pocket with as many as he could.

'Hadn't you better wrap them in something, to protect them from the heat?' asked Tilly, dryly. 'You're just about to embark on a journey around London hours before the Great Fire begins, and Tom's marching into it with a pocket full of fireworks.'

Tom looked accusingly at Will, as though this were some outrageous prank too far or an assassination attempt. Will shrugged and muttered something about it being a jolly good point, and that Tom should go and wrap the fire crackers up in silver foil and put them in his backpack, not in his pocket. 'Just in case!' he added, nervously.

'There's not a lot of room in here, you know', said Tom, trying to find space in his haversack. 'I'm not a pack animal – I don't have unlimited carrying capacity.'

'You'll be absolutely fine,' said Will, unsympathetically, marching over and stuffing the firecrackers down one side of the bag, adding with a grin, 'your discomfort is an important part of the illusion of you as my servant. Right, well I suppose we've got everything we need.'

'Are we insane to be even thinking about doing this?' asked Tilly.

'Yes, of course, but that's why it's so much fun,' Will replied. 'Destiny calls – or at least we'd better all hope it does!' he added with a forced laugh.

'Agreed!' said Katherine and Tom in unison.

'OK – Boffin, you're flying top cover, right? So we'll get you and Tilly up into the belfry first, and then you get the drone up overhead. You'll be the eyes and ears of the operation. Tilly will stay with you, navigating with the maps and helping cover the radio. Once we've done that, Tom and I will try and get close to the Tower of London, and hole up somewhere to keep Traitors' Gate under observation whilst waiting for the Archbishop's boat to appear.'

'Oh yeah, one last thing,' Katherine said, handing round small squirty bottles Tilly thought she recognised from Mufasa's private supplies cabinet.

'What's in these?' asked Boffin suspiciously.

'These, my dear family, are bottles of high strength flea repellent. And you need to *cover* yourselves in it. As Will said, don't forget that London's in the middle of a Great Plague, and it's the fleas spreading it. This stuff should keep you safe. Fleas of the 1660s won't ever have been exposed to it, either, so it should be especially effective.'

'You are marvellous,' said Will, beaming, and lathering himself up in the repellent, even running his fingers through his wig as though applying conditioner. The others followed suit.

'Gosh, you're even more repellent now than you were before,' Tom said to Will, much to everyone else's amusement. Even Will managed a laugh.

Despite her contribution, Katherine looked sullen, as did Cousin Angus. 'And what am *I* going to be doing during all this, exactly?' she enquired in a sarcastic tone.

'You're our back-up little sis,' said Will, firmly. 'You, too, Angus. I'm sure we'll need you at some point.' Quite how Katherine and Angus would be providing the back-up was left rather vague, and they seemed understandably unsatisfied. 'Look, Kate, we need someone here to cover things at this end. You won't even notice we've gone because, judging by previous forays down through the portal, time spent in the past does not mean time spent in the present.'

'Logical enough, if the time has already been spent,' mused Boffin, rhetorically.

'Fine then,' said Katherine, sounding slightly more upbeat. 'Just look after yourselves,' she added, as they filed into the Beehive and on into the elevator laden with kit and supplies.

'All for one. . .' said Will, turning to face Katherine and Angus, '. . . and one for all,' as everyone repeated the famous refrain of the Three Musketeers. The boys offered mock salutes, twisted the dials to the pre-agreed year, month, day and hour, pulled the brass lever to the "down" position and disappeared from view as the lift doors closed and the familiar rumbling began.

The South Front of Old St Paul's Cathedral. The spire is missing: it burned down in a lightning storm in 1561

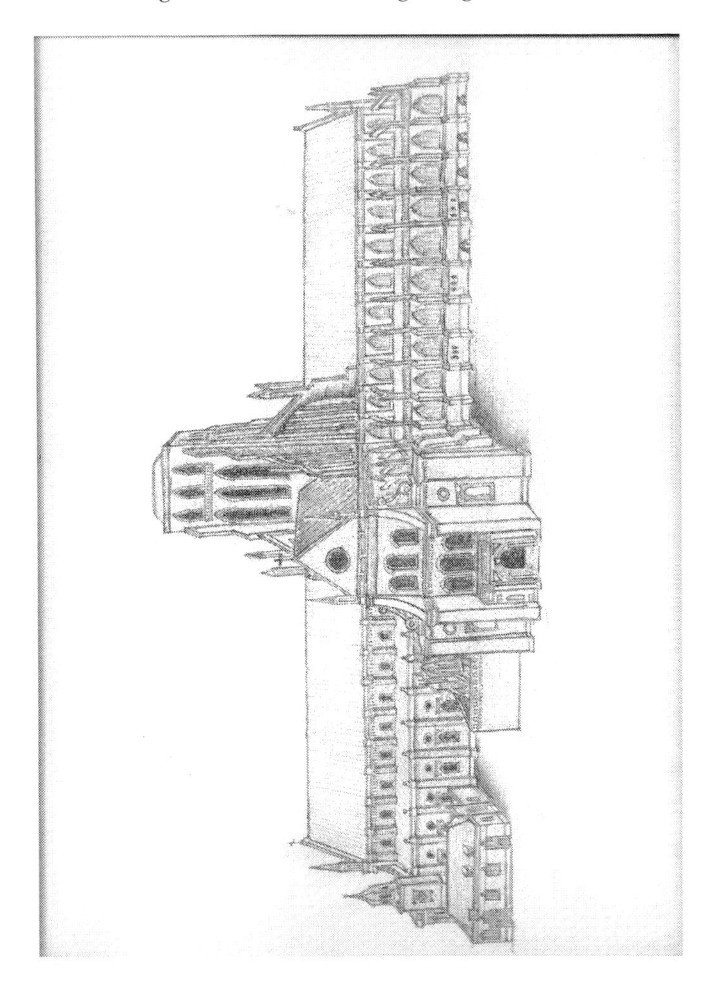

24 EYE IN THE SKY

The lift jolted to a halt with its familiar clunk, and the doors slid open to reveal total darkness. There was not a speck of light to be seen, save that emanating from the open lift itself.

'Torches on,' said Will, drawing the metal gate aside, and four beams flicked on after some fumbling noises. The light showed the Beehive to be much as they remembered it, with only a slightly different – less extensive, and rather more moth-eaten – selection of robes, cloaks and disguises hanging on the pegs around the walls.

'See if there's anything else useful here,' Tilly suggested. Tom rummaged through the selection and pulled out a couple of helpful additions to their outfits: a long cloak for Tilly, and something similar for himself.

'Onwards and upwards,' directed Will, checking that the false facial hair Kate had given him was still stuck in place, and motioning to the closed door into Hades. 'Careful now . . . Let's try and avoid running into anyone.'

Hades, too, was enveloped in total darkness. Like the Beehive, it looked remarkably unchanged, though similarly lacking in electric lights. Torchlight revealed tallow candles, partially burned, in the wall–brackets and more primitive iron chandeliers suspended overhead. The tapestry hangings, however, were much clearer, their colours less faded with age. Now the explorers could see legendary scenes from British history depicted in exquisite detail. Will recognised King Alfred the Great of Wessex amongst the characters, but they had no time to investigate more closely.

Making their way toward the entrance to what they hoped would still be the St Paul's tunnel, the team noticed that the door was different. Altogether older, it was made of tightly fitted thick wooden plank sections, held together with heavy ironwork.

'No lock,' said Boffin.

The door swung open, creaking so loudly that they feared anyone within a hundred yards would hear it. Trekking up the passageway which was lined with much older, darker stones in place of the carefully–laid red brick to which they were accustomed, the party came eventually to the ascending stairs, rising inexorably toward Old St Paul's. The heavy stones forming the walls on either side told them that they were passing through the ancient foundations – comprised of Caen stone, shipped from Northern France – up into the belly of the vast building.
Reaching the end of the passage, they arrived at a spiral staircase, and an extremely narrow one at that. About two minutes of climbing brought them to the first door, which they assumed to be an exit into the crypt.

'But we don't want this one . . .' Tilly reminded everyone, leading the way past it, already somewhat breathless under the weight of all her bags and provisions. The staircase rose up and up and up, twirling around so tightly that Will was starting to feel slightly sick. This sensation was made considerably worse when Boffin let out a series of loud retching noises directly behind him.

'Boffin, if you're sick, I will be too!' Will warned, only half-joking. 'And I'm ahead of you, so that won't be good for either of us.' Boffin drew a dramatic breath; then continued.

They passed half a dozen other small doors on the way up, but kept climbing. Each one of the adventurous four carried a portion of the equipment and supplies, and they sweated with the weight of it all, squeezing themselves up in the tight space, the buckles and bags scraping against the dirty stone walls. The fact that they wore heavy period costume over normal clothes didn't help either. Eventually, after what seemed an eternity, Tilly reached the final small wooden door, and the stairs wound no further.

'Here goes . . .,' she said, turning the iron ring handle gently. The door opened easily enough, and they were through. Everyone looked around for signs of life. They had arrived at the end of their trek, near to the top of the central tower of Old St Paul's. The structure was open all the way up to the flattish stump roof now above them, and a strong breeze whistled eerily through the high gothic arches, three of which punctuated each side. Glancing back at the door, they realised that it was faced with a thin layer of the same stone as the surrounding structure, making it blend almost invisibly into the wall.

'The gigantic old spire burned down in a lightning strike of 1561,' wheezed Will, gazing around from a doubled-over position as he fought to regain his breath following the exhausting climb. 'Before that it was the tallest building in Europe. Four hundred and eighty-nine feet – that's over one hundred and twenty feet taller than our own St Paul's . . . Phew, I'm knackered.'

A walkway, about ten feet wide, ran around the tower at this level. In the opposite corner from the one where they had emerged, the four of them could see a door where another, non-secret, staircase must emerge and provide access for regular cathedral staff. An internal stone balustrade prevented them from plunging into the bells at least a hundred feet below, but such was the darkness of the lower portion of the tower that it was like standing at the edge of a huge, deep well from which light could not escape. All they could see of the tower seemed to be in a parlous state of structural repair, as did the rest of the building.

'It's crumbling anyway,' said Will, looking around at the battered old stonework and managing at last to stand upright, having deposited his load of bags.

'Guys, look at this,' said Tilly, also puffing hard, and staring out of one of the enormous gothic arches, probably twenty feet high, which faced south across the Thames.

'Oh my . . . ,' Boffin didn't even finish the sentence.

More than three hundred feet below them, seventeenth century London spread out, bathed in bright moonlight. Only a few twinkling lights and torches were visible outside residents' houses and shops. Other than that, there was no general street lighting of any kind, and of course the discovery of electric lighting was still a century and a half away. The river banks teemed with small rowing boats, and larger sail contraptions, though these mostly hugged the north side. 'Of course, south of the Thames isn't London at all at the moment,' Will explained as they looked out over what appeared to be an expanse of farmland on the other side of the silvery serpent which wound past the capital. 'It's still controlled by the Bishop of Winchester'.

It wasn't entirely barren, however. Buildings followed the edge of the river on the opposite bank, in some places several rows deep, and a larger built-up area could be seen at the southern end of London Bridge, almost like a small town in itself. Shakespeare's famous whitewashed Globe Theatre stood amongst a cluster of other entertainment centres, including the Rose Theatre and a bear-baiting arena. Yet many fields were still visible in the moonlight beyond Old Father Thames which, unembanked, was much wider and flowed more slowly.

'No bridges at all, then,' said Tom, 'apart from – oh wow, guys, look at Old London Bridge!'

To their left, Old London Bridge towered above the

dark swirling waters beneath, packed nearly its whole length with houses and other structures, except for a gap in the buildings right at the northern end where a previous fire had left a void which had yet to be rebuilt. Many of the structures looked very grand in the half-darkness.

'Smells a bit, doesn't it?' Boffin commented after a while, sniffing the air loudly to drive home the point. Even up in the tower, the combination of dung, putrefying rubbish, livestock, and a lack of personal hygiene or any proper sewage system filled their nostrils with a ghastly stench.

'You could look at this forever,' Tilly said wistfully, struggling to take in the view. 'I even studied this at school.

'If only all history teaching was this engaging!' she added, with a sigh.

'You could,' agreed Will, breathing more evenly now, 'but, ironically, time's not something we've actually got a lot of this evening, so let's help you two get set up here and then Tom and I will steal off to establish ourselves near the Tower somewhere.'

At that point, Tilly turned back to her older brother and immediately snorted with laughter.

'What is it?' asked Will, clearly anxious to get on.

'It's just –,' said Tilly, now laughing hard, 'you do look very silly with that fake – ha, ha – fake moustache. Captain Hook, eat your heart out.'

Will grinned. 'Needs must,' he replied, stroking his upper lip theatrically.

Boffin at last tore himself away from the view to set down his vast and unwieldy backpack and holdall, both crudely disguised with patches of hessian sacking. Everyone began unpacking.

'Sleeping bags over here . . .,' directed Tilly, 'and put the gas camping–stove in this corner, where it can't be seen from below. Food here . . . and radio base station here . . . '

Nearby, Boffin was delicately unloading the drone equipment. 'Careful,' he hissed at Tom with a paternal glance at his proprietary technology, 'that's very fragile, you know.'

Gingerly, he laid out his baffling array of cables, boxes, video screens and control panels, until it presented some semblance of order. It was as though they'd bought along Brains from *Thunderbirds*, up to and including the geek-chic glasses. 'OK, looks like we're all go,' he said, flicking on various switches, and watching lights on the dashboard come to life, accompanied by the gentle hum of a cooling fan hidden somewhere in the equipment.

'Game on,' he added, clearly relieved, as Tom took a few photographs from the tower's edge for the historical scrapbook.

'Really weird to be up here and not be able to see our house,' said Tilly, looking down towards the south west.

'I think I can just make out the medieval deanery,' Will said, squinting in the direction of where their home now stood. 'See, there's the great hall, and the chapel extending from the side of the wing. The old Bishop's Palace is down there,' he added, pointing toward the north-west corner of the cathedral. 'Those were the days when we could actually have said that we lived in St Paul's! Or perhaps I should say these *are* the days . . .?'

'Let's do a final test of the radios,' suggested Tom.

Boffin flicked on the base unit Tilly had set up and radioed Will's earpiece. 'Are you receiving me, over?'

'Argh! Yes I'm receiving you. Crikey – that's jolly loud. Can we turn it down?' Will asked, hastening to remove the earpiece until it was set at a quieter level.

'Of course,' said Boffin defensively, reaching over and fiddling with something on the console in front of him. 'Tom, check yours please.'

Tom's was also fine.

'OK, the final thing I want to check is the direction finder I've fitted up for you both, hidden in these crosses,'

Boffin continued, handing the boys what seemed to be simple metal crucifixes.

'The magic ingredient is a tracker, which will tell us where you are if you get lost, and we can't find you. Don't let go of it under any circumstances.'

'What's the range on the transmitter?' asked Tom.

'From up here,' mused Boffin, stroking his chin for effect, 'probably a minimum of two miles, so you're both covered as long as you don't go much beyond Westminster. Anyway, we'll be tracking you with the drone overhead, so there shouldn't be any difficulties.'

'Perfect. Ace, Tom, final checks. All OK?' Tom nodded. And we're off!' said Will, turning back to the concealed entrance to the stairway. 'I think we'll be reversing down here,' he went on, rhetorically, climbing in backwards. 'Easier this way!'

'Keep in touch' said Tilly, hugging them both as they disappeared through the narrow doorway.

'Roger that,' Tom replied into his sleeve-mounted walkie-talkie mouthpiece, which was rather unnecessary as he could still see both Tilly and Boffin less than five yards away.

'Remember,' echoed Will's voice back up to them, 'if things get too hot, literally, or you think you're going to be caught, get out of here. Just make sure you let us know so we can scram, too! And remember the London Stone – if for any reason you can't get back to the future, find it, carve the date and time on it, and someone'll come and get you. God speed,' he concluded, his voice by now muffled and echoing slightly as he descended out of view down the narrow spiral stairs.

And with that they were gone, leaving Boffin and Tilly to soak up the atmosphere, and the stink, with a growing sense of foreboding at the prospect of the events that were fated to unfurl right in front their eyes.

'Drink?' asked Boffin, squatting down next to a small hamper and lobbing Tilly a can of ginger beer.

'Sure – thanks, Boffin.' Tilly caught the can one-handed and yanked off the ring pull. The can emitted a satisfying hiss and the contents bubbled over slightly, obviously shaken. Tilly jumped up to avoid being covered.

'Oops,' said Boffin. 'Sorry about that.

'Right, let's get the drones up and running,' he continued, matter-of-factly, turning back toward his control station. That they were perched atop a crumbling belfry – one of the highest points in Europe, possibly the world, at the time – looking out over a city that was about to be consumed by an inferno of truly Biblical proportions did not seem to have fazed him in the slightest.

A strong, dry breeze blew in from the east, whistling gently through the arches around them. Tilly slurped quietly as Boffin set about his business, loading what looked like large battery packs, checking that the control transmitters were working, and that the video feedback was, also.

'Made this one myself,' said Boffin, proudly, clipping various struts into place. 'Designed to stay up for hours on end. It's not exactly a US Air Force Predator drone, but it'll do. I call it Chewbacca – after the Star Wars character,' he added, noting the totally blank expression on Tilly's face.

'Oh, I see,' said Tilly, who had never seen a Star Wars film in her life, and had no intention of rectifying that.

'It's basically just a flying wing, except that it's also a kind of dirigible,' Boffin continued, clearly enjoying himself as he pumped the drone full of compressed helium he'd pulled out from somewhere.

'Where on earth did you get that gas bottle from?' Tilly asked.

'Oh, I, er, borrowed it on a sort of permanent basis from the clown we had at Estella's last birthday party,' he said somewhat sheepishly. 'He was blowing up all these giant balloons and I thought I could make much better use of it, so, erm . . . I borrowed it. Because the drone's so light, it hardly needs to move at all to stay up. That means less drain on the batteries, and way longer endurance. The flying wing shape means it can cope with a reasonably high wind level. In fact, if the wind's strong enough it can simply glide on that. Plus I can hang a decent camera off the bottom – see . . .' and he pointed to a complicated-looking assembly on the underside of the drone. 'You'll note the propellers are housed in casings within the wing itself. I based that on the Horton Ho229,' said Boffin, beaming. 'You know, the secret World War II German experimental aircraft?' he added.

'To be honest, Second World War secret planes are not so much my thing, Boffin, so no . . . It's quite large when it's inflated though, isn't it?' Tilly ventured tentatively, watching Boffin handling something that was by now larger than he was.

'There's no problem,' said Boffin in a muffled tone from somewhere behind the huge wing he was having to manhandle forcefully to prevent it from drifting off into the night. For a moment, Tilly worried the drone might drag Boffin away with it.

'Here, let me help you,' she said, grabbing the tether cord and holding it tight.

'Phew, thanks a lot,' said Boffin, relaxing slightly.

'The good news is that it looks like the camera's working all right,' he went on, toggling a joystick on his control panel. The camera swung around through 360 degrees on the gantry underneath the drone.

'All systems are . . .,' he flicked a few more switches, and the propellers began whirring softly, '. . . go,' he finished.

'Amazing, well done Boffin,' Tilly said encouragingly, marvelling at her cousin's ingenuity. Fully assembled, Chewbacca looked like a huge and sinister bird of prey.

'Now the great thing about this beast,' Boffin explained, furiously jabbing at a tablet-type screen attached to his control panel, 'is that I can set it to autopilot – so we can just sit back and have it circling overhead somewhere high up; and if we need to we can even get it to follow the boys, using those trackers I've attached to them. All right, I've currently set it to stay at about six hundred feet above them. Hopefully high enough not to draw attention to itself, but close enough for us to see everything going on. 'Right, you can let the tether go I think . . .'

'Sure?' asked Tilly, grinning, but doubting whether a larger than human-sized bird flying over London in the second half of the seventeenth century could really escape notice entirely.

'All right then. Off – we – go . . .,' she said, giving Chewbacca a gentle push out through the middle of the three gothic arches on the south side of the tower, as the engines revved higher and the drone began to soar gently into the night. Now they just needed to hear from the boys that they were in position, and their trap would be set.

25 THE BOYS ARE BACK IN TOWN

Reversing down the narrow secret stairs hidden in the tower of Old St Pauls was, in fact, much easier than anticipated, and the brothers made speedy progress back towards street level. Their head torches gave some light, but occasional beams of moonlight which cut across their path from narrow vertical slits (in lieu of windows) in the stonework also helped.

'Ouch! Watch it will you?!' Will protested in a muffled voice.

'Sorry, but why have you suddenly stopped?' asked Tom, climbing back up a couple of stairs to remove his pack from Will's face. His brother rubbed his nose angrily, checking to see if it was bleeding and repositioning his hat and headlight.

'This is the level of the Norman triforium,' he said, his pupils contracting sharply as Tom's headlight shone into his eyes. Will pointed to a location mark on the wall to back-up his claim.

'Yep, right and . . . ?' replied Tom.

'Well, don't you just want to have a quick look? This is a once in a lifetime opportunity!'

'Yeah, go on then – a few minutes can't hurt.'

Will shuffled towards the door they had stopped beside, and pushed.

'Un-bally-believable,' uttered Tom after a while, looking around them. The boys were in a part of the triforium at the intersection of the long nave and transepts of the cathedral. Above them, darkness hid the base of the tower, many feet overhead. The huge volume of the cathedral was lit only by a few candles around the high altar at the far eastern end, and by moonlight streaming through the tall, pointed gothic windows.

'I think it's even longer than our own St Paul's,' estimated Tom.

'You're right, it is, or, er, was – well, maybe still is,' said Will, correcting himself, still somewhat confused by which tense to use from their position in the past. 'Old St Paul's was longer, wider across the middle, and taller than our St Paul's – at least, it was until the spire burned down. But it had a smaller overall volume.'

Above the nave and transepts, vaulted ceilings rose a hundred and fifty feet from the ground, supported by massive masonry columns with their distinctive curved Norman arches which stood like a tall line of forest–height giant redwood trees running the full length of the church. Tom took a couple of photographs.

'Turn the flash off you muppet,' snapped Will. 'Anyway, time to move, I think. The others will be waiting for us to check in.'

Stealing a last glance at the awesome sight, they continued their descent of the staircase, and jogged back into Hades down the winding secret tunnel. Finding their way out proved somewhat tricky, since the building over their heads was actually the medieval deanery, their own home having not been built yet.

'Let's use that window,' Will suggested, after they found the nearest door to be locked. 'You go first.'

'Oh, thanks very much,' Tom responded, sarcastically. 'Very generous of you as always . . . '

'I'll help you with a boost; give me your foot,' said Will, ignoring his brother's tone.

'By the way, have I seen you in Pirates of the Caribbean?' asked Tom, looking pointedly at his older brother's outfit.

'Shut up and hurry up, you menace!' replied Will, boosting Tom up and through the window from the vaulted undercroft in which they had found themselves. Tom slipped through easily, emerging into a rectangular courtyard in front of the house, flanked on all sides by other buildings, with a large masonry archway leading out toward St Paul's Churchyard. He stood up and brushed himself down. Behind him, a substantial stone house rose out of the ground. It looked incredibly old. In the centre was obviously a great hall with high windows, which sat above the undercroft he had just been in. The rest of the building had two principal storeys and a gabled second floor, and Tom could make out the outline of a chapel roof hidden to the rear. His inspection of the remarkable twelfth century dwelling was interrupted, however, by a cry for assistance.

'Help! I'm stuck!' Tom heard from somewhere behind him.

He turned to see Will wedged in the window, which wouldn't open far enough for him to get his ludicrously square shoulders and extravagant outfit through. Tom snorted with laughter, and yanked his brother's outstretched arm to pull him free.

'Phew, thanks,' said Will, re-setting his hat at a jaunty angle and making sure his feather was positioned correctly. He pushed at the lead-lined window behind him until it looked closed.

'Now for the river,' he commanded, seemingly too preoccupied with the mission to be interested in what the medieval Deanery looked like, and the boys set off through the archway and into the warm, windy night as a nearby bell struck midnight.

Ahead of them, the old cathedral rose like a vast ship atop the crest of a huge wave of earth, its lead rooves glistening in the moonlight. Inigo Jones' porch of tall classical columns was impressive, but looked rather odd against the backdrop of a cathedral which was primarily Norman and Gothic in its style and construction.

'Looks a bit like Salisbury Cathedral, don't you think?' Tom suggested, in hushed tones.

Turning left out of the arch, they walked smartly down Ludgate Hill, leaving the cathedral behind them. The streets were cobbled, in varying degrees of (dis)repair. Ahead, the Lud Gate stood halfway down the hill, a fortified stone gateway guarding the western entrance to the old City. A grim statue of King Lud himself stood in an alcove over the gate looking up towards the cathedral. Swinging left before they reached it, the boys darted down Creed Lane and from there onto St Andrew's Hill, left again past the church of St Andrew by the Wardrobe, and then on to Knightrider Street.

'I can't cope with the smell,' Will said, weakly, clutching his frilly collar to his mouth to use as a primitive mask.

The boys made their way through the warren of overhanging buildings, with sometimes four or five storeys above them stepped progressively closer to those on the opposite side of the street. In some places, the buildings very nearly touched at the top, creating dark alleyways and lanes with only occasional beams of moonlight penetrating to ground level, rather like a dense, man-made forest. Underfoot, the detritus of everyday living littered the streets, from pools of putrefying liquid and the contents of chamber pots to animal bones and straw.

'Oh cripes!' said Tom, practically jumping out of his skin, and moving quickly to the other side of the street, as a drunk man slumped on a pile of hessian sacks snorted loudly in his sleep.

'I think that's the parish constable,' said Will,

disapprovingly, 'look at his badge.' He stifled his laughter. 'So much for local law enforcement. And someone should really write to the Corporation about litter collection!'

Recovering his purpose, Will radioed the team in the tower as quietly as he could using his walkie-talkie microphone hidden in the cuff of his sleeve. 'This is Broadsword calling Danny Boy, do you read me? Over.'

'Er, this is Danny Boy, I guess – we read you. Over… and in fact we see you, too. Give us a wave, will you? By the way, since when have been codenamed Danny Boy?'

Will and Tom looked up on hearing Tilly's reassuring voice, but could see nothing between the narrow gables of the tightly packed buildings despite knowing that the drone was soaring stealthily overhead.

'I believe you!' said Will, 'but we can't see you . . . Oh, and since just now.'

'Probably for the best,' she replied, crackling back over the radio. 'The next street looks clear to me. Keep going, chaps. Everyone's gone to bed.'

From her vantage point up in the tower, Tilly was poring over her maps under a red light so as not to damage her night vision. She traced the route her brothers needed to take to get closer to the Tower. On her right, Boffin sat on his camping chair staring intently at the displays in front of him, one of which showed two infrared figures moving quickly through deserted streets, with occasional other centres of heat indicating where households had set the required lantern outside their properties to light the streets, though few seemed to observe the rules. Perhaps the plague had simply killed off many of the residents, or scared them away.

'OK, guys, once you're down St Peter's Hill you'll be on Thames Street, and then it's basically straight along to the Tower,' she continued.

'Got it,' came Tom's reply.

'Hang on . . . ,' said Boffin, urgently, 'there's some activity close to you, on the river bank.'

Hundreds of feet below, the boys dived into the nearest smelly doorway. 'Please confirm, over,' said Will, breathing hard, 'what exactly can you see?'

26 CONTACT, ENEMY

'Looks like a dozen people or more on the quayside,' said Boffin over the radio. 'They seem to be preparing a boat by the looks of things. Lots of activity, anyway.'

'Maybe smugglers?' Tom suggested, his eyes visibly lighting up in the gloom as though this would be a positive development.

'Maybe,' Will said, biting his lip, 'but let's hope not. Are we OK to keep going, guys, or are we walking straight into them?'

'You're practically on top of them, Will – they're right down at . . . what's the name of the place, Tilly?'

'Broken Wharf,' confirmed Tilly, also over the radio loop. 'Down the alley toward the river, right next to your position.'

Nobody spoke for several seconds. Then voices could be heard, growing louder and echoing down the lane adjacent to where the boys were hiding.

'I think they're moving towards us,' said Tom, tugging anxiously at his brother's frilled sleeve.

'Several of them are moving toward you, guys,' Boffin confirmed, sounding as if he was also trying to keep calm.

'Yes, all right, we know. I'm thinking,' said Will

irritably, looking hastily around them.

'Quick, Tom – down here,' and he dragged his brother down a dark alleyway just to the side of the warehouse building in whose doorway they had been hiding.

'Son Eminence a dit que nous devons être prêts à l'aude. C'est essential que personne ne sait que nous sommes ici. Comprenez vous?' said one, his authoritative tone suggesting he was very much in charge.

'Oui, Capitaine! Nous cacherons jusqu-au matin' came the smart response.

'They're speaking French', said Will as quietly as he could and stating the blindingly obvious. 'I think they said something about being ready by dawn, but you will recall my French teachers have all been total pants so I'm really not sure. What the hell's going on here?'

'You don't think they're the Cardinal's agents do you?' asked Tom.

'I think that's exactly who they are,' replied Will, sticking his head cautiously out of the end of the alleyway to try and snatch a glimpse of what was going on. Given that his hat had a large brim, it quickly became apparent that it was impossible to do this subtly whilst in disguise, and he rapidly recoiled. 'Why else would anyone be working by moonlight only, with no torches? Suggests to me they're hiding something. Plus I reckon "Eminence" refers to the Cardinal. That at least confirms that the story is true, anyway. His henchmen are here tonight. And perhaps he is here somewhere, too. No doubt we'll find out in good time. Still, it's a bit odd. He's been officially dead for five years, after all!'

But their deliberations were cut short. From somewhere behind them, they heard growling. Loud, snarling, bone-shaking growling, followed immediately by furious barking and gnashing of ferocious, shark-sized teeth.

'Oh merde!' yelled Will. 'Run for it!'

The boys darted out of their hiding place like rats chased from their hole, followed by an enormous Bandog which had obviously been snoozing whilst on guard duty in the alley by the warehouse. The hound, which looked akin to a giant and especially hideous English Mastiff with a fawn coat, reached the end of the alleyway in double-quick time, but almost immediately ran out of chain. The monster yelped as it was yanked back and was reduced to straining and barking aggressively from a distance. The boys prayed the chain would keep it there as they made their getaway. The hound was so large that it seemed unlikely anything would hold it in place for long against its will.

'Sacré-bleu – qu'est ce que c'est?!' shouted one of the Frenchmen, only yards away, wheeling around to face the landward side of the lane.

'Agent ennemi!' cried another, and the two set off in hot pursuit, rushing to light torches, and brandishing thuggish-looking clubs. .

'I'm pretty sure one of them just said enemy agent, Will!' gasped Tom frantically, as they tore along the street, 'so we need to run rather faster – like rather a lot faster!'
'Oh, Lordy,' said Boffin over the radio into the boys' earpieces. 'Um guys, you've got company.'

'We bloody well know that Boffin, why do you keep telling us things we know, tell us something we don't already know!' shouted Tom, panting, as the boys skidded round a corner off Thames Street, away from the river and back into the mass of the City's narrow winding lanes. They could hear shutters being slammed back overhead as the commotion woke wary local residents. Mercifully, the shadows concealed them from those looking down, but the French agents were still on their tail, as evidenced by the glow of their torches, visible not far behind.

'Give us an exit,' panted Will into the radio as he pushed himself off a filthy wooden wall to allow him to corner more quickly, and stumbling over a particularly badly set cobblestone which nearly sent him flying across the narrow street.

'Errr, errr . . .,' said Tilly, thinking a little too slowly for the boys' comfort, 'take the next right, then left, then right again.'

Tom looked back just in time to see a large hand swing for his bag and miss narrowly. He could hear the swoosh followed by another curse as his pursuer missed him.

'They're right behind us, Will, and they're not at all polite, these damned Frenchies – faster, faster, faster!' said Tom. 'And please don't worry about me and the heavy bag or anything, I'm absolutely fine,' he added, his voice dripping sarcasm even as he panted furiously, the sack swinging around wildly on his back, repeatedly knocking him off-balance.

'Delighted to hear it!' said Will, accelerating round the next bend and looking fairly ridiculous as his large, frilly lace collar bobbed up and down stupidly around his neck, the sword clattering at his waist. They were passing down a street which seemed to be dominated by shoe shops, judging by the signs flashing by above their heads. Will slowed slightly, and waited for Tom to draw level. As he did so, he yanked out the bottom crate of a teetering tower of soiled wooden boxes which promptly came crashing down behind them, and over which their pursuers stumbled and fell, buying them precious seconds to make good their escape.

'Nice one,' said Tilly out of nowhere, watching the action intermittently through the drone's camera directly overhead as and when gaps in the gables allowed, and seeing one of their pursuers go flying.

'Where next?' asked Will, as the boys ran past a gaggle of unsavoury, if surprised-looking men huddled sinisterly in a doorway, stinking of alcohol.

'Left, then right,' said Tilly. Minutes later, they came to a halt some streets away, to recover their breath.

'I think you've lost them, guys,' said Boffin. 'Can't see them anymore, at any rate.'

'Phew,' replied Will, completely breathless. 'Well, the good news is that only about twelve streets know we're here – so that's absolutely fine,' he added, sarcastically.

'Relax,' said Tom, panting, and clearly having actually enjoyed the experience thus far. 'No one really saw anything.'

They looked about them. They were at the top of a shallow hill. 'That's a really terrible smell,' said Tom, sniffing the air.

'Do you realise where we are?' asked Will, conspiratorially, grabbing Tom's arm and turning him to face south.

'Nope.'

'We're on Pudding Lane, aren't we? Look, that's Farynor's Bakery right over there. Just look at the sign. Unmistakeable. This place is going to be burnt toast in a few minutes', went on Will. 'We need to make like a stone and roll.' He chortled appreciatively to himself at the lame witticisms.

'Let's head down the lane,' suggested Tom, managing a slight sycophantic chuckle. 'We need to get over to the other side of the river to keep an eye on Traitors' Gate from the south bank, anyway. Are we going to risk London Bridge?'

'I doubt we can at this time of night – I bet the gates will be shut,' Will replied. 'But let's go and make certain of it. If not, we'll find a ferryman to drop us over on the opposite bank, and look for a good place to lay up for the night. What do you make the time?'

'I reckon it's about 12.30 am,' said Tom, consulting his digital wristwatch.

'Righty-ho – after you,' and Will gave a mock bow. 'No, wait! I'm the master, so I'd better go first,' he amended, thinking better of his offer. And with that he led off down the lane toward Farynor's Bakery with a swish of his piratical cape.

Seconds later Boffin's vice crackled over the radio earpieces. 'Er, boys, I don't want to be the bearer of bad news yet again but it looks like your favourite seventeenth century hoodlums are back,' he said, watching his infra-red monitor as two sets of people bearing what appeared to be flaming torches headed towards either end of Pudding Lane.

'From where?' asked Will urgently.

'Two bogeys moving at speed along Eastcheap, heading for the top of the lane by the look of things,' replied Boffin, 'and another two coming back along Thames Street at the bottom of the hill. I don't think it's a welcoming committee, either.'

'What are we going to do?' said Tom, suddenly afraid again, 'we're trapped like, er, toads in a hole or something.'

'Toads in a what?' hissed Will, irritably. 'Look, stop panicking, I've got an idea.' He scrabbled around under his various layers of costume and pulled out four EG Burst smoke grenades. 'Here, lob these two about halfway down there, I'll do the same at this end', he said, turning to face the Eastcheap junction. Within moments, the street was filled with a thick green smoke. Each grenade could produce around twenty thousand square feet of smoke in only thirty seconds and, because the street ran north-south, with an easterly wind, it was not easily dispersed.

'They're confused!' said Tom triumphantly, hearing the muffled surprise of their pursuers echoing round the walls of the lane, although now of course the boys couldn't see the French agents either.

'Let's see if any of these doors are open,' whispered Will, moving hurriedly from doorway to doorway, trying the handles as quietly as he could.

'Damnit, no luck,' said Tom, speedily doing the same on his side of the lane.

'Quick, in here,' Will hissed to Tom, 'I don't believe it – the bakery's actually unlocked. We certainly don't want to linger here, but we can hide out for a few minutes.' Tom closed the door a little too loudly behind him, stirring up a light cloud of flour and dust from the dirty floor. Suddenly, a face appeared at the mullioned window, peering inside. The boys froze, lurking just beneath the window but with a good view of the Frenchman's nose, their hearts beating faster than ever. Then Tom sneezed.

'Ici! Ici!' yelled the voice, as the agent heard him. Seconds later, the door burst open as one of his companions kicked it in. More flour and dust billowed into the air, adding to the confusion.

'Oh fudge, run for it!' yelled Will, darting across the shop floor to the back entrance which opened up behind the smelly stables of the Star Inn on Fish Street.

'Oh sod it, this door's actually locked. Get it open will you?' he shouted at Tom, while grabbing a bench from against the wall and wheeling around to drive it against the three villains who had by now followed them into the bakery.

'Done – just a bolt. Quick!' shouted Tom from the open doorway.

Two of the Cardinal's agents had fallen over, one of them dropping a flaming torch which almost immediately set off an intense blaze near the beehive-shaped ovens next to which it landed. Will dropped the bench, which landed on the foot of the third man, who howled in pain, hopping around comically.

Legging it out of the shop as fast as he could, Will escaped just as a loud boom heralded an explosion of glass and wooden splinters as the lead-lined windows were blown out all over the alleyway behind them, as the inn's horses neighed and reared up in fright.

'You muppet, you just started the bloody Great Fire of London,' Tom shouted as they pelted down the lane.

'No I didn't, it was the sodding Frenchman wasn't it? And what the hell is that ungodly smell?' Will continued, as they emerged from the bottom of the lane, looking around frantically for any sign of their pursuers.

'Yuk,' seconded Tom, panting heavily once again. 'Smells like rotting fish.'

'Must be Old Billingsgate Fish market just over there' said Will, gesturing to one side of the street ahead of them. 'Maybe we could hide there. It was on that site for nine hundred years, you know.'

'Now's not the time for a history lecture, brother!'

'Oh, right, yeah, fair enough. This way . . . ,' and they found themselves back on Thames Street, and directly ahead of the great fortified north gate of Old London Bridge.

'It's shut, I knew it,' said Will, cursing and skidding to a stop. He only barely attracted the attention of a half-asleep – or, more likely, drunken – night watchman slumped against a corner of the gate. 'There's only one thing for it, we need to get a ferry across. It'll be easier to see what's going on from the south bank anyway, because we'll have an uninterrupted view of Traitors' Gate across the river, and we'll put some distance between us and the Cardinal's men. We'll also be safer from the chaos that's just about to grip the City. Plus, on a slightly touristy note, I rather want to see the old Globe theatre up close!'

'Good plan,' Tom agreed, as the boys set off at a quick jog again and the sounds of crackling and shouting grew from somewhere behind them. Up a street to their right, men pulling a cart called for householders to bring out their dead.

'Oh cripes,' said Tom nervously, 'the plague carts.'

The men working on the cart wore floor-length robes of coarse material, and had strange, beak-like masks giving them the appearance of the ancient Egyptian sky god Horus – who was always depicted with a bird's head – only with much longer beaks. They had stopped at a door with a dripping red cross daubed on it, just visible by its sheen in the moonlight. But the cacophony of shouting and the smell of burning wood now attracted their attention, and they looked round to see which direction the disturbances were coming from.

'I think we'll steer clear of that,' Will remarked with dry understatement, and they jogged smartly on down Thames Street, constantly looking over their shoulders to check for pursuers.

In the distance, muffled peals indicated that church bells were 'ringing backwards' – the first general warning of the fire. The stench of the streets was almost unbearable, made worse by the dry summer's heat which accelerated the rotting process.

'The sooner we get across the river, the better,' said Tom, holding his nose. 'Tilly, can you see anyone on our tail?'

'Not at the moment, boys, but it looks like a lot of people are stirring,' she replied, glancing up from her monitor to look over the tower parapet and see if the fire was already visible from where she stood. She thought she could just about discern a faint glow.

As they ploughed on, Will and Tom passed various bodies slumped, passed out, in doorways – *at least, I hope they're passed out*, thought Tom to himself, gathering his clothes more tightly around him and readjusting his heavy sack.

'Tilly, which one is Puddle Dock?' enquired Will into his concealed radio microphone.

'Uhmmm, it's about . . . sixteen alleys away.'

'Sixteen?' groaned Tom, as Will quickened the pace once again.

'Can you see if there's anyone on the dock?' he asked, breathing hard, 'just so we don't run all the way down there pointlessly. There aren't any ferries waiting at the steps nearer to us.'

'Hang on. Yes, there is,' said Boffin a few moments later, having reoriented the drone over the river so as to be able to zoom in on the dock from a distance. 'And it looks like your French chums from the nearby wharf have done a runner.'

'Or have completed their preparations and are up to no good,' Will suggested, ominously.

Ahead, another cart-team plied its trade, collecting the bodies of those who had succumbed to the plague.

'I think I'll be quite chuffed when we get home,' said Will.

'Me too!' Tom agreed fervently, sticking close to Will's elbow.

'Stay overhead, guys,' requested Will, 'we're heading across the river.'

'Roger that,' Boffin replied. 'Good luck chaps.'

27 ONTO OLD FATHER THAMES

Three hundred feet up in the tower of Old St Paul's, the highest manmade point in the land, Tilly and Boffin had a good view of the scene unfolding around Pudding Lane to the south east, as the warm wind fanned the flames which were now clearly visible from their perch.

'It's so dry,' observed Tilly, 'the houses are just waiting to burn.'

The two of them watched for some minutes as the flames continued to grow. In some places, licks of fire now extended perhaps twenty feet into the air.

'Look at it go,' said Boffin, whistling under his breath, keeping one eye on the others' progress on his monitor.

'At least we know from history that Thomas Farynor and his family made it out of the bakery in time,' consoled Tilly, 'although I seem to remember their maid servant was less fortunate as she couldn't face the jump to the building next door.'

'Yeah, you can't really miss it I suppose,' replied Boffin. 'It is already rather a large fire after all! At least people will have plenty of time to make a dash for it. The crackling is so intense that the inferno's hardly going to be sneaking up on them.'

Every so often, Boffin or Tilly felt a puff of air that was distinguishable from the by now familiar tempo of the warm wind which whistled through the rafters. After a while, they realised the top of tower was home to an enormous, seething colony of black bats.

'That's just great,' said Tilly, pointing her torch up into the eaves overhead and recoiling as the beam picked up row after row of furry, fearsome-looking bats hanging upside down, their small, fanged and pug-like heads visible despite being wrapped in their own wings, so that they appeared to be swaddled in dark cellophane. 'Juuust great, because I hear bats and long hair go really well together.' She put her glamorous locks up into as tight a bun as possible, ducking instinctively as yet another bat swooped low past her head. 'I really *hate* flying rats.'

Boffin, however, seemed rather enamoured by all the bats, gazing up and around and making strange cooing noises as though he were trying to communicate with them in their own ultra-sonic language. Snapping back to reality after catching Tilly's unimpressed eye, he returned to his screens.

'OK, guys, you're nearly at the dock,' he said.

Down at street level, the boys slowed their pace to a quick march as they approached Puddle Dock. 'What on earth is that ahead on your left, Will?' came Tilly's voice over the radio.

'Ah, yes, that's Baynard's Castle,' he whispered back, looking up at the heavy stone walls of a large fortified building immediately abutting the riverside. 'It was originally a Norman fort, I think, but this one's more recent – thirteenth century if I recall – and was lived in by two of Henry VIII's wives, Catherine of Aragon and Anne Boleyn. And get this, it's also the place where Mary Tudor was declared to be Queen of England, ditto Lady Jane Grey I think. She was queen for only about a week you know. It's now home to some terribly grand aristocrat or other. The previous occupant rather fell out of favour with the Crown after supporting Parliament during the Civil War. Not a great long-term call,' smirked Will, knowing that he would certainly have been on the King's side.

'What happened?' asked Tom.

'Well, obviously King Charles II – who's the king now, by the way – wasn't too keen on people who had supported the Parliamentary campaign against his father, the king and martyr Charles I, and subsequently chopped off his head in 1649. So lots of them lost their property – and considerably more than that, in some cases – when Charles II was restored to the throne in 1660. In fact, those who were to be punished but had already inconveniently died were dug up and executed posthumously!'

Passing the castle on their left under the watchful gaze of a night watchman stationed by a sturdy gate at the top of a broad flight of steps, the boys came at last upon Puddle Dock, the old disembarkation point for the monastery of the Black Friars, whose high-walled compound stood nearby, shrouded in darkness.

'Yeah, a few people here,' whispered Tom over the radio, 'mostly asleep by the look of things,' he added. 'We're going to make contact.'

Will puffed himself up, tweaked his hat to make sure it was at just the right commanding angle, pressed his moustache firmly into place, and strode forward towards the nearest boat lying alongside the uneven wooden jetty which jutted out into the river. The tide was going out, so the water level was already quite low, and clearly receding quickly.

Will had to call down to the boatman, who was talking in hushed tones with another man in an adjacent boat.

'A fine night it is, sir,' Will began. 'What be your name?' he added, in the deepest, most convincing seventeenth century voice he could muster.

'A fine night to yer good selves, sir. The name's

Stokeld, Rob Stokeld.'

The man couldn't be any older than Will and – despite his extremely thick and shifty eyebrows which made him appear constantly cheesed-off, and which Tom thought made him look a bit like one of the Angry Birds – he had a friendly enough demeanour.

'Where be ye heading to, good sirs?'

'We are travelling yonder,' said Will, pointing extravagantly toward London Bridge, 'past the bridge, and to the south bank.'

'By God, sir, that'll be dangerous,' said Stokeld, taking in Will's costume, which was almost comically over-the-top, even by the standards of the time. 'It be dark, the water be cold, and the tide's going out, so the water under the bridge be treacherous indeed, sir.'

'So be it, my good man, but will you take us?' said Will, more urgently, the smell of fire once again reaching his nostrils.

The ferryman paused for a moment. 'There's an extra charge, sir, for work beyond the bridge, and seein' it be the small hours of the mornin',' he said finally.

'How much extra?' asked Tom, indignantly. Stokeld looked taken aback that his potential customer's servant was speaking out of turn.

'Silence, Baldrick!' Will said, thumping Tom on the upper arm. 'Remember you may only speak when spoken to!'

Tom saw his brother's evil grin flash across his face momentarily beneath the fake moustache, before he turned back to continue his negotiation with the boatman.

'At this time of night and through the bridge, I'll say one shilling fer the pair of ye,' said Stokeld, looking slightly perplexed by his new charges but sensing the opportunity to make good cash.

'Done,' said Will. 'Payment once we reach our destination' he added curtly, stepping awkwardly down some slimy steps and into the small boat, which rocked violently as he did so, and positioning his sword with a gentle clatter so that it lay comfortably alongside him. Tom followed, smarting at his lot in life as a seventeenth century serf. *Will's enjoying this far too much*, he thought to himself, making a mental note to even the score once they were back in the twenty-first century.

The ferryman bade farewell to his colleague, who smelled even worse than he did, and pushed the ten–foot boat away from the jetty, unhitching the rope tether from an upright post as they went and pulling the slimy cable on-board. The bench on which the boys sat side by side was barely six inches deep. 'Jolly comfortable,' said Tom sarcastically under his breath as he wriggled uncomfortably.

One end of the vessel had a battered old covering, in case of rain, though Will doubted how effective it would be with all the holes in it. Stokeld sat in the middle of the boat, manoeuvring them out of the backwater and into the stately main flow of the river.

'Yer jus' in time, sirs,' he went on. Another half hour or so and you'd have to wait until mornin' to make the crossing . . .'

'Beggin' yer pardon, sir,' he added, addressing Will, 'but you do look mighty familiar. Are you from aroun' 'ere, part of the Corporation per'aps?'

'Er,' said Will, forgetting his low voice for a moment, then swiftly correcting himself. 'Er,' he repeated again, but lower this time, 'I am, er, Sir Richard de, um. . .'

'Sir Richard de Um?' repeated the ferryman, confused.

'No, um, Sir Richard, er. . .'

Starved of inspiration, Will looked subtly around them as they rowed into the main flow of the river. His eyes fell first upon the silhouette of Old St Paul's behind him. Looking to his left he saw the red glow of the growing fire and the large mass of London Bridge.

'Just Sir Richard?' asked the ferryman, getting

suspicious.

'Of course not. Sir Richard de Fire . . . bridge,' snapped Will, defiantly.

'de Firebridge,' mused the ferryman. 'I didn't realise you were a knight, Sir Richard, I do beg yer pardon.'

Will could hear muffled sniggering on the bench next to him, and he elbowed Tom in the ribs as subtly as he could, rocking the boat a little in the process.

'But you may call me simply Sir Richard,' added Will, grandiosely with a dismissive gesture of his hand.
'Thank ye, Sir Richard,' said Stokeld, with a sardonic bow of his head.

By now they were moving closer to the south bank of the river, evidently making for the slower water on the inside of the bend. From their new vantage point, Will and Tom could see the huge, congested expanse of London on the north side – by the 1660s, a city of nearly half a million souls. A boat just like the one in which they were seated bobbed by, being dragged east by the current. A man's body lay slumped back over the seat.

'Plague,' said Stokeld, matter-of-factly, using his left oar to push the unfortunate craft further away. 'It be devilling everyone,' he added. 'Still, not as bad as the year that passed,' he said, recollecting 1665 which saw the beginning of London's Great Plague that had killed off around a quarter of the capital's population in only a year and a half. Worst of all, the city was still infected. The boys were aware that Stokeld was keeping a close eye on them.

'Why so few large ships in this part of the river, my good man,' asked Will, trying to keep the conversation light.

'That'll be the quarantine for foreign ships, sir,' said Stokeld. 'By God, the plague has come upon us from foreign shores, so it has. No doubt a plot by those heretical devils, the French. Bit late for a quarantine if you ask me, sir.'

They made slow progress at first but, as they neared

London Bridge, the current quickened noticeably and the boat picked up pace.

'Hold on tight,' said Stokeld, as they approached one of the stone arches. The boys could hear the roar of the water dropping down beyond the bridge – clearly the large islands on which the arches were built constricted the flow of the tidal river, leaving the water level much lower on one side of the bridge than the other when the tide was moving in or out.

'Might get a bit rocky, sirs,' said Stokeld, rowing more industriously now.

To their left, and past the northern end of the bridge, they could see the faint red glow of the fire, a fact still oblivious to Stokeld from his rearward-facing seat ahead of the boys. A plume of white smoke was rising into the night air, fanned westwards by the winds blowing from in front of them.

'What in the name of the Good Lord is going on over there,' asked the ferryman, finally twisting where he sat to look over his right shoulder as they heard a loud explosion.

'By God, it looks like an inflammation of the City, so it does!' replied Will in his best Shakespearean voice.

They were moving really quite fast now, drawn inexorably towards the bridge, the imposing shapes of the buildings which spanned nearly its entire length looming up quickly overhead. The fire already seemed to be moving toward the bridge's northern end, although a sizeable gap between the north gate and the first house – the legacy of another fire in 1633 – would save the remainder of the bridge in the firestorm to come, Will reminded himself. He and Tom exchanged nervous glances. The ferryman had stopped paddling now and was merely using the oars to steer, allowing the current to do the hard work for him, but looking repeatedly over his right shoulder to study the reddening, pulsating skyline and align the boat with the centre of the bridge's arch.

Tom was impressed to notice that Stokeld's outfit

was not all that different from his own. *Well done, girls*, he thought quietly.

'Easy now,' the ferryman said to himself, evening up the angle of the boat. Tom, moving his eyes from left to right along the bridge, counted nineteen arches, with all manner of buildings above them, including what appeared to be a chapel halfway along the bridge's length.

'Safer under the ones without private 'ouses,' said Stokeld, nodding upward to indicate that the risk of having a chamber pot emptied on them was much reduced by not passing beneath anyone's bedroom window. The little boat slid between two large piers which guarded the bottom of the arch through which they passed. The four- or five-foot drop in water level from one side to the other meant that the experience was like going down an adventure park's mini log-flume. The boat rocked violently from side to side and foul-smelling water sploshed in over the sides.

'Easy girl,' the ferryman said to himself. 'Easy, now.'

The water effectively slingshotted the boat through the arch, and they made swift progress for the next couple of hundred yards, the ferryman simply dipping his oars in to the Thames to control direction as the boys tried to keep their feet clear of the foul water which had by now collected in the bottom of the vessel.

'Here, if you please,' said Will, pointing to a small jetty not far from the bridge's southern gateway.

'Right ye are, Sir Richard,' said Stokeld.

'We have some business here for a while,' said Will, mysteriously. 'I shall pay you your shilling now, but I want you to wait here for us until daybreak. Do not under any circumstances accept any other business – you will work only for us until I say otherwise. In return, I shall pay you a retainer of five shillings per day. If you do as I ask, there will be a further bonus of five shillings at the end of our engagement. Are we agreed?'

'Yes indeed, sir, thank ye kindly,' replied Stokeld with a small bow once more, his eyes widening. 'Most generous.'

The boat drew alongside the appointed pier. Will handed Stokeld the promised coins, and reiterated the offer of more. 'Come back at sunrise and wait for us, then,' he added firmly.

The boys left the boat and walked along the short jetty onto the embankment before marching swiftly up a lane which lay alongside some kind of long, rectangular dock. The south bank was much less densely developed than the north. In some places, only one or two roads running parallel to the river stood between the water and marshy countryside, although the area where the boys landed was much more tightly packed with gabled houses, shops and taverns. From where they stood, they could see the outline of the heads of executed traitors on top of the southern gate of London Bridge.

'Bit grisly, isn't it?' said Tom, wincing as he tried hard not to imagine how the various heads had ended up in the arrangement.

'Let's find somewhere to lay up,' said Will, his mind on the more pressing question of shelter, 'and sharpish. We don't want to be wandering around in the small hours for any longer than we absolutely have to. Keep your eyes peeled – the south bank's even more dangerous than the north after dark, and there are no police to call. This is the Wild West.'

28 THE GEORGE & DRAGON

'Where exactly are you going?' crackled a voice over the radio.

'Ah, we'd almost forgotten about you, Boffin,' replied Tom. 'We're going to find somewhere to lie-up and observe. Can you see anywhere suitable? Obviously we need a view of Traitors' Gate . . . '

'This map marks a large coaching inn about fifty yards ahead of you on your left-hand side; by the look of things, it overlooks the river. In fact, I think I can make it out on the screen, too.'

'It's probably quite dodgy,' said Will, looking furtively about them. 'But then where's not, I suppose.'

To their right, vistas of fields could occasionally be glimpsed between rows of houses and down-at-heel shops, while the patchy paving underfoot and generally muddier roadways were a far cry from the more carefully laid cobblestones of the City. Following another lane towards the river, they arrived a minute or so later outside the promised coaching inn. The large sign above the battered old wooden gates announced it as the 'St George & Dragon,' with the name emblazoned over a faded colour rendering of St George slaying something that looked to

Tom more like a seriously overweight serpent than a dragon.

'Looks lovely,' he said, sarcastically, by now feeling the weight of his pack digging deeper into his collarbones. 'In we go,' said Will, pushing on the pedestrian door which sat within the larger gates that were obviously designed to allow coaches in and out. The pedestrian door, however, was locked.

'Bother, it's shut. Ah – wait, it's OK,' said Will. 'The sign here says "Knock Loudly", although the spelling leaves something to be desired,' he added, as the sign actually read "Nok Lowdlee".

The boys duly hammered hard on the door. After some minutes, a panel shot back just below Will's eye level. 'Why be ye disturbing us at this late hour, gentlemen? It's well past midnight, by God it is,' said the aged night watchman. As the old man spoke, a haze of alcoholic breath wafted over Will, who tried hard not to gag and pretended he hadn't noticed.

'We seek shelter for the night,' said Will, coughing slightly and raising his hand to his mouth. He felt his fake moustache coming loose with the sweat on his upper lip. He stroked it meditatively to make sure it didn't slip. The old man looked them up and down for a moment, evidently suspicious. The boys tried to look as innocent as possible. The sound of bolts being shot back on the other side of the door suggested that the doorman thought they weren't too much trouble, and soon the portal swung open.

'God be praised,' said Will. 'Thank ye kindly good sir!' he added, as he and Tom stepped over the threshold. The boys were shown through the gate and in via another door to the dark interior of the inn. An all-wooden building with low ceilings and little natural light, it was not completely dark on account of the moonlight struggling through the grubby windows. Their host, who held a small lantern containing a solitary candle, beckoned them further into the long, low-ceilinged room. Will nearly bashed his head on a particularly prominent beam, stooping just in time, and grabbing his hat and wig to prevent them coming off, too.

'There be strange goings on this night,' said the man, burping abruptly, then rubbing his mouth with the back of his filthy sleeve. A nearly empty bottle of something extremely pungent stood on a nearby counter-top. 'Some kind of trouble over in the City,' he finished, swaying slightly and clutching the side of the counter for balance. For a moment it looked as though he'd topple over regardless.

'We did see signs of a monstrous fire,' said Will, sensing a response was required.

'Aye, I too saw the glow,' replied the man, hiccupping. 'Looked like a bad 'un. Will yer servant be sharing yer accommodation, sire, or would you like me to show him to the stables with the other servants?'

A broad smile creased Will's face as he turned to look at Tom, who stared back with an expression which clearly read *If you dare send me to a plague-ridden seventeenth century stable with a load of stinking serfs I'll do unspeakable things to you.*

Will pretended he was seriously considering the idea. 'No. No, that won't be necessary,' he said eventually. 'Baldrick will stay in my room to remain in attendance.' Tom looked incredulous that there might have been a moment of doubt about his accommodation with the livestock.

'It be sixpence a night, sir, paying in advance,' said the night-watchman, burping obviously.

'Here,' Will slid a coin across the counter-top at the bar by which they now stood, 'and a view of the river if you please.'

'This way if you will, good sirs,' said the man, pocketing the coin in a flash, and leading them off up some rickety and deeply uneven stairs to the first floor.

The passageway emerged onto an open gallery, on

one side of a large internal courtyard in which were arrayed a range of heavily worn carriages and wagons. Veering right onto another landing across the north side of the yard, the man showed the boys to a room far towards the back of the decrepit building and overlooking the river.

'The room be to your likin'?' enquired their host, lighting a miniscule candle on the table near the door with the flame from the small lantern which he carried, and evidently not much fussed by the answer.

'It will suit our needs very well, thank you. I wish you a good evening,' finished Will, signalling the man to leave. With that, their host disappeared off along the landing in the opposite direction to that from which they had come. The boys listened to his footsteps creaking into the distance. Then silence fell, for a few moments anyway.

'Is that a *pig*?' asked Tom eventually.

'I'm sorry to say it's someone snoring – or possibly more than one person. There's no way one normal human being can snore like that,' Will laughed.

'We'll have to keep it down,' Tom replied quietly. 'Looks like these walls are little more than a few planks with plaster over the top.'

'True enough.' Will pushed the bolt across the door and, moving a crude wooden chair behind it, propped the back of the seat against the horizontal spar of the door to slow the entry of anyone trying to get in to their modest chamber uninvited.

'Great view though,' continued Tom, rubbing the glass of the bay window in front of him to remove some of the filth. Some way to their left sat the outline of London Bridge, the pointed gables of the houses and other buildings which lined its length clearly visible in the moonlight. Near the far end of the bridge, they could see flames jumping above the level of the structures beyond the gatehouse.

'Pudding Lane must be just cinders by now,' Will speculated, guiltily, as he took off his hat and wig and itched his scalp vigorously. Further to the right sat the vast hulking, defiant structure of the City's ancient fortress, with William the Conqueror's White Tower at its heart almost radiant in the moonlit darkness. Between that and the boys' observation post lay the dark, malodorous, flowing mass of Old Father Thames, effectively London's open sewer. There were larger vessels on this stretch of the water – some with three hefty masts – which evidently didn't venture further upstream, but sat bobbing as menacing silhouettes. Already, there seemed to be an increase in the number of other boats and lighters out on the river, and in the number of people shouting to one another on the north bank, desperate to get themselves and their possessions clear of the oncoming inferno.

Looking down to his left and straining his eyes, Will saw Stokeld's boat tied up close to the jetty where he'd dropped them off, the dark shape in the bottom of the boat presumably Stokeld asleep under a cloak.

Will let out a sigh of relief. 'OK Tom, get some sleep, I'll take first watch,' he said aloud.

'Looks fairly rat-free, actually,' said Tom, sounding remarkably upbeat as he toured the room with his torch, inspecting the skirting-boards for possible rodent runs. He got out his flea repellent anyway and squirted it around the area of floor he planned to bed down on. 'The "bed" seems a bit of a risk, don't you think?' he said by way of explanation, taking off his cloak and using it to create a half-decent pillow. A blanket from his sack provided some protection from splinters on the old floorboards.

Will nodded, settling down in another chair by the window. 'Broadsword calling Danny Boy, over,' he whispered into his microphone, groaning as the nearby snoring grew louder and louder.

'Danny Boy receiving you. Over,' replied Tilly's voice. 'We're at the George and Dragon and have set a watch. I'm on for the first couple of hours. Tom will take over around 3am.'

'Sounds sensible,' said Tilly. 'Boffin's put the drone on autopilot over your position – circling at 1,000 feet – and is going to get some sleep. I'll take first watch up here and let you know if anything comes up.'

'Fine. Just make sure that, whatever happens, you guys are out of there on Tuesday morning,' said Will, gazing at the flames which seemed to grow more intense by the minute. 'History tells us that the cathedral burned on Tuesday evening – but don't take any chances. Even the heat before that could be fatal.'

'Got it,' said Tilly. 'We'll let you know if we see anything,' she added.

'Likewise,' said Will. 'Sleep tight little sister,' though he knew there was absolutely no chance of a decent night's sleep for him.

He pulled out the night vision scope to get a better look at Traitors' Gate across the river. On the floor to his right, he heard a small gurgle from Tom, which meant he was asleep already. Will sighed. It was going to be a very, very long night.

29 WATCHMEN

The dawning of Sunday morning was heralded by the incongruously upbeat sounds of the bells of nearby St Mary Overie – modern-day Southwark Cathedral – set against the cacophony of panicked noises and explosions which were now emanating from the City. By this time, Tom was in the chair by the river, keeping a weary look out for boats moving to or from Traitors' Gate at the Tower of London.

Will had overslept his allotted two-hour rest break and awoke from his extremely uncomfortable fitful first sleep of the night on the uneven wooden floor. Groaning, and stiff in seemingly every joint, he sat up and threw his pillow – part of Tom's disguise – back to his brother, who got to his feet and tied it back on. 'You've been drooling on it you foul creature,' Tom exclaimed, crossly.

'Oh don't fuss, it makes it look more realistically soiled. Did I miss anything?' Will asked, bleary-eyed.

'Nothing in particular, but the fire's really spread. Looks like it's at the north end of the bridge now and spreading west with the wind. There are loud bangs every so often, sounds like gunpowder.'

'It almost certainly is,' said Will, forcing himself to

stand up and stretch. 'Remember that the Civil War between forces loyal to King Charles and those of Parliament only ended fifteen years ago. The wharves along the river front are still filled with gunpowder from Parliamentary stocks. London was a Parliamentary power base after all. As the fire goes on, the diarist Samuel Pepys relates that the bangs just get bigger and bigger. Where's the loo by the way?' he enquired, returning to more mundane matters.

'Go along the landing to the stairs at the end and out towards the river. There's a sort of disgusting outhouse with a long drop that's cleaned out by the tide. You won't be able to use it though, the smell's just unspeakable.'

'I'll have to take my chances,' said Will, already looking fairly desperate. Removing the chair against the back of the door and unbolting it, he headed off to sample the 350-year old lavatory facilities.

'Told you,' said Tom, seeing the disgusted look on Will's face when he returned several minutes later looking like a victim of shellshock from the First World War trenches.

'Let's never speak of it again,' said Will, quietly, only half in jest. 'Did you bring some of that anti-bacterial hand wash?'

Tom nodded. 'Ah great, thank God,' said Will as he rubbed his hands together furiously. 'Let's see how the others are doing. Boffin, Tilly, do you read? Over.'

'We hear you boys,' said Boffin. 'Sorry about the snoring by the way,' he added. 'Tilly said I kept accidentally depressing the 'Talk' button on the console when I was asleep.'

'No worries, Boffin,' said Tom chortling, 'it was very funny.'

'We had to recall Chewbacca to fit a new battery pack, but it's on the way back over to you as I speak. Honestly, guys, the chaos over this side is insane,' and Boffin related the scenes playing out from his bird's-eye view. 'We can feel the heat of the fire from here already.'

'I saw a team of nearly thirty men dragging what must be a primitive fire engine on a sled along by the cathedral earlier,' added Tilly, describing what sounded like little more than a hot-tub-sized water container with a feeble-looking hose barely a few feet long.

'Anyway, I don't know why they're not pulling down houses now around the fire,' said Boffin, looking closely at his monitor. 'They really need to create a big enough fire-break, but they're just doing – well, not a lot. There are a few bucket chains operating from the edge of the river and involving scores of people, but that's like trying to use a water pistol to put out a blaze on an oil rig.'

'The Lord Mayor, Thomas Bloodworth, is resisting calls for demolitions of property,' explained Will. 'He won't order the creation of large fire–breaks until later today, by which time the firestorm will be completely unstoppable as burning embers spread the fire rapidly with the assistance of the wind.'

'On the plus side, it looks as if, for the most part, people are having time to get out of the way,' observed Tilly. 'Also, looking down at the north side of the cathedral there are loads of people bringing things into the building for safekeeping – lots of books and papers for a start.'

'That would also be right,' said Will, his continuing history lecture almost as unstoppable as the flames themselves. 'The area around the cathedral is where all the booksellers are based, and they're moving their stock into the cathedral crypt because it's mainly stone and they think it'll be safe in there. Big mistake, of course.'

'Little do they know their books will help make the blaze especially intense,' chipped in Tilly.

'Exactly,' replied Will. 'We're going to go and check on our friendly neighbourhood ferryman. I need to make sure he's hanging around, or we'll be a bit stuffed when we do see some activity at Traitors' Gate and we don't have a boat to do anything about it. Boffin, can you position the drone so that you can see the Traitors' Gate entrance as well, just to keep an eye on things for us?'

'Sure can,' said Boffin over the radio, piloting Chewbacca back out over the river in a wide arc.

Up in the belfry of Old St Paul's, Tilly was setting up a solar charger for the batteries. 'Sorted,' she said. 'Fancy some breakfast?'

'Don't mind if I do,' Boffin answered. Tilly unwrapped some sausage and bacon rolls in tin foil. 'Now we're talking,' enthused Boffin through a mouthful, crumbs spewing out over the control panel. 'Oops, sorry,' he said. 'Got any brown sauce?' he added hopefully.

'Fraid not, Boffin,' said Tilly. 'It is the seventeenth century you know.'

30 CITY OF FIRE, CITY OF CHAOS

It was a tense waiting game. South of the river, the boys had left the inn and were walking back toward their landing point nearer the bridge. There was no sign of the night-watchman who had let them in, but they'd met the rather more respectable innkeeper and told him that they thought they'd be staying for a second night.

Despite the small crowd of people assembled on the riverside near the jetty to watch the unfolding disaster in the City from a safe distance, Rob Stokeld was still asleep in his boat, snoring loudly and muttering in his sleep. 'No, James, you lazy. . . James, I said no! For goodness. . . .' the sentence tailing off into indecipherable mumbles. Tom kicked the boat. Nothing.

'Good morning!' said Will, loudly.

'Eh?!' Stokeld lifted his hood back slowly, and saw the boys standing there. 'Ah, good morning Sir Richard,' he said, realising who it was and scrambling to make himself look a little more presentable. 'A fine Sunday morning it is, too' he added, squinting in the early light.

'Notwithstanding the apocalyptic conflagration afflicting the City, I suppose,' pointed out Will, dourly.

'Well indeed, sir, I meant no offence,' said Stokeld,

sheepishly looking towards the City to check on the progress of the fire.

'I came to check that our arrangement remains, Stokeld,' continued Will.

'It does indeed, sir. I'll be here for yer whenever yer need me. I've already turned down business this morning in good faith.'

'Very good,' replied Will, thinking this story was highly unlikely given that he'd only just woken the snoring ferryman. 'We shall return later on. Be ready, mind, as we may need to move very swiftly.'

'Thank ye, sire, I'm the fastest ferryman on the water. Don't you worry abou' nothin'. Ye shall find me here.'

'Better yet,' replied Will, 'there is a landing point next to the George and Dragon inn – do you know it?'

'I do indeed,' said Stokeld. 'Good ale,' and he licked his lips at the thought of it.

'Good, well wait for us there if you please. In fact, you might as well take us back there if you're going,' said Will, stepping down into the boat with Tom following.

'Your wish is my command, sir,' and Stokeld kicked off from the pier, untethering his boat as he went.

As the ferryman rowed them the two hundred yards or so back to their accommodation, the boys could see that London Bridge was jammed full of people and carts at the few intervals without houses and presumably, therefore, along its entire length. All had a single aim: fleeing the fire which had now cut off the northern end of the bridge.

Just as the boys disembarked at the green, slime-covered steps near the inn, a huge explosion rocked the boat from the north, nearly sending Tom flying into the Thames. Wheeling around, the three of them saw a huge fireball rising from where a gently smoking wharf had stood only seconds before.

'One of the old powder stores from the Civil War,' said Stokeld, looking worried, as the fireball gave way to smoke, and bits of debris began falling back to earth, some splashing dramatically into the waters of the river not far away from them. People on boats closer to the fireball threw themselves into the river.

'At the rate the fire's goin' it'll get the Tower 'n' all the City's powder stocks with it,' added the ferryman.

'As I say, we shall return,' said Will, handing Stokeld another coin to steady his nerves.

'Thank ye, good sir.'

Will and Tom rushed back to their room as quickly as they decently could, realising that the threat to the Tower was crucial.

'This is it,' said Will. 'The archbishop's troops will be on their way shortly, now that the Tower itself is under threat. The whole complex must be stuffed full of the royal powder supplies. They'll be worried that embers from the fire could jump the moat, burn the wooden buildings within the curtain walls and set off the gunpowder stores. Then perhaps even the White Tower itself wouldn't be safe. Keep your eyes peeled for anything suspicious.'

The boys' breakfast of biscuits and bottled water from Tom's large sack proved predictably unsatisfying, especially after Tilly revealed what she and Boffin were feasting on in Old St Paul's.

As the day wore on, the flames continued to grow, as did the flood of refugees onto the river. Small boats teemed around the northern bank, as hapless residents loaded everything they possibly could into them. Where no suitable craft presented themselves, some people were throwing large items of furniture directly into the filthy water of the river in the hope that they would float.

Listening to some of the conversations that drifted over the water toward them, Will became aware that some ferrymen were being extremely unscrupulous, charging astronomical fees for moving people and property to safety, and he felt a bit guilty that Stokeld was sitting idle in his boat. 'Needs must,' he justified to himself under his breath.

Further biscuits and water for lunch did little to improve the mood in the boys' Spartan room at the George and Dragon, nor did the apparent absence of any sign of the archbishop's expected rescue vessel.

'Maybe the story's wrong?' Tom mused despondently. 'Or maybe they actually went over land and not down the river at all. We might have missed it all for all we know.'

'Well, Tilly and Boffin haven't seen anything suspicious yet. Keep the faith, brother.'

Mid-afternoon there was a false alarm as Boffin spotted a likely-looking ship, only to realise that it was King Charles II's royal barge making its way downriver so that the monarch could personally inspect the fire in his capital city. It returned upstream, presumably to the Palace of Whitehall, shortly afterwards.

Amidst all the chaos, however, around early evening, another smart-looking vessel flying a flag from the prow and rowed by at least a dozen oarsmen appeared at speed through one of the middle arches of London Bridge. Various other uniformed men stood in the central section of the wooden boat, which was at least twenty-five feet long.

'This might be us,' said Tom, suddenly interested again and sitting up straight to get a better view.

'Guys, can you see this?' he called over the radio.

'We see them,' said Boffin. 'Looks like they're heading for the Tower, too,' he added, as the ship steered a course for Traitors' Gate and began to slow down. Yet another loud explosion rattled the windows. The boys ducked briefly, worried that the force of the blast might have blown them in. This time, they needn't have been concerned.

'Can't see a wharf blowing up,' said Tom, sitting back up and scanning the opposite bank.

'Then it's probably the Tower garrison blowing up houses to create a firebreak before it reaches them,' Will surmised, keeping his eyes fixed on the boat now bobbing outside the Tower, and occasionally inspecting it through his binoculars.

'Bingo! I recognise the flag – it's the Archbishop of Canterbury's coat of arms.'

After a couple of minutes, the huge iron portcullis of Traitors' Gate began to lift clear out of the water, green slime and weeds dangling from the crossbars. It took some time to raise and, slowly, purposefully, the boat moved inside.

'They're in!' said Will. 'I think it's time to go to and see our friend Mr Stokeld, don't you, Tom? Bring the kit bag will you? Who knows where we'll end up tonight.'

'We're heading to our ferryman, team,' said Tom, over the radio.

'Roger,' Tilly acknowledged.

'No, actually, he's called Rob,' replied Tom.

'Very funny,' said Tilly, unamused. 'I can see those men from the boat moving inside the Tower. Yep, half a dozen of them have just gone straight into the White Tower itself.'

'Up to the Conqueror's Chapel,' said Will. 'Action stations, people, this is it. The trap is set. We're on.'

The Chapel of St John in the White Tower – also known as the Conqueror's Chapel

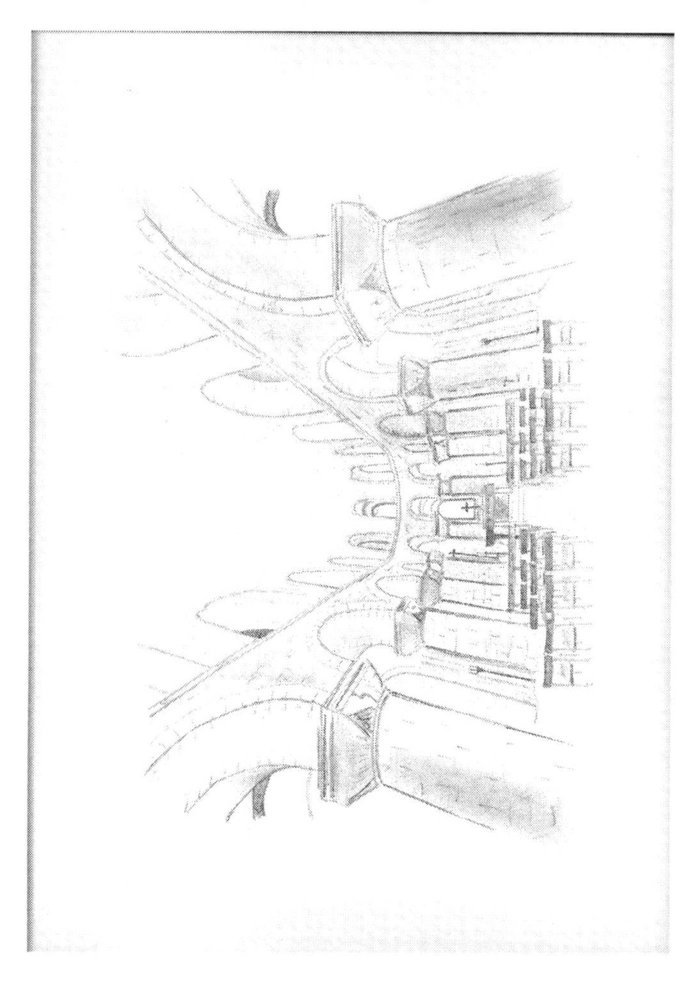

31 A VERY HOT PURSUIT

'What's taking them sooo looong?' Boffin asked Tilly up in the belfry, tapping his foot in an agitated fashion and leaning closer to his screens to make sure he wasn't missing anything.

'Not sure, but if the case is well hidden, it may be taking them some time to extricate it. Perhaps it's buried under the floor, or stashed in a wall, and needs to be excavated. A couple of those chaps did seem to have tools.'

'Have you seen anything else, guys?' came Tom's voice over the radio.

'Not yet,' replied Tilly, 'although it is getting a little smoky up here! Not too bad yet, although it is making life quite tricky for the battery solar charger.'

7pm, thought Will looking at his watch. Where were they? He was beginning to get anxious that perhaps the case had left the Tower by a different route after all. At least the tide had begun to turn so that it would carry boats up river quickly – that would help them.

'Are you two certain no one's left the White Tower yet?' he enquired impatiently.

'Pretty certain,' came Boffin's reply. 'It's hard to be

sure because there are so many people running in and out of the east gate to tackle the fire, but we haven't seen any of the distinctive uniforms emer . . . oh, wait! I think we've got something now.'

'What is it?' asked Tom, urgently, as the boys hurried out of the front gate of the inn and towards where the ferryman had tied up the boat nearby.

'Yup, we've got two men carrying what looks like a small box – maybe a chest, or case, or something – out of the White Tower, back towards Traitors' Gate. The others are following closely behind. Hard to see as the light's going a bit, but it's definitely them. I can tell from the uniforms,' said Tilly, zooming in with the camera that was mounted on Chewbacca's belly.

'OK, look,' said Will to the team up in the belfry, 'we're going to get in the boat with our ferryman, so we're not going to be able to talk into the radio. We'll be able to hear you through the earpieces, but not talk back. So I'll try and use taps on the radio with the channel open to answer any questions. One tap for yes, two for no. Got it?'

'Got it,' replied Tilly, just as the boys reached the landing stairs.

'A very good evening to you, Stokeld,' said Will, approaching the small boat.

'Evenin' Sir Richard, and – er, what was the name of yer valet again?'

'This is Baldrick.'

'An' evenin' to you, Baldrick,' said Stokeld. 'Me ol' father was called Baldrick, so he was.'

'Isn't that a happy coincidence,' said Tom dryly through gritted teeth, jabbing Will in the small of the back as they once again stepped down into the unstable boat.

'We have special business on behalf of the Crown,' Will explained, getting creative. 'We will wait here a short while and I will give you the signal when we need to move. We will be heading up river with the direction of the tide – I think, anyway,' he hedged.

They sat in silence for a short while, as Boffin gave them a running commentary through their earpieces: 'OK, the boat's out on the river again, you should be able to see it now heading back west . . .'

'Towards Westminster, if you please, Mr Stokeld!' instructed Will.

'Right you are, Sir Richard!' and the boat started moving off from the steps. By this time, the river was a frenzy of activity. 'We might 'ave some difficulty getting' through the bridge, mind, so many are sheltering from the heat under the arches,' explained Stokeld.

Ahead of them, the boys saw that many of the nineteen arches of old London Bridge were playing host to dozens upon dozens of small river craft, each loaded to capacity with people and possessions, all desperate to escape the flames, but clearly with nowhere to go. Looking round to his right, Will saw the archbishop's vessel picking up speed as it approached the middle of the Bridge, all six sets of oars working in perfect unison, the flag fluttering at the prow as it cut through the choppy water on this side of the bridge.

'A little faster if you please, Stokeld.'

'Right you are, sir,' and the ferryman heaved more energetically on the oars.

Negotiating their way through an arch at the southern end of the bridge, Stokeld had to push back with his oars against other craft jostling for space, slowing their progress. The archbishop's boat – which, at closer range, the boys could now see bore the name *Manticore* – forged ahead, picking up speed and leaving them some way behind.

'If they get too far ahead for us to track you both properly, do you want us to follow the boat?' Boffin enquired over the radio.

Will replied 'yes' with a single surreptitious tap of the squawk button hidden in his cuff.

As they progressed under the bridge the shouting and

chaos on the road above became all too obvious. Boom! Another warehouse on the north bank exploded at ground level, the upper floors collapsing down upon it and cascading into the river, just missing a barge which had pushed off from the nearest wharf only moments before. The *Manticore* continued to put clear water between them as the boys' small ferry craft made only modest progress up the river.

'Looks like we've got company,' said Tilly's voice over the radio after ten minutes or so. 'Suspect vessel moving at speed to close with the archbishop's boat from the north bank – I think it's just come out of that dock where you two had the run-in with the Cardinal's heavies when we arrived.'

In the fading light, Will and Tom strained their eyes to identify the craft. Then – yes, there it was, perhaps four hundred yards ahead: the same silhouette that they had glimpsed the Frenchmen loading shortly after their arrival the previous evening.

'It's them,' said Will, forgetting the ferryman was present. Stokeld looked confused, but continued rowing. The French vessel was about the same size as *Manticore* but an altogether rougher creation, though closing the distance with its target at speed.

'See if you can get closer,' said Will, pretending to talk to Stokeld and gesturing at the boats ahead, but depressing the radio talk button so that Boffin and Tilly could hear the instruction, too. Boffin manoeuvred Chewbacca lower and closer to the impending clash, the direction of the gusting wind for once helping the drone's progress, rather than impeding it.

By now, Will was practically standing, just to get a better view. 'I don't think they've spotted them yet, Baldrick,' he said quietly to Tom, who was also gripped by the unfolding drama. It was as though a great battle of ancient Roman triremes was about to play out in the middle of the river Thames, albeit on a modest scale. The

French boat was within fifty yards of the *Manticore*, then forty, thirty, twenty. . .

'They must think it's just another ship fleeing the fire,' said Tom holding tightly to the side of their own boat as though they were the ones about to be rammed. 'Amongst all the other ships on the river, it would be an easy mistake to make.'

Suddenly, one of the men standing on the *Manticore* looked right and, seeing the impending collision, braced himself against the cabin at the back of the boat. The other standing officers were not so lucky. Crash! The French ship impacted the *Manticore* exactly amidships, ramming it hard, shattering oars on the starboard side and knocking those who had been upright straight into the water some distance from the boat. Quick as a flash, several others jumped from the French ship onto the *Manticore*, and the sound of gunfire crackled across the water, only partially disguised amidst the sounds of chaos from the north bank. 'They're using pistols!' said Boffin, horrified, as two of the Frenchmen grabbed what appeared to be the box that had been removed from the Tower and lifted it into their own boat. Once all the Cardinal's agents had returned to their vessel, barely sixty seconds after they had rammed the *Manticore*, they furiously backed it away from the archbishop's crippled boat.

One of the Frenchmen threw something into the Manticore, whose remaining crew promptly threw themselves into the cold water just before what remained of their boat exploded behind them. The surviving soldiers swam as best they could to a nearby barge, whose crew, having seen the explosion, helped them out of the water.

'Did you just see that!?' said Boffin excitedly over the radio. 'Right, we've got them anyway, but it looks like they're not heading back to the dock they set off from. No, they're not. They're heading up river, boys – keep going.'

'Faster, Mr Stokeld, if you please,' said Will, tersely. 'I

remind you that we have urgent business on behalf of the Crown.'

By now the ferryman was wheezing unhealthily, and Will felt a bit guilty for pushing him so hard, but they badly needed to close the gap on the escaping agents, otherwise they might never see the case again and the whole adventure would be for nothing. Having narrowed the gap between them to barely two hundred yards at the time of the ambush, the distance was once again opening up rapidly.

'Stay on them,' commanded Will hopefully, as they passed through the debris field of the shattered *Manticore* just as its once proud prow slipped beneath the surface of the water.

32 THE PALACE OF WHITEHALL

'They're making for the shore,' said Tilly. 'Looks like they're going to dock at one of the landing stages of the private palaces along the Strand. No – wait, they're not stopping yet.'

Having passed Baynard's Castle, the entrance to the old Fleet River (a tributary of the Thames), and the Temple – the legal heart of London, with its ancient crusader church and courtyards which daily teemed with barristers still just visible in the last of the evening light – the Cardinal's agents now made for the royal centre of London: the old Palace of Whitehall.

'Can you set us down somewhere by the Royal Palace, Stokeld?' asked Will.

'Right ye are, sirs,' he said, manoeuvring the boat painfully slowly towards the north bank.

'Quick as you can, please,' Will added, urgently.

Ahead, the French ship pulled alongside a smart stone pier which jutted out into the river. A cloistered walkway extended along it from the rambling range of palatial buildings beyond.

'The great ancient royal heart of London,' Will explained to Tom under his breath, confidentially.

'What on earth are they doing marching into the palace?' asked Tilly over the radio.

Tom was tapping his feet impatiently against the wooden hull of their boat, seeing how much of a head start their targets now had.

The ferry bumped up against some stone steps not far from the French boat with a gentle thud. Will handed the ferryman another coin and promised to return, as Stokeld tied the boat to a metal ring on a stake. The boys scrambled as quickly as possible out of the shaky vessel and onto the slimy steps, running through a series of passages and out along a stone parapet which guarded the riverside of a formal garden.

'This is a part of the palace,' said Will. 'We must not get caught. The punishments for intruding on royal property are – not pleasant, shall we say!

'Let's hole up somewhere and get the Bug out to see what's going on,' he suggested.

'Guys, I think they're in the range of buildings to your north-west,' said Boffin over the radio.

'Thanks, Boffin, we'll be deploying the Bug shortly to have a look inside.'

'Good idea,' came Boffin's reply.

'In here,' hissed Tom, opening the door to a fine but empty brick-built garden room with a pointed slate roof which overlooked the river. He began to rummage around furiously in his sack, clipping together bits and pieces. Moments later he revealed under torchlight a small, black contraption about the size of a Scalextric car. 'This is the Bug,' he said proudly, flicking the "On" switch and watching the screen on the controller come to life to show a large picture of Will's nose.

Will put the gizmo down. 'Very cool. Let's get to work.'

The Bug made a gentle humming noise as it set off out of the window into the night.

'How does it even work?' Will asked.

'No idea,' replied Tom. 'It's Boffin's creation, so incomprehensible to non-techy people, but I think there's some kind of high-powered lift fan in it.'

The camera allowed Tom to pilot the Bug shakily towards an open window at ground floor level in the red–brick range of buildings which Boffin had identified.

'Thank God it's hot this evening,' said Will. 'It means plenty of open windows for us to make the most of.'

In the distance, further bangs suggested yet more powder supplies, or perhaps some other explosive substance, had been consumed by the inferno. Thames-side warehouses were piled high not only with explosive powder, but other highly flammable materials such as pitch and tar. These, too, contributed to the inferno and to the explosive intensity of the blasts.

Elevated women's voices suddenly drifted into earshot near the boys' hideout.

'The point, my dear Georgiana,' said one, 'is that I do not think that is a very sensible idea. The other ladies at Court will not be amused at all.'

'Please, my dear Genevieve, you're not my governess…'

'She's right, though,' said a third.

'Thank you kindly, Eleanor, but neither are you!' said Georgiana, sounding increasingly irritated as the footsteps passed, crunching into the distance along the gravelled pathway.

'Gently does it, gently does it,' said Tom allowing himself to breathe once more, and talking the Bug through the mullioned window.

'Boom – we're in.'

'Good work,' encouraged Will. 'Now, let's have a good look around.' The Bug's rotating camera peered around the room it had entered, picking up wood-panelling and large hanging tapestries on the walls.

'Go through that door,' Will gestured at a point on the small controller screen, 'that should be a hall.'

Tom guided the Bug through the broad doorway ahead, whose door was standing ajar. Sure enough, they found themselves in a large hall with a stone-flagged floor, wooden panelling rising to the level of the base of the high gothic windows, and portraits covering the walls above. Overhead, a hammerbeam wooden roof soared into the air.

'There . . . there they are!' said Tilly. Up in the tower, she and Boffin were also watching the feed, relayed by Chewbacca which, by circling overhead, could pick up and boost the weaker signal from the Bug.

'See if you can settle on a window sill, or a mantelpiece or something, and see what's going on,' said Will.

At the far end of the hall, on one side of a great table positioned widthways to the length of the room, sat a man in elaborate crimson robes with a skull cap covering his receding hairline, flanked on either side by some unpleasant-looking characters in dark blue formal clothing. That this was the Cardinal there could be no doubt. He was elaborately moustached, while his beard was trimmed to a small, particularly pointy goatee. Even through the Bug's limited vision, the children could clearly discern his penetrating, almost ghostly stare. Opposite the Cardinal and his henchmen, in a different style of clothing with very large white lace collars, sat three other men whose pointed beards were more developed.

'Can you turn up the volume?' asked Will. 'I want to hear this.'

'Your Excellency,' said one of the men, who was obviously English. 'We are most grateful for your visitation, but we cannot agree to your demands. They are unacceptable to His Majesty. France must agree to reasonable peace terms. We will defeat the Dutch in short order, and then you will be left to fight England alone. At that point, it will be only a matter of time until victory is ours.'

'We have been very generous,' said the man in the purple robes with a slow shrug and sounding as though he was not in fact at all disappointed. He let out an exaggerated sigh. 'My king will not allow me to make any furzer concessions. I must return to Versailles to speak wiz 'im at once. I regret that we 'ave not found more acceptable grounds for agreement.'

'Very well, your Eminence. We shall await word from you. You know our terms.'

'I am truly sorry about ze fire,' added the Cardinal in his curious French-Italian drawl, rising to leave, and not sounding sorry at all.

'He's ballywell masquerading as the French Ambassador!' said Will. 'Don't you see? In 1666, the English are at war with the Dutch and the French. The Cardinal's obviously pretending he's an emissary from King Louis XIV of France, sent to negotiate a peace settlement. After all, who would know one Cardinal minister from another? It's not as if, in the seventeenth century, you can just go on the internet and check what someone looks like. But it's only a cover for him to be in London

'Mazarin was at the heart of French power when he was Chief Minister of France, so he'll know just about all the tricks of the trade. And of course the terms are unreasonable – they're designed not to be acceptable. As soon as the English government ministers turn him down, he's got the perfect excuse to leave London, taking the case with him. And then he'll be off to retrieve the Grail, and it'll all be over.'

'We've got to stop them!' said Tom, practically shouting, 'and before they open the case.'

'What's going on, boys? Talk to us,' said Tilly, over the radio.

'We're cooking up something big and bold,' replied Tom. 'Stand by for action.'

33 HIT AND RUN

'I'm hungry,' said Tom a few minutes later.

'What, now?!' replied Will, flabbergasted, you've just told the others that we're cooking up something big. I didn't think you meant *literally* . . .'

'Yes, now! We haven't eaten for hours,' Tom went on, rummaging around in his sack for a chocolate bar. 'All we've eaten are stupid biscuits. I could literally kill some chicken nuggets right about now.'

'Oh, *sure*, nuggets. Let's just head over to McDonalds and . . . Oh, wait, that's right, no chicken nuggets for the next three hundred years!' said Will, sarcastically. Ignoring the protest he radioed the tower from their hiding place.
'Tilly, can you guys give us a rough idea of the layout of this corner of the Palace? It looks like the Cardinal's going to be moving on with his entourage soon, now that the sham diplomatic discussions have broken down, and that means the case will be going with them. We might not be able to keep up, so we're going to have to grab it, and I think better to do it while they're still sitting around talking than when they're on their way and on their guard.'

'Agreed,' the reply crackled back over the radio. 'You're about twenty yards across the formal garden from what looks like the main riverside entrance to the range of buildings in which the hall sits. I guess that the Cardinal's heavies are lurking somewhere in there, masquerading as his retinue.

'On the other side of the building is a long brick quadrangle extending inland, three storeys high by the look of things.

'Wait. . .' she added, 'it looks as if some carriages and wagons are being drawn up. Boys – quick, it seems the horses are being saddled . . . I bet those are for the Cardinal's delegation. You need to strike now, or else the game's up! Needless to say we don't have a handy carriage of our own . . .'

'Uh ooooh,' said Tom, through a mouthful of chocolate crumbs which flew everywhere. He got the Bug airborne as the Cardinal rose from the table in the large hall and glided towards a door on the west side of the room. His henchmen followed in his wake, as did the Bug, lurching all over the place like a drunken humming–bird and barely missing a chandelier which was filled with lighted candles.

'Have you been drinking? Can't you keep that thing steady?' asked Will, testily, feeling a bit airsick just watching the performance on Tom's diminutive controller screen.

'*Sooorrrry*,' said Tom, 'but Boffin only gave me a half-hour lesson, and the controls are jolly sensitive.'

'We've got more movement in the courtyard,' said Boffin, 'maybe half a dozen of the . . . Yes, I recognise one from the boat, definitely. A great troll of a man with that appalling beard. He's got a bit of a limp now. Ha, serves him right.'

Will looked out of the window over the small, ornately manicured hedges. 'Nothing else for it,' he said to Tom, opening the door with a dramatic swoosh and looking each way for any sentries. None were to be seen.
'And where exactly are you going?' asked Tom,

indignantly, polishing off the second finger of the chocolate bar.

'We've got to get that case!' replied Will.

'That's your plan is it? "We've got to get that case!"' mimicked Tom. 'The Cardinal has maybe twenty henchmen with him, and they're all armed with pistols. You can't just walk up to them and take it, Will. That's a bit over-confident, even for you.'

'I'll improvise,' Will said, with an impish grin. 'Keep me posted on what you see with the Bug, will you?'

'All *riiigght*,' said Tom, dubiously. 'But don't do anything too dumb.'

Closing the door behind him, Will followed the edge of the building until he reached the same open window through which Tom had flown the Bug a short while earlier. Tom watched as his brother squeezed himself through, knocking his hat off in the process.

'Very dignified,' he said to himself sarcastically, as Will's disembodied arm emerged once more from the window to recover his hat from the flower bed beneath it.

'I'm in,' Will said over the radio. 'Status update please.'

'Nothing new from the courtyard,' replied Tilly, 'just a few people milling around, waiting.'

'The Cardinal's still in the room talking to some of his agents,' said Tom, looking at the monitor on his control, and watching the Cardinal gesticulating energetically in front of a large hearth where a fire blazed despite the heat of the night. 'But they're talking in French and I can't understand it.'

Now that the Cardinal was standing, they could see that he was a tall man, thin and somehow ghostly as his expression had earlier suggested. Yet all his actions were precise, the actions of a man who knew exactly what he wanted and how he was going to get it.

'He's talking to them about a diversion,' said Tilly, listening in from the cathedral belfry. 'But does that mean the carriages, I wonder? Maybe they're going back down the river?

'Wait – there's something else. He's quite agitated. He's just told them that someone or something called Adrasteia has set a deadline for the case to be recovered. This is the only opportunity, or – yes, he's saying this is the one chance. No going back. Hang on, the other man's now asking about the King.

'Nope, Adrasteia, whoever or whatever that is, is not King Louis. But Mazarin says he has his orders. All very strange indeed – it sounds like he's working for someone else,' she tailed off.

By now, Will was next to the door into the great hall, only a few dozen yards from the Cardinal. 'Can you see the chest from the Tower anywhere?' he whispered into the microphone. Tom rotated the Bug to all corners of the room. Nothing.

'Hang on, I'm going through into the next chamber, and the Bug lurched forward again, attracting the attention of one of the henchmen.

'He thinks it's a bat,' said Tilly, amused, listening to the excited shouting in French.

'Wait,' said Tom, 'I've seen it. One of the men in the room with the Cardinal is actually sitting on a small case. I bet that's it. He guided the Bug to land on top of a large cabinet on one side of the room to have a better look. I'm certain that's it, Will,' he added, zooming in. 'I guess it's not a surprise that the Cardinal would be keeping it that close, but it's going to be a bit tricky for you to get hold of.'

Will looked around the deserted great hall. The representatives of King Charles II had long disappeared. He dashed the forty feet or so across the floor to another doorway where he waited for a few seconds to see if he'd been spotted. Again, nothing. All was calm. He could hear raised French voices now.

'What are you doing?' hissed Tom over the radio.

'I'm going to give the horses a bit of a fright,' and Will pulled out a couple of packs of Chinese firecrackers from beneath his disguise. Heading through the door behind him, he found himself in another ante-chamber, overlooking the courtyard which lay some feet below on the other side of the hall. Only moonlight illuminated his surroundings. 'Perfect,' he thought, quietly opening one of the leaded windows.

The sounds of horses stomping and snorting impatiently greeted him, as did a waft of pungent air, a mix of filth, horse manure and burning wood. Igniting the three blocks of firecrackers simultaneously with a lighter, he lobbed them towards the three principal carriages below, closing the window smartly afterwards.

About ten seconds passed and then . . . ratatatatatat! It sounded as if several Thompson submachine guns had opened fire at the same moment. Chaos unfolded. The horses all bolted in different directions, veering violently all over the courtyard, unable to escape. The carriages they pulled were dashed against one another and the walls of the buildings. One carriage overturned entirely, and its horses, having dragged it some way along the surface of smooth cobbles, broke free.

'Nice show,' came Boffin's voice over the radio, watching admiringly via the Chewbacca video feed.

But Will wasn't hanging around to watch. Darting out of his hiding place, he made his way past two suits of medieval armour which stood guard against the wall of the hall, toward the next room, where the Cardinal was.

'Sacré-bleu!' The sound of agitated French voices wafted out of the room. To Will's delight, as he peered around the door frame, he saw all the men in the room gathered by the window, gripped by the unfolding drama in the courtyard below, the Cardinal's crimson robe fluttering slightly in the evening breeze which flowed through the open windows.

'Now's your chance,' said Tom's voice over the radio,

'while they're all distracted . . .'

Will reached into his disguise again and pulled out two more EG Burst smoke grenades. The colour labels declared the smoke to be red.

'Appropriate for a cardinal,' thought Will. 'Dad would be proud,' and he pulled the rings and tossed the grenades on to the floor in the middle of the Cardinal's chamber. In seconds, the room was filled with thick red smoke. Will dashed in, having to estimate where the box might be since he now couldn't see it himself.

'What's going on?' hissed Tom urgently over the radio, also unable to see anything through the smoke. Will ran headlong into someone stocky, shoving them forcefully back. The man swore in French, choking on the coloured smoke and crashing into the fire irons by the hearth. Then Will accidentally stubbed his toe against the corner of the heavy wooden box, and swore himself. Two metal handles, one at either end, presented themselves. Will picked it up, turned around, and walked awkwardly as fast as he could out of the room. Unfortunately, he walked straight into the wall and had to grope his way toward the door, still wreathed in red smoke. As he darted ungainly across the hall and back to the room whose window opened on to the garden, he heard a coughing, spluttering Cardinal yell in French that the case was missing. His voice was curiously high-pitched and ringing when agitated.

'Tom, come to the window to help me with the box – quick, it's jolly heavy. The damn scroll must be made of lead or something.'

'On my way,' said Tom stuffing the control into his bag and dashing out of his hiding place across the garden, reaching the window just as his older brother did.

'Here,' said Will, passing through the simple but sturdy case, which only just fitted. He was just about to hop through the window after it when a large, powerful hand reached around his midriff and yanked him violently back into the room.

'Run for it!' shouted Will to Tom. 'Run to the boat,' he added, as he furiously lashed out at whoever had caught him. A well-aimed backwards kick between the Frenchman's legs and his captor buckled over as two of his friends appeared in the doorway behind him. The man still had hold of Will's cape, which tore as he finally dived through the window and into the hedge below. He swiftly caught up with his younger brother who was labouring loudly with the heavy case along a gravel path.

'Thanks a lot for waiting,' wheezed Will sarcastically.

'You told me to run!' said Tom, puffing indignantly, waddling under the combined weight of his pack and the case.

'Obviously I was being heroic,' said Will, 'I didn't *actually* want you to leave me with some vile agents of the Cardinal in mid-seventeenth century London.'

'Consider it payback for calling me Baldrick,' said Tom, as Will grabbed one end of the case to help him along.

They ran as fast as they could, back through the winding passages of the palace complex toward the landing steps, where they hoped against hope that Stokeld was still moored up at the Whitehall Palace Stairs.

'Please be there, please be there,' Tom was repeating over and over again to himself.

'Well, we're completely stuffed if he's not.'

34 OUT OF THE FRYING PAN, INTO THE FIRE

'Chaps, I'm sorry to be the bearer of bad news all the time but I think you've got more company,' said Boffin over the radio, trying to sound calm, and feeling anything but. The picture on the monitor in front of him revealed half a dozen soldiers bearing halberds running the length of the long, rectangular courtyard where the horses were still being pacified. Boffin was in no doubt that they were headed out in hot pursuit of Will and Tom as they beat a hasty retreat.

Crash! Tom had run straight into a kitchen maid, who went flying into a large shrub. 'So sorry,' shouted Tom over his shoulder, 'but can't stop.'

'A plague on your house!' shouted the girl with long curly hair in a thick Irish accent from her new position seated in the shrub. They were back out on the landing stairs now. 'Oh, thank the Lord, he's still there,' said Tom, seeing the ferryman Stokeld bobbing around absent-mindedly at the bottom of the steps as he inspected his revolting fingernails.

'Stokeld!' shouted Will at the top of his voice,

'Stokeld! Untether the boat, right now!'

The ferryman looked round in surprise, his shifty eyebrows shooting rather comically further and further up his small forehead as he saw the boys racing down the stairs towards him, pursued by a gaggle of thick-set French agents who certainly did not look as if they had the boys' best interests at heart. Stokeld didn't need much encouragement, and immediately slipped the mooring-rope from its rusty iron ring on the steps and kicked back hard off the lowest exposed stair.

'Jump!' shouted Will, as the boys neared the end of the pier. Tom duly did so with Will giving him a helping shove in the back to propel him the necessary distance. Clutching the unwieldy case and with his own bag hanging over his shoulder, Tom nearly capsized the small ferry boat as he landed, crashing into Stokeld at the oars, and just saving the case from flying off into the Thames. Tom's high-velocity landing had the effect of pushing the boat much further from the shore, leaving it out of reach for Will, who wobbled precariously on the edge of the steps. He looked over his shoulder to see the Cardinal's men bearing down on him at speed. He had perhaps five seconds to decide what to do, and few options.

'Oh fudge,' he said, turning back toward the Thames and diving headlong into the stinking waters of the river.

For a moment, everything went dark as he disappeared beneath the glinting black surface of the water. Kicking furiously, he resurfaced thirty seconds later only a few yards from the ferryboat which was by now ten yards or so from the landing stairs.

'Help!' he shouted, feeling the weight of his costume dragging him down once more to the icy depths, his sodden wig matted to his head. Stokeld extended a long oar toward him, and dragged him closer to the boat, as Tom ineffectually tried to counter this move by paddling ferociously in the opposite direction, merely creating much splashing.

'Thanks a lot,' Will gasped, as Stokeld and Tom heaved his sopping frame into the rocking boat. 'Thought I was a goner for sure – er, I mean, praise God for my deliverance from those beastly devils!' he added, glancing at Stokeld.

'Why be ye gentlemen scurrying from the royal palace at this hour?' asked Stokeld, suspiciously, evidently wondering if he had now been implicated in some dastardly, treasonous plot against the king.

'Those are French agents, my good man, and they're up to no good,' replied Will, matter-of-factly. The loud French swearing of the Cardinal's men on the quayside seemed evidence enough for Stokeld, who began rowing fervently in the opposite direction.

'French, you say? By God, they be always up to no good, sirs! Where to, Sir Richard?'

Will was dripping wet and stank of all the grotesque contents of the river which, in the seventeenth century, was essentially a gigantic cesspool. His fake moustache was long gone, as was his treasured hat and the old family sword in its scabbard, although somehow his wig had stayed plastered to his head. Mercifully, in all the commotion, Stokeld didn't seem to have noticed the missing moustache, no doubt in part because Will's face was now so dirty.

Tom was making faces at Will to indicate that he was very much aware of the smell, obviously enjoying divine justice in revenge for his older brother having despatched him to the sewers back in the twenty-first century to collect their historic cash. Fortunately, as Will patted around to see what else might have gone missing, he discovered that he still had the large coin purse tied to his belt.

'Lambeth House, as fast as you can, Stokeld,' he said.

'Right ye are, sir. Off to see the Archbishop of Canterbury, are you?'

'Something like that,' Will replied as they struck out

for the middle of the river, the boys paddling with their hands to help the boat to move faster. By now, the halberd-armed royal guards had acquired flaming torches and had joined the Cardinal's agents at the end of the steps, all shouting and gesticulating wildly, but all equally reluctant to take a dip in the river.

'I suspect they can't swim,' shouted Will, triumphantly, offering a very obvious 'V' sign to the assembled would-be pursuers.

'What on earth is going on?' asked Tilly's voice over the radio. Will didn't respond. Tom realised he must have lost his earpiece in his dip in the water, and tapped his ear to let Will know that the team in the tower were communicating.

'Are you both OK?' she persisted, sounding very alarmed. One squawk from Tom on the radio confirmed that they were.

Looking behind them, they could see their massed pursuers retracing their steps back in to the palace. Moments later, they reappeared at the landing pier at which the French agents had arrived earlier, and began piling into the boat in which the Cardinal's agents had travelled.

'We're not going to be able to out-run them,' exclaimed Tom anxiously. 'Row harder, man! Row, row row!' he shouted at Stokeld.

'Well, we probably don't need to,' said Will, looking as if he didn't entirely believe what he was saying. 'Look how low it's sitting in the water already, compared with an hour ago. My bet is that they holed it somewhere below the waterline when they rammed the *Manticore*. With that many people in the boat, they're dangerously overloaded anyway. They'll never make it to us.'

By now it was past 9pm, and in the distance the crackle and roar of the fire was clearly audible. A shower of glowing embers could be seen descending from the heavens, twinkling like stars in the night sky. These spread the fire far and wide, rendering the belatedly–established firebreaks next to worthless. Even this far up river, puffs of smoke drifted past them, with flecks of ash and burned wood occasionally falling around them, hissing as they kissed the surface of the Thames.

'Lambeth House is just over there,' said Will, gesturing to the much darker south bank of the river for Tom's benefit. 'You can see the windows of the chapel are illuminated.'

By now mid-river, the boys enjoyed watching the overloaded pursuing boat slowing as it took on more water, before turning sluggishly for shore once again. In the distance, the figure of the Cardinal stood alone on the pier, his fine crimson robes rippling in the wind. Perhaps it was the effect of the shadow which fell across his face from the torch he held aloft in his left hand, but even at this range his expression looked murderous. Suddenly, he turned on his heel and marched smartly back into the palace, apparently exasperated at the incompetence of his own agents.

The river itself still teemed with boats, lighters and barges making good their escape from the flames, and soon the boys felt safer, knowing that their movements were better disguised by all these other vessels crowding the waterway.

Half an hour later, Stokeld manoeuvred them to the edge of Lambeth Steps, a little upriver from Whitehall. Such was the volume of waterborne refugees from further east that they had to walk across half a dozen boats which were also vying for space at the landing stage, just to reach the stone walkway to the bank. Balancing precariously with their precious cargo, Will left the usual instructions with Stokeld to wait, and offered a further financial inducement. He was very cold now, the water having comprehensively soaked everything he was wearing, and the wind chilled him further.

A short walk across a road that was little more than a

muddy track, and they arrived at the huge brick-built Tudor gatehouse of the London home of the Archbishops of Canterbury, Lambeth Palace.

'Will,' said Tom suddenly, 'why are we giving this to the Archbishop at all? I thought we were going to take it home and, you know, look at the clues and stuff to find the Grail ourselves.'

'We're taking it to the Archbishop,' Will chattered back, rubbing his chest with both arms, 'because that's where it was meant to go. And some things are better left hidden. What are we possibly going to do with the Grail anyway?' he added. 'We'd only have to go and hide it ourselves, probably somewhere much less safe.'

Tom didn't respond, obviously disappointed that their quest wouldn't have the expected ending. Will hammered on the pedestrian gate, adjacent to the large carriage gates, which were also closed.

'What's going on?' asked Boffin over the radio, which crackled with static. Tom explained. Boffin, too, was disappointed, but Tilly thought it wise and backed Will's decision.

For a nervous minute, the boys stood, Will's teeth chattering audibly, waiting for a response. Then the viewing port of the pedestrian gate shot open.

'Who goes there?' asked the gatekeeper, who had a gnarled nose.

'We have an urgent delivery for the Archbishop,' said Will

'What is it?' said the man disbelievingly.

'Tell him it's from the Tower, he'll understand,' Will replied.

The gatekeeper considered him for a moment. 'Very well then, wait there.'

A small puddle had appeared on the ground where Will stood. Tom looked down. 'Um, Sir Richard,' he said sarcastically, 'you appear to have lost control of your bladder, by God!'

'Very amusing, Baldrick, it's obviously the river water dripping off me, isn't it!'

The boys looked around furtively, conscious that the Cardinal's agents might appear again at any moment. Outside the gatehouse, they were boxed into a corner, with nowhere to run if any nefarious characters should emerge from the gloom. Nearby, a small crowd had gathered, discussing the progress of the fire in heated tones.

'It's at Garlick Hill, Mr Renouf,' said one, hysterically. 'Jersey must be the only safe place in these accursed isles, now Mr Hemms,' replied the bespectacled Renouf, clutching a baby tightly.

'Garlick Hill?!' repeated Will, overhearing the talking, 'that's barely five minutes' walk from St Paul's. Tom, get on to the others, and find out what they can see.'

'Broadsword calling Danny Boy,' said Tom, quietly. 'What's the status of the fire? Over.'

'We can't see all that much now, to be honest,' Tilly replied. 'The fire's much closer, and the heat is phenomenal. I'm not sure how much longer we should wait up here. The smoke's making it more and more difficult to see anything, and there are burning embers being fired up into the air by the force of the blaze. Crews seem to have created a bit of a firebreak to the south east of us so that might hold it off for a while, but every time they pull houses down, the fire just leaps across.

'People are literally using long hooks to pull down the buildings, and bucket chains to bring water up from the Thames,' she continued, disbelieving how primitive the firefighting techniques were.

Tom relayed the conversation to Will. 'You've got to get out as soon as you think you should,' Tom replied to Tilly. 'Don't hang around. Start packing up so you're ready to go at any time.'

'Roger,' came Boffin's response.

At that moment, the solid pedestrian gate creaked open on its massive ancient hinges. Alongside the gatekeeper stood four soldiers of the Archbishop's personal guard in their fine maroon livery.

'Come with us, please,' the sergeant said, solemnly. 'We've got some questions for you.'

35 PRISONERS

'What the hell's going on?' asked Tilly urgently over the radio, watching the monitor as the guards picked up the case, and frog-marched the boys inside the curtilage of Lambeth House (as it was then known).

Tom crossed his arms in front of him to show that he couldn't speak freely.

'It doesn't exactly look like they've got a friendly reception, does it?' said Boffin, sounding worried.

'No, it does not!' replied Tilly. 'Keep a close eye on where they're taken. We may need to spring them.'

Several hundred feet below the orbiting drone, the boys passed through the Tudor gatehouse and into an inner courtyard, bounded on the riverside by a long brick wall, and on the right by a huge hall with large buttresses. Two of the escorting guards peeled off through a doorway on their right with the case. Will made to go after it, but was held back by the sergeant.

'And where exactly are you taking that?' asked Will, angrily.

'You said it was for the Archbishop, so it's going to wait somewhere safely for him. Keep moving.' The man prodded Will in the small of the back with his halberd.

'No need for that,' said Will, reluctantly walking as directed.

The boys were shepherded through the porch of the large hall, and into its cavernous interior. Despite its ancient appearance, Will realised that this was what Samuel Pepys had described as Archbishop Juxon's 'new old hall', which had only recently been built to replace the earlier version destroyed by Parliamentarians during the Civil War. It was a magnificent space. The roof rose over forty feet to the highest point: a glass lantern which would offer light by day. After dark, brackets on the walls held flaming torches which cast a shadowy light over the long tables that filled the Great Hall.

At one of these, another group of the Archbishop's guard sat round talking animatedly, falling suddenly quiet when they saw the sergeant and his new charges arrive.

'Who've you got there, then, sergeant?' asked one.

'Special guests of the Archbishop,' replied the sergeant, with an unpleasant laugh. 'They returned the case, Collis, you'll be very relieved to hear. The Archbishop *will* be pleased.'

'They 'ad the case?' exclaimed the man whom, the boys realised as they got closer, looked rather damp, as did a number of his colleagues. The familiar stench of filthy Thames water drifted freshly in their direction.

'How the hell did you get that then?' asked the man, standing up and lurching towards Tom, who was closest to him. Tom recoiled, saved by the intervention of several other members of the guard who rose to restrain their colleague.

'Where is the Archbishop?' demanded Will, practically shouting. 'I must see him right away!'

'Oh, you'll see 'im all right, boys, you'll see 'im,' said the sergeant. 'But he's with 'is Majesty the King at the moment, locked in Privy Council. You might have heard there's a little fire on, over in the City. Bit of a national crisis, you see. So the Archbishop's otherwise engaged at the moment.

'I'm sorry he doesn't have time for a nice fireside chat with you. But don't you worry, we've got a comfy little room all ready for you to wait in while he's out on business. I know he'll be delighted to hear how you got your hands on that special case.' The sergeant laughed nastily again.

'We rescued it from the French agents, didn't we?' said Tom.

'What do you mean, French agents?' asked the Sergeant, sceptically.

'We mean the Cardinal's men,' interjected Will, as they wound their way through a warren of passages and were directed to start climbing a broad wooden spiral staircase.

'I see,' said the guard, evidently unconvinced. 'Well, you'll have plenty of time to explain this in person. You're not going anywhere in a hurry are you?' he asked again with that unpleasant cackle.

'Actually, we are,' Will replied. 'I am Sir Richard de Firebridge, a knight of the realm, and I demand – '

'My backside, you are,' said the sergeant, getting nasty, and shoving him on. 'Now be quiet before we really give you something to complain about.'

The small party reached the top of the stairs. Ahead of them was a narrow wooden door, iron-studded, complete with viewing hatch. Tom and Will exchanged nervous glances. They were both thinking the same thing: this is a prison cell.

The junior guard stepped forward and lifted a large key from a hook on the wall a few feet from the door before unlocking the room. Moving to the fireplace within, he used his torch to light a small fire with the measly logs that were already in the grate.

'After you, *Sir Richard*,' said the sergeant with a mock bow, pushing the boys inside the room, as the other guard retreated and locked them in.

'We'll come and get you when the Archbishop's good and ready to talk to you,' he called through the inspection hatch, 'but I don't want to hear a peep from you before then.' With that, he slammed the hatch shut. The guards' guffaws echoed around the stairwell as they beat a retreat.
The boys were locked in a room about ten feet square with a fireplace on one wall, slightly offset from the centre of the room. Thick, crude wooden panels lined walls of brick, otherwise visible above the panelling, which didn't quite reach the ceiling. Ominously, large metal rings protruded from the walls on all sides, with fragments of rope hanging off them.

'Well, at least they didn't chain us up,' said Tom, trying to find a silver lining to their predicament. 'And we've got a fire, so you can dry off.'

'Ah yes, *brilliant*, a nice toasty fire. Perhaps some marshmallows and hot chocolate and a sea shanty to while away the night? Yes that's right, because we're not stuck in a grotty prison in the seventeenth century. Fabulous. You're right, Tom,' Will added, every word dripping sarcasm, 'so much has gone right it's difficult to know where to start. This was not part of the plan!'

He sat down in front of the fire, and began rearranging the wood with his booted foot to get a better blaze. 'I've actually been to this place before,' he went on. 'It's the Lollards' Tower. The Archbishops use it to lock up heretics. What a bitter irony for a loyal Anglican,' he continued, talking mainly to himself.

Tom peered out of one of the two small windows of the room. 'We've got a decent view of the City, as well,' he said, ignoring Will's pessimism. 'Or what's left of it.'

'Guys, what on earth is going on?' asked Tilly again through Tom's earpiece.

'Ah ha, forgot you were there for a moment,' said Tom, responding via the radio. Will looked round, suddenly more cheerful.

'Bloody idiots,' he said, 'they've also left us with your

bag, Tom.'

Tom unhitched it and handed it to Will before relating to Boffin and Tilly what had just happened. 'So, basically, we've been locked in a prison for our trouble,' said Tom, matter–of–factly.

'Hey, I've got an idea. The Bug is still in the Palace of Whitehall, isn't it?' said Will, excitedly.

'Yeah, but I'm sure we'll be out of range,' replied Tom.

'Doesn't matter. Get Boffin to fly Chewbacca over the Palace and take control of the Bug remotely. Maybe he can fly it across the river to us. It can only be about a thousand yards or so. Then we can sce what's going on downstairs, and our best way out of here.'

'Good thinking,' said Tom, relaying the idea to Boffin, who immediately set Chewbacca on a course back for the Palace of Whitehall over the river.

'We might not have enough juice to get the Bug back over to you,' said Boffin. 'But it's definitely worth a shot. Better if it finished up at the bottom of the river, anyway,' he added, 'rather than being found on top of some random cabinet in the Palace where it might prompt quite a lot of tricky questions later!'

'Will you give me the radio for a moment?' Will asked. 'Thanks.'

'Tilly, can you hear me?' he began. 'Great. The way I see it, the main problem is that, even if we can convince Sheldon we've done him a mass- '

'Who's Sheldon?' interjected Tilly.

'He's the Archbishop of Canterbury, *obviously*,' said Will, irritably.

'Anyway, even if we can convince him we've done him a massive favour,' he said, ploughing on, 'the fire will most likely have engulfed St Paul's and the Deanery by the time we get out, blocking our access back to the future for – well, God only knows how long. You and Boffin will be able to get back, but Tom and I could be stuck here for a very long time. I mean, imagine how much debris and rubble is going to be covering the site, and think how many people are going to be swarming around after the fire's blown out. We'll be totally stuffed.'

'I don't much fancy hanging around here much longer, Will,' said Tom, suddenly looking agitated as he listened to Will's end of the conversation.

'So we've got to get out and make it back to the elevator before the fire hits, or all bets are off,' concluded Will.

'Agreed,' said Tilly. 'Boffin's nearly got the drone back to the Palace, so hopefully you'll have the Bug soon enough, and then we can make a proper escape plan.'

36 SISTER ACT

Through the small north-facing window of their prison cell high up in the tower, Will could see the hungry flames devouring ever larger swathes of the old City. Occasional explosions still rang out, the last gasps of a growing number of unfortunate wharves along the river.

'Just remember that insurance doesn't exist,' he explained to Tom, slipping back into moonlighting history lecturer mode. 'Every church, house, shop, warehouse, livery hall – absolutely everything, will have to be rebuilt with fresh funds. There are no insurers covering this. It's actually the Fire that really helps to kick–start the insurance industry.'

Tom joined him at the window. 'Will, you're really not the Archbishop of Banterbury, are you?' he said, chuckling appreciatively to himself at the terrible pun. 'But you do stink,' he continued, holding his nose.

'Thank you for that profound observation,' replied Will, sardonically. 'At least it's a rather drier stink than earlier.' Several of his disguise garments lay on the floor sizzling gently in front of the meagre fire which burned in the grate.

'Boffin, how are you getting along?' Will asked,

anxious for action.

'Nearly with you,' Boffin responded. 'The wind is just too strong for the Bug. It's only really meant to be used indoors, or outside but with very little breeze. So I've had to hitch a lift.'

'On what?' enquired Will.

'On Chewbacca,' said Boffin, proudly.

As the drones drew closer, the screen on Tom's controller grew less fuzzy and more focussed, and they could make out the silhouette of the top edge of the larger machine, with Lambeth Palace hoving into view as the Bug piggybacked its way toward them.

'Nice work Boffin,' marvelled Tom, suitably impressed.

'OK, Will, I think I've got it,' he added, as Chewbacca neared the Lollards Tower in which the boys were holed-up. Tom poked the aerial out of a hole on one side of the window frame.

'Alright, Boffin – Tom's picked it up now,' Will said. 'Thanks a lot.'

'I'm going to have to bring Chewbacca back to the cathedral one last time, Will,' Boffin responded. 'I'm low on juice again, and it's getting seriously hot at our end. I'm not even sure I'll be able to get the drone back up here – the flames now are a bit like a jet engine, and they're creating their own super-heated wind. It's gusting gale-force up here. The drone's really going to struggle to fly close enough.'

'You should see the state of the streets, boys,' added Tilly, looking down through binoculars at the scene unfolding around the cathedral's churchyard and surrounding lanes. 'People are saving literally anything they can. I saw one family pulling a bed down Ludgate Hill earlier – with somebody still in it! It looked as though the occupant was too old or ill to walk. And by the look of things people are still bringing stuff into St Paul's for safekeeping.'

'OK guys, understood,' Will replied. 'Hope to have you back overhead later on. In the meantime, we'll try and get ourselves out of here.'

Humming to himself, Tom piloted the Bug down until it was level with the window at which he was standing, and he could see himself in the camera monitor. 'Smile, stinky,' he said to Will, prompting his brother to wave with a nudge of his elbow.

'Oh, do just get on with it will you,' exclaimed Will, annoyed but quietly amused.

The drone floated down out of sight, looking for an open window or door to enable access to the building. The cell's own windows were sealed shut. The Lollards Tower was situated at one end of the Archbishop's private chapel, which itself sat at a right-angle to the river.

'There we go,' said Tom, identifying an unglazed window at the base of the staircase they had recently climbed to their prison tower. 'Don't you feel like Rapunzel up here?' he went on, beginning to get acclimatised to his imprisonment.

'No, I do not feel like a glamorous blonde woman,' said Will flatly. 'Have you found anything useful or are you just timewasting? That battery's not going to last for ever you know.'

'Patience, patience,' admonished Tom, knowing this would irritate Will more than almost anything else. 'Bother,' he added.

'What is it?'

'They've put a guard at the base of this tower on the courtyard side. Damnit!'

'Fly up to the outside of the cell door and see if there's anything we can do there ourselves,' instructed Will. Tom directed the drone up the stairs; it bounced periodically off the walls as it went.

'Ooops, oops – whew, missed that one, ooooops, oops,' Tom said, monitoring its progress, the battery indicator sinking perilously low. A thorough inspection of the outside of the door revealed no obvious means of escape, although fortuitously no guard was stationed there. 'Set the Bug down somewhere so it can save power and keep an eye on the stairs, will you?'

Tom obliged, moving the sturdy little machine down several levels to a window ledge, to offer some early warning of any return of their captors.

'This is Broadsword calling Danny Boy. Over,' said Will.

'We read you,' replied Tilly.

'Look, I'm not going to lie,' began Will. 'We're in a bit of a tight spot here. How do you fancy coming to the rescue, sister?'

37 MIDNIGHT EXPRESS

'Oh sure, no problem, boys,' responded Tilly sarcastically. 'Great, I'll be over in a few minutes, across the river whose only bridge is on fire at one end, and, um, where every boat in sight has been commandeered for the rescue effort. But really no problem at all. I'll just hope on a Tube train. Oh wait, that's right – the Tube doesn't start to get built until the 1860s so are you OK to hang around for a couple of centuries? By the way, my emergency disguise of a series of hessian sacks with some holes in them looks really good, too. Looking forward to trying this one out on the catwalk. Super chic! Thank God none of my friends can see me. Gawd.'

'Great, thanks a lot,' said Will after the furious diatribe was over, and choosing to ignore the difficulties. 'Um, by the way, do you have any cash, you know, for bribes and stuff?' he ventured nervously.

'No, you big fat hog!' replied Tilly. 'I wasn't supposed to be going on a shopping spree if you remember.'

'*She's not taken it very well!*' Will hissed to Tom in an exaggerated whisper. Tom rolled his eyes.

Returning to the radio conversation, Will continued: 'Look you're a smart girl, you'll think of something.'

'Don't patronise me, William!' his sister warned. 'I guess I'll have to come and bail you out as usual.'

'Boffin,' she went on, turning to her cousin, 'will you be all right up here on your own for a bit? Well, you and the bats. Looks like my incompetent brothers need a bit of a helping hand.'

'Er, I'll be fine,' Boffin agreed, 'but what on earth are you planning to do?'

'Oh, I'm sure I'll think of something,' Tilly replied. 'Remember, Father always did say I was a talent lost to the Metropolitan Police.'

'Um, right, OK,' said Boffin doubtfully, not quite sure how this qualified her for a solo trek across Great Fire London. 'You've got your radio, right?'

'Yup, right here,' she confirmed, patting her side.

'Maybe take one of the flares or something, and a smoke grenade, just in case.'

'Thanks Boffin, good idea,' and Tilly hid the items under her fairly poor disguise, together with a small tablet computer which would enable her to watch the video feed from both Chewbacca and the Bug.

'Once you've refuelled the bird,' she said, referring to Chewbacca which was on its way back to their hiding place on a long, circuitous route to avoid the worst of the extreme heat, 'start to pack up, and make sure you're ready to go at a moment's notice, OK? When the heat and smoke get too intense, go back down to Hades and hide out there, because we know that's safe from the fire.'

'Will do,' replied Boffin, eyeing the approaching blaze with trepidation. 'Look after yourself, coz.'

With that Tilly hurried off down the hidden stairs of Old St Paul's tower, to the increasingly desperate scene hundreds of feet below. Opening the lowest door on the hidden stairway, she slipped out into the vast, unfamiliar crypt of the ancient cathedral. Emerging from behind a large monument to some long-forgotten grandee of the medieval City, she surveyed the scene before her. The columns and vaulted ceilings stretched out in both directions as far as the eye could see, only discernible because of the streams of moonlight that cut into the heavy darkness through the lower windows, periodically fading as dense clouds of smoke drifted past outside.

The crypt itself was a hive of activity. Everywhere she looked, people with arms or wheelbarrows filled with papers and books were stacking their wares on ever-expanding piles and precarious towers which teetered under the strain. Using the frenetic activity as cover to make good her escape, Tilly darted for a large archway at the far west end of the crypt, where a couple of lanterns could be seen disappearing up what must be a flight of stairs.

Emerging from the stairwell into the main body of the cathedral, a similar scene presented itself, only several times more frantic. The Great West Doors of the cathedral were standing wide open, and a flood of people and possessions was making its way into the perceived safety of the church. Tilly darted out through the vast entrance and found herself in Inigo Jones' colonnaded portico. Running down the steps, she had to navigate hordes of people, some shouting for missing family members who had become separated in the flight from the fire, others jostling to escape the coming flames with their most precious possessions.

'Miss Pillsbury!' called an anxious servant. 'Miss Pillsbury, Miss Pillsbury where are you?' A family tried to regroup after having been dispersed by the crowds, 'Binghams over here!' shouted one of them, but the call was lost amidst the cacophony of desperate pleas from other families, Joneses, Prices, Summers, Meads and Millers amongst them.

You're all smelling fairly ripe, thought Tilly, who was even more sensitive than her older brother to bad smells, as she barged through the tightly-packed crowd. As she fought her way out of the flow of human traffic, she tripped on an abandoned chair and sprawled across the filthy street. Seemingly uninterested or unaware, passers-by failed to stop, all except one girl who crouched down and helped Tilly to her feet.

'Thanks a lot,' said Tilly. 'You saved me, I could have been trampled.'

'Don't think anything of it m'dear,' said the feisty-looking girl.

'Katie Law, hurry up or we'll leave you behind,' shouted an older version of the girl, evidently her mother. 'Good luck,' Katie winked at Tilly. And with that, she was off into the crowd once more.

Dusting herself off, Tilly shoved her way through the chaos and made for the relative calm of Deans Court, or Deanery Yard as it was then called.

'Excuse me, excuse me,' she said, jostling aggressively. The intense heat from the blaze surged through the narrow streets and lanes, as though the mouth of Hell itself had opened up. Tilly, naturally a creature of the sun, was reminded of the baking heat on a Greek island – *except I wouldn't want to be sitting on a sun-lounger right now*, she thought. A quick glance at her watch, however, brought her thoughts back to earth with a jolt. 'It's 1am,' she radioed to Boffin. 'We really don't have long at all. I've got to get across the river, sharpish.'

Running west down Carter Lane and darting left onto Blackfriars Lane, she made it to the river bank. 'No boats, bother,' she cursed. Looking up and down the river, now an extended traffic jam of panic-stricken shipping, she noticed several vessels being loaded at Whitefriars, on the other side of the Fleet River. Running back up the hill she found her way to the Lud Gate. Usually, the City's gates were closed at night, but on this occasion the portcullis was up and the heavy old gates sat wide open as the flood of refugees from the fire flowed down the hill away from St Paul's and over the Fleet Bridge. Tilly mingled with them, caught up in the flow, at times practically carried by the press of bodies, so that she had to fight simply to stay upright.

To her horror, she saw looters smashing up the fashionable shop windows only yards from where furtive sentries stood on the Lud Gate. The guards couldn't care less, it seemed, and were apparently preparing to abandon their own positions. Criminals confined in the prison cells over the gatehouse peered anxiously out of the barred window slits, waiting for their opportunity to escape. It was a free-for-all.

Running up Fleet Street, she forked left into Water Lane and found her way back down to the river, where a solitary barge still lay alongside the quay.

Time for my best acting, ever, she thought to herself, rubbing her eyes furiously to redden them, and welling up as she approached one of the men who was hurriedly loading the boat. He wasn't tall, about the same height as Tilly, and was in a serious rush.

'Hurry up Barclay, you lazy oaf,' shouted the man. 'Are your feet capable of co-ordinated movement? And you, too, Cadbury. I'm not paying you to dawdle, y'know!!' 'Yes, sir, Cap'n Wilmot, sir,' said the hapless Barclay, heaving another crate onto the barge, wheezing loudly as he did so.

'Please, sir,' said Tilly, tapping the foreman on the elbow. 'My family's gone over to the other side of the river and left me here. We got separated in the evacuation. I don't know where to go and I'm all alone. Will you please help me?'

The man appeared unmoved. 'No room,' he grunted, returning to his shouting.

Tilly was undeterred, and several minutes of her sob-story appeared to annoy the man so much that he caved in. 'OK, get on the barge, but just quit your whining, by God!'

That was easy, she thought, climbing over a pile of sacks and sitting down to enjoy a brief moment's respite, but still pretending to sob loudly for the benefit of her fellow passengers. Several minutes later, the boat pushed off from the shore.

'No, Dykes, you knave!' shouted the foreman, thumping a blonde man who was trying to shift a crate around, 'you'll unbalance us! Marlow-Thomas, get over here and show Dykes how it's done!'

Tilly stifled a laugh as a manically gabbling Welshman, no doubt Marlow-Thomas, steamed into view and started lecturing the unfortunate Dykes on the appropriate way to heave crates around mid-river. It was going to be a long night, for all of them, it seemed. Especially Barclay.

38 RESCUE

Up in the Lollards Tower, Tom was whistling noisily to himself. Will kept throwing irritated glances in his direction, making it clear that the musical accompaniment was not welcome.

'Oh, do be quiet, will you,' he snapped finally, after his visual objections had been ignored.

'*Sooorrryy*!' said Tom. Will returned to his supper of Mars bar and bottled water, which was by now running very low.

'This one's pretty much finished,' he said, shaking the remaining drops at the bottom of the bottle.

'Mine, too,' Tom agreed, holding up another. 'Well, Tilly's on her way, so I think I'm going to get forty winks.'

'Likewise,' said Will.

'Which end of the bed do you want?' he asked, looking around at the empty chamber, and they both laughed.

Tilly's passage across the river was proving agonisingly slow. Having set off from the Whitefriars quayside, the modest barge which carried her was picked up by the current and propelled sluggishly towards

Lambeth. The incompetent Barclay had struck again, steering the barge too close to another vessel, entangling some netting hanging off the side of the barge with the boom of the sailing boat and sending a bespectacled blonde passenger by the name of Mays and a lolloping giant called Sinclair tumbling into the brown waters below with an enormous serious of splooshes.

'You oaf, Barclay!' shouted the angry foreman Wilmot, rushing up to inspect the damage and hauling the unfortunate passengers out of the river with a rope and boat hook. After what seemed like hours, the boating mess was disentangled, with Barclay receiving a clip round the ear from Wilmot, who then himself seized control of the rudder.

The scene unfolding back in the City almost defied description. Flames in excess of one hundred feet high roared up into the night sky above the level of the buildings, now casting such a powerful light on the river that it might as well have been sunrise. Tilly could see people jumping into the Thames from various wharves closer to the inferno, where no marine craft presented themselves and the fire had cut off landward escape routes.

Along the south bank, spectators gathered to watch the unfolding show, mesmerised by the kaleidoscope of colours as different materials burned together in the awesome pyrotechnic display.

'Mind out!' yelled another of the men navigating the barge as a nearby boat knocked into them, nearly repeating the earlier episode.

The central and southern parts of the river were carpeted with a thick layer of waterborne craft. Like the bankside spectators, many of those on the river seemed to have been hypnotised by the spectre of the flames, and the hiss and crackle of the burning buildings not far away. No doubt some had nowhere to go while others simply sat in tragic silence watching their homes burn.

Only a couple of streets to go, Tilly thought, seeing how close the fire now was to the cathedral. 'Hurry up, Boffin,' she added, under her breath.

By 2am the barge had covered perhaps only a mile, but it was now opposite Lambeth Palace. The giant man called Sinclair had passed out after his ordeal, utterly drunk, on the pile of sacks beside Tilly and was mumbling in his sleep. To her horror, however, on drawing level with Lambeth Steps the barge made no attempt to dock.

'Excuse me sir,' she said to the man on the tiller, 'are we not docking at Lambeth? I think my family is over there.'

'Tough, little missy,' snarled the man. 'You're mighty lucky to have been given a free ride at all. And anyway, there's no space there to dock' – he gestured to the gathering of boats around Lambeth Steps. 'We're going further up river to the next pier. Should be more space.'

It was 4am before the barge arrived at the promised landing stage on the south bank, which was also jammed with refugees. As soon as the pier was within range, Tilly took a running jump off the vessel and sprinted back down the river bank into the night.

'You're welcome,' the bargeman yelled sarcastically after her, shaking his head in disbelief, and turning back to howl once again at the incompetent Barclay, who had just fallen off the barge and plopped noisily into the river after trying and failing to throw the landing rope around a post, and losing his footing.

'Are you back overhead Boffin?' Tilly asked urgently, puffing as she made her way along the riverbank.

'Chewbacca's circling over the boys' prison cell,' said Boffin. 'I've put it on autopilot to follow those trackers I gave them so it'll keep doing that until the batteries go dead, but the smoke up here is unbearable Tilly, I've got to head back down.'

'Yes, of course you must,' she replied.

'I should be able to lay a long wire down part of the

stairs and out of one of the window-slits, so I could probably operate Chewbacca from Hades,' added Boffin hopefully. 'We'll soon find out, anyway.'

'OK, do it, great thinking,' she agreed.

Noting the radio silence from the boys in the jail room, Tilly wagered to herself that they were asleep.

'Absolutely sodding typical,' she thought as she ploughed on through the night, her blonde hair below her cloth hat gleaming in the moonlight. This section of the Thames was barely developed, with only a narrow line of ramshackle houses clinging to the river bank for the mile or so upriver from the palaces of Whitehall and Lambeth. Even here, exiles from the City were taking shelter wherever they could, under trees, or carts, or outhouses. Every now and then Tilly caught a snippet of a conversation hinting at the personal tragedies of those affected by the fire.

'Don't worry, Saul,' said a mother to a particularly short boy who must have been about Will's age. 'We've still got each other.'

At least it's a warm night, thought Tilly, trudging on in her servant-girl disguise and feeling hungry. The sun was coming up by the time she sighted the distinctive red-brick gatehouse of Lambeth Palace ahead. With every step she took back towards the City, the congestion and chaos increased. The scene in front of the archbishop's palace was of total confusion.

Perfect, she thought, hoping it would provide some cover for her illicit entry to the compound. The walls of the archbishop's residence sat just above the high water mark of the river, with a strip of exposed land perhaps only five or six yards separating one from the other at the current stage of the tide.

Spotting a tree clinging to a slight mound in the river bank and overhanging the outer wall of the fortified compound, Tilly made straight for it.

'Will, Tom, can you hear me?' she hissed over the

radio loop. 'I'm outside.'

Silence.

'So *lazy*,' came Boffin's voice in reply. 'I think they're still asleep,' he added, with a loud yawn of his own just to make the point that he'd been working through the night.

'Boys,' she hissed, more loudly this time.

Still nothing.

'I don't believe it,' Tilly said to Boffin, 'you'd think they didn't want to be rescued.'

Dashing across the muddy bank, she had to be careful not to trip over large animal bones embedded in the stinking sludge, or get her feet stuck. She reached the overhanging tree and began to climb.

'Huh, huh, hello,' said an obviously sleepy Will, just waking up. 'Oh God, we're still in the seventeenth century. I was beginning to think it was all a bad dream.'

'Well, a very good morning to you too!' said Tilly, heaving herself out onto the large bough of the tree. 'And this *will* turn into a nightmare if you we don't get you out of there pretty darn quickly.'

'Great,' said Will, rubbing the sleep from his eyes and lifting himself onto his elbows, 'what's the plan?'

Tilly shinned her way cautiously along the long, outstretched bough of the tree overhanging the Palace garden wall – not the easiest manoeuvre wearing thick skirts – and looked around.

'I'm just about over the wall,' she replied. 'There doesn't seem to be anyone about.'

Groaning, Will stirred himself and moved to the window to inspect proceedings. When he relayed the news of Tilly's arrival to Tom, the latter immediately activated the Bug, now on the last bar of battery juice on the control, and sent it whizzing down the staircase to wait for her.

'Hang on,' said Will. 'Tom's just going to check out the bottom of the stairs and your approach route. We don't want any nasty surprises after all, hey?!

'And I really think we need to get a move on,' he added, urgently, noting that from their perspective St Paul's in the distance was now almost entirely obscured by flames.

'What exactly do you think I'm doing here?' Tilly enquired tartly, getting out her mini-tablet so she could see for herself the feeds from the Bug and Chewbacca overhead. 'Boffin, are you still with us?' she asked hopefully.

'Yup, still here,' he said, breathing heavily after his dash down the secret staircase and back into Hades. 'Looks like you've got some movement in the front courtyard behind the main gate. I think they're getting ready to welcome someone, because part of the guard is forming up in two lines.'

'Bother, I bet the archbishop's about to return from Whitehall,' guessed Will. 'We need to move now, before he gets here and they come to collect us for interrogation!'

'The guy at the bottom of the stairs on the cloister side is asleep at his station,' said Tom. 'Go now!'

'Go now, Tilly,' relayed Will on the radio. Stashing the tablet back into her clothing Tilly let herself gently down off the bough of the tree, which was at least fourteen feet above the ground, until she was suspended only by her arms. Having reduced the distance she'd have to fall into the flower bed below, she released her grip and landed almost silently in the morning half-light amongst the small shrubs and flowers which looked rather parched after the long, hot summer. Crouching down, she looked about her again, just to make certain she hadn't been spotted.

'So you need to move to your right, along the wall,' directed Will from his viewpoint at the window four storeys up, watching his sister moving catlike through the undergrowth. Tilly crept along the wall, staying in the flower bed which afforded a little extra cover, until she reached the garden wall of the chapel. Seeing the empty window frame through which Tom had originally flown the Bug, she moved closer and, using a small buttress for a foothold, pushed herself up and through the narrow opening, to land on the flagged stone floor within.

She now found herself at the base of the wide spiral stairs up to the boys' cell. The fact that she could clearly hear the snoring from the guard only feet away gave little comfort. Boffin's voice crackled over the radio again. 'Er, guys, I think the archbishop's nearly back,' he said, watching an ornately carved barge flying the by-now familiar flag move closer to Lambeth steps, having travelled the short distance from Whitehall Palace. Boffin watched as the cluster of smaller boats around the landing stage frantically moved out of the way.

'Yup, it's definitely him,' he said, as Archbishop Sheldon and his entourage swept off the boat. Passers-by ran up to the archbishop to ask for his blessing, and he stopped to offer it, buying the children precious time.

Back in the palace, Tilly froze as, only feet away, an unfamiliar voice shouted 'Wake up yer lazy pig!' The sound of an impacting kick followed by a loud 'oomph' announced that someone had received an unwelcome blow.

'You were bloody asleep weren't you, Marshall?'

'No, Sergeant Mossop, I was just resting me ol' eyes.'

'Do you take me for a fool, Mr Marshall? And you're drunk, as usual. I can smell the cheap ale from 'ere. Get upstairs and check on the Archbishop's guests. He's sent word ahead that he wants to interview them as soon as he's back, so you've got less than ten minutes to make 'em respectable for His Grace.'

'Right you are, sergeant,' said the guard, whose heavy footsteps now headed towards Tilly.

Up in the prison room, the boys had been listening-in to the whole conversation via the Bug's microphone, which sat on a sill near Tilly. She looked at it in wild panic and mouthed 'help' at them, before darting into a darkened alcove to the side of the staircase only seconds before the guard rounded the corner and charged past, up toward the prison room.

'Fudge, fudge, fudge, fudge,' said Will. 'Tom, throw me your bag, quickly now!'

Scrabbling around in the bag Will pulled out a block of Chinese firecrackers and snatched a smoke grenade from the bandolier round his midriff, hoping that it hadn't been ruined by his brief dip in the Thames. The seals appeared to be intact.

'Tilly,' he said urgently on the radio, as the sound of the heavy footsteps on the stairs grew louder and louder, 'put a trip-wire of some kind on the stairs about half-way down if you can. We're going to give our friend a bit of a show.'

'What on earth are you going to do?' she asked, tiptoeing up the stairs after the guard as fast as she could without giving herself away, wincing as every other step was met with a sharp creak. 'And where on earth am I going to magic a trip wire from?!'

'Just do it, will you? And remember, the guard may well still have the key on him and we'll need it to get out of here so you cannot let him get away under any circumstances.'

'OK, if you say so,' she replied, sounding totally unconvinced, and looking about her for anything she could use to lay the trap.

Outside the door, the boys heard the sound of a keyring jangling as the nervous guard fumbled with the lock, breathing hard and clearly rather unfit. Evidently anxious to get his charges up and moving ahead of the Archbishop's visitation, the guard opened the observation hatch to issue orders.

Will was ready for him. Waiting to one side of the door below the level which could be seen through the hatch, he lit the fuse of their final block of firecrackers and slipped it through the small gap under the cell door.

'What devilish sorcery is this?' cried the guard, standing back from the door, as the blasts of the firecrackers rattled off in rapid succession. Screaming dementedly, the man turned and ran down the stairs as fast as he could, practically falling as he went.

'Devils! Sorcerers! Beasts!' he shouted at the top of his voice, just as a leg emerged from a doorway and sent him tumbling head over heels down the stairs.

'Oops, sorry,' said Tilly, stepping coolly out of her hiding place and not sounding sorry at all. The guard was knocked out cold, but he'd made such a commotion that the team was certain they wouldn't have long to effect their escape.

'Come on, come on, where are they?' asked Tilly, frisking the unconscious body of the balding guard. 'The keys aren't on him, Will.'

'I think he's left them in the door,' replied Will, urgently. 'Come up and check . . .'

Dashing up the stairs at top speed, Tilly reached the cell door. The key ring was on the floor in front of her.

'They're here,' she said on the radio, relief washing over her.

'Er, you don't know the half of it,' interjected Boffin. 'Guys, you've got a lot of company. Looks like the whole guard turned out by the gatehouse heard the commotion. Half a dozen of them are on their way toward you. I guess you've got about a minute to escape, maximum.'

39 A GREAT ESCAPE

'Hurry up will you!' demanded an agitated Will through the bars, rattling them like a demented chimpanzee in a zoo. Behind him, Tom was hopping nervously from foot to foot, his bag already strapped to his back. Tilly was trying each of the keys in turn.

'Nope, nope, nope . . . yes! There we go.' The door was suddenly flung open.

'Thanks, sis,' said Tom as the three siblings plunged off down the stairs with the shouts of the archbishop's troops echoing up towards them.

'Dash it all, they've beaten us to it,' said Will, rolling a smoke grenade down the stairs to buy precious seconds.

'Through here,' said Tilly, leading the brothers through the doorway she'd hidden in just above the still unconscious body of the first guard. They found themselves in the gallery of the chapel.

'Where now?' asked Tom, shutting the door quietly behind him just as another member of the guard found his colleague's unconscious body through the haze of green smoke. But Tilly was already stepping over the edge of the wooden gallery and testing the strength of a wall-hanging which covered one side of it.

'This should do us,' she said, using it like a fireman's pole to drop the fifteen feet or so to the stone floor below. The boys followed, suitably impressed. The muffled shouts of their pursuers rang around the building.

'I think they've realised we're missing,' said Will, with a grin. 'We've got to get back to Lambeth Steps,' he added. 'That's still our best chance. Rob Stokeld should still be waiting there with the boat.'

'Still?' whispered Tilly, sceptically.

'I ruddy well paid him enough,' Will retorted.

'OK then, this way,' instructed his sister, heading for a small door at the end of the chapel. 'If I'm right, this leads . . . Yes, perfect,' she continued, pushing the door open and beckoning the boys inside. They were in a dim chamber, lit by a solitary window looking out over the garden. Opening the window, Will helped Tom out, then Tilly, and finally followed himself.

Retracing Tilly's route along the outer wall, pausing occasionally to look over their shoulders and check that they hadn't been spotted, they passed the overhanging tree Tilly had used shortly before to break in and reached the furthest end of the garden, where a small gate was set into the perimeter wall.

'Sorry, archbishop,' said Will taking a short run up to smash it open, 'but needs must.'

He threw himself against the door, which failed to move at all. 'Ooowww,' he said, nursing his shoulder and staggering back from the door, doubling over with the pain. Tilly turned the handle and opened the gate.

'Oh for God's sake!' Will exclaimed, witnessing the manoeuvre. 'Who on earth leaves a perimeter gate of a fortified compound unlocked anyway?'

'Who knows,' said Tilly, 'but it pays to try the simple things first. It's a woman's touch you know. You boys just want to smash everything up all the time.'

Will looked seriously peeved. Tom was barely able to conceal his amusement, quickly turning his laughter into a hacking cough after catching his older brother's eye and fearing the repercussions. Making their way back along the outside of the wall along the slippery riverbank toward the gatehouse, they approached Lambeth Steps.

'Careful, they've probably got a look-out for us,' said Will wincing, obviously still in some pain. 'Can you see Stokeld, Tom?'

'Um, no I can't,' Tom replied, scanning around like his brother. 'Oh, wait – yes, he's still there! Unbelievable.'

'Good old Rob, hey!' said Will, suddenly buoyed up and forgetting about his throbbing shoulder. 'I think we're just going to have to make a dash for it. Everyone ready? OK – GO!'

40 A CARDINAL'S VICE

'Sir Richard!' said the ferryman Stokeld looking up and seeing the three siblings hopping across neighbouring vessels towards him. 'I was just about to head off for some food. Good job you came back. I've been working up a terrible hunger, by God I have,' he said, rubbing his stomach, theatrically, no doubt angling for a bonus payment for his loyal service, which Will provided as he, Tilly and Tom stepped into Stokeld's boat.

'We are most grateful you're still here, Stokeld. But we must move fast now. Time is of the essence.'

'Who is this fair maiden?' asked Stokeld, staring at Tilly.

'This is my sister, Lady, er, Fifi,' said Will, who received a scowl from Tilly.

'Fifi?' she mouthed at him. Will shrugged apologetically.

'Lady Fifi,' said the obviously smitten ferrymen, with a slight bow. 'I am at your service, your loveliness.' Tilly recoiled at the smell of the man but responded with a small bow of her own all the same.

'Whitefriars quay, if you please, sir,' said Will.

'Right you are, Sir Richard,' said Stokeld, going through the by now familiar routine of untethering the boat and pushing it out into deeper water.

'I saw you disposed of your moustache, sir!' observed Stokeld.

'Ah yes,' said Will, 'It was, um, getting a bit itchy,' which was at least partly truthful.

'I understand,' said Stokeld sympathetically, briefly taking a hand off an oar to scratch his own stubble.

'It's been mighty chaotic round 'ere,' the ferryman continued. 'Even saw the archbishop 'is self, comin' back from seeing 'is Majesty over at the Palace.'

'Is that so?' asked Will, gazing anxiously down river in the direction of their prospective landing point, the ferryman's conversation washing over him slightly. It was already 8am. Would they make it in time to beat the flames back to the future, or would they have to spend yet more days – perhaps weeks, or worse – in the seventeenth century?

'Will,' began Tom, unthinking. Will glared at him. Stokeld looked perplexed. 'Erm, *will* you, erm, be needing anything, sire?' Tom asked, realising his mistake and trying rather unconvincingly to cover it up.

'No, thank you *Baldrick*. I have everything I *need* – except competent *staff*, of course,' Will muttered. Tom felt a bit stupid.

'Sir Richard,' said Tom quietly after a while, 'I think I saw one of the Cardinal's men on the quayside.'

'So did I,' replied Will under his breath so the ferryman couldn't clearly hear what was going on. 'But do you think he saw us?'

'Isn't that a type of one-eyed dinosaur?' joked Tom. Will did not look amused.

'Not sure,' continued Tom, furrowing his brow and suddenly looking serious again as the joke panned. 'But I think he might have. He was obviously there on a lookout for us.' They both looked around together, Tilly wondering what they were searching for.

'Oh no, what is it now?' she asked, wearily.

'I think we might have some company,' Will answered, curtly. 'One of the Cardinal's men.'

'What about him?' asked Tilly.

'We spotted him as we piled into the boat. He'd obviously been on lookout duty by Lambeth Palace, which means that they had correctly guessed where we'd gone. That also means that they'll have realised the case is safe with the archbishop by now.'

'So what do you think they want with us?' she continued. 'Won't they just try and steal it from the Palace?'

'Well, they might,' said Will, looking pensive. 'But as you saw it's well protected against an assault – at least by anything other than a super-subtle secret agent from the twenty first century,' he said, gesturing towards Tilly. 'And they know that the case was ambushed once – in other words that someone's after it – so the archbishop's guard won't be taking any chances with protection for it. If the Cardinal really is just a treasure hunter, I think we've foiled him.'

The three of them digested this as they bobbed painfully slowly over the surface of the water. 'So that means,' continued Will . . .

'. . . that the Cardinal's bent on revenge against us now,' finished Tom, the colour draining from his dirty face.

'I'm sorry to say that's probably right,' agreed Will, looking around them again as Stokeld navigated the boat through yet another cluster of refugee vessels on the river. 'So, for obvious reasons, it's all the more essential that we make it back to the portal today. We really don't want to be hanging around post-fire London anyway, but especially not with an enraged Cardinal and his henchmen on our tails.'

As their ferry slowly rounded the great arcing right-angle of the Thames, the full horror of the flaming City spread out before their eyes.

'Oh my . . . ,' gasped Tilly, unable to finish her sentence. The fire had spread even further, engulfing most of the buildings between the cathedral and the river. Though the sky itself was quite clear, huge black clouds of smoke billowed over the City, stretching miles to the west, driven on by the brisk easterly wind which continued to whip the flames ever higher, perhaps now as much as a hundred and fifty feet into the air in some places.

'Fudge,' said Will, 'it's got farther than I thought it would have done by this stage. We're going to have to make a run for it, guys, as soon as we get to the bank.'

He turned to the boatman. 'Stokeld, can you go any faster?'

'I'm trying, Sir Richard!' replied the beleaguered ferryman, straining on his oars, 'but the tide's against us, and so is the wind.'

'And so is the time,' finished Will under his breath.

41 HOME STRAIGHT

'Guys, it's total carnage on the north side,' said Boffin over the radio, using the daylight camera under Chewbacca to zoom in on the scene unfolding on the Fleet Bridge and up the hill towards the Lud Gate. He watched as people jammed through the ancient gateway in a bid to escape the oncoming flames. 'People are abandoning things on the roads around the cathedral,' he continued, 'because they can't get through, and the fire's already caught the wooden scaffolding around the east end of St Paul's – it's moving fast now.'

Will surveyed the quayside at Whitefriars, perhaps only thirty yards away. Were any of the Cardinal's men waiting for them, he wondered. They'd have had plenty of time to ride the mile and a half from Whitehall to Fleet Street in the time the three of them had been afloat. Their best hope was that, amidst the ongoing chaos on the river, it would be difficult for anyone trying to keep track of them to do just that.

Tilly stole a glance at her watch, which read 9.30 am. Now that they were nearing the north bank, the heat from the fire was considerable, even out on the water and with a decent wind.

'Getting pretty hot around 'ere,' said Stokeld, nervously, as he looked over his shoulder to guide them in the final few yards.

'Thank you, Rob,' said Will, dropping his character, Sir Richard, for a moment. 'Here –' Will handed Stokeld a large pouch of coins.

Stokeld was gobsmacked. 'This is far more than a year's earnings for me, by God it is,' he said after flicking briefly through the cash.

'You've earned it, my friend,' said Will. 'You don't know how helpful you've been.'

Will helped Tilly off the boat, then hauled Tom up onto the quayside. Shaking Stokeld's hand he added, 'see you in another life, I hope. Good luck.'

'Thank ye, Sir Richard!' came Stokeld's voice after him, as the three siblings fought their way through the crowds of refugees. Struggling up Water Lane against the flow of the exodus, they battled on.

'This is exhausting,' panted Tom, breathing hard and crashing into yet another person. 'Ouch, watch it you oaf,' he exclaimed, angrily.

Emerging from the top end of the lane onto Fleet Street, the siblings were hit by a blast of hot air mixed with ash as glowing embers fell all about them.

'Bloody hell, it's like being at the back end of a rocket engine,' said Will, brushing a smouldering ember out of his filthy wig.

'We're nearly out of time,' said Tilly, looking worriedly across the Fleet River and up towards the cathedral, which was now hard to make out through the screen of smoke being driven towards them.

'Nothing for it but to make a dash,' said Will.

'Boffin, are you still there?' asked Tilly.

'Still here,' said Boffin's voice, but the radio crackled so badly it was difficult to make him out.

'I think the fire's making the radio play up,' said Will. 'Look Boffin, we're nearly back with you. Get ready to go fast, the fire's advancing quickly now. It's going to be touch and go whether we make it back in time.'

'Roger,' crackled Boffin, getting ready to move out. 'I'm going to crash Chewbacca into the fire,' he added, a note of sorrow just detectable over the distorted radio. 'We can't take it back, and we . . . we obviously can't leave it hanging around for ever,' his regret more pronounced.

'Probably for the best, Boffin,' said Will slightly curtly, and not even bothering to hide the fact that he was speaking into a radio. Given the chaos around them, he figured that no one would think twice. In fact, it seemed that no one noticed anything other than their immediate surroundings in the collective, but surprisingly ordered, panic.

From upper storeys of houses overhanging the street, families threw down valuable possessions to the road below as they prepared to make their own exit. In some cases, random passers-by made off with choice items if no one was waiting to receive the objects, or the receiver looked the other way.

Nearby, a large mob set upon a pair of gilded carriages loaded with the valuable belongings of a well-to-do City merchant's family, some of whom cowered in the passenger cabins as their progress stalled amongst the throngs on Fleet Street, and opportunists simply began pillaging their belongings. Law and order had broken down entirely.

Amidst the chaos, however, Will noticed a pretty blonde girl with large eyes leaning out of the near side of the finer of the two carriages, holding one of her sturdy-looking shoes in her hand. With this she proceeded to ferociously assault the thronging mob, repeatedly shouting 'hands off my baggage you vile hoodlums!' and 'That one's from Paris you vagabonds. Get your hands off my potions.' Thwack, crack, thump. Men several times her size recoiled under the girl's onslaught, backing off to find easier pickings as she ordered the coachmen to whip up the horses, regardless of who was in the way.

'Quickly now,' said Will to the others, regaining his composure and fighting a path down the hill toward the Fleet River. Though barely a couple of hundred yards ahead, it took many minutes to get through since they were the only people heading toward the fire, rather than away from it. Except, they soon realised, that they weren't quite alone after all.

'Tom, do you see those two guys on the other side of the street?' Will asked, glancing repeatedly over his left shoulder.

'Where?' queried his brother.

'Outside the apothecary's right now,' Will replied, looking at the shop sign overhead which swayed in the breeze.

'Oh cripes, yes I do!' agreed Tom, quickening his pace and jostling more aggressively towards the river.

'They're two of the guys who followed us when we escaped the Palace of Whitehall,' said Will, 'and one of them is the chap who was waiting outside Lambeth Palace for us – you know, the really thickset, ugly one.'

'Which means that he went across the river to raise the alarm,' added Tom, wide-eyed.

'Precisely, and that means that they're almost certainly not alone,' Will went on, looking behind them, nervously. 'Tilly, those. . .'

'I heard,' she said, interrupting him.

'Look,' said Will. 'If for any reason we get into trouble, whoever else is free just needs to get back to the elevator as soon as possible. If you're back in the present you can plan a rescue, and anticipate anything that happens. But if none of us makes it back we're totally stuffed, so promise me now that we will all run for it if the situation calls for it?'

Tilly and Tom exchanged dubious glances. 'OK,' they agreed.

'Fine,' said Will. 'That's settled. Ready to leg it?' he

added with a smile.

'No time like the present. . .' said Tilly

'. . . or the past!' Tom added with a grin. Stealing another look over their shoulders across the street at the menacing agents who were by now working their way through the flow of people separating them, the three siblings ran for it, seeing a narrow gap in the crowds open up ahead.

'They're following!' shouted Tom, in a trying-to-be-calm sort of voice, glancing round as the two Frenchmen barged a group of bickering people out of the way, sending them sprawling across the cobbled ground.

'Go, go, go, go!' shouted Will, helping Tilly up on to the stone balustrade at the edge of the Fleet Bridge in order to bypass the choke point where half a dozen horse-drawn carts had become trapped, wedging one another in. Their furious owners were exchanging brutal words and occasional blows as they sought to escape the jam on the bridge.

Tom jumped up on to the balustrade after Tilly. Will followed. His balance wasn't as good as he remembered, and he nearly plunged into the stinking red-brown waters of the River Fleet which ran below, filled with the by-products of the tanners and butchers whose shops lined the banks further upstream.

Ludgate Hill was now less busy than Fleet Street – clearly many of these residents had already made themselves scarce. An abandoned refectory table sat randomly in the middle of the hill, its owners – or possibly thieves – nowhere to be seen. The heat was intense, and down the middle of the road ran a shimmering silver stream with steam rising from it.

'What on earth is that?' panted Tom as they skirted it warily.

'The cathedral's lead rooves must be melting,' said Will, looking up to see flames licking out of windows half-way along the length of St Paul's. 'Lead melts at low temperatures – say, only about 330C,' he added.

'Who actually knows that?' asked Tilly incredulously, jumping from one side of the molten lead stream to the other to reach the right-hand side of the hill. The three were sweating profusely, both from the strain of running under heavy clothes, and the increasingly intolerable heat from the fire.

'Nearly there,' she added, encouragingly, as a loud shriek followed by a satisfyingly loud splash announced that one of the Cardinal's agents behind them had involuntarily entered the Fleet River.

The children had a lead of perhaps fifty yards on their pursuers, who had now been joined by others from side streets, as they dashed toward the Lud Gate halfway up the hill toward St Paul's. The gate's sentries had long gone, and the shattered remains of carriages and carts which hadn't made it through the gate lay scattered behind it, awaiting their fate. Only the molten lead now flowed through it, together with the odd straggler clutching their worldly belongings.

'They're going to catch us!' gasped Tom, looking round. 'They're much faster than we are outside the confines of the crowds.'

Will was rummaging around under the remaining pieces of his costume as he sprinted up the hill. 'Ah ha!' he exclaimed, pulling out a pair of smoke grenades, his large coin purse bashing noisily against his leg as he ran. They were only two hundred yards from the Cathedral's steps, now one hundred and eighty, one hundred and sixty . . .

'They're flagging,' said Tilly, triumphantly, looking over her shoulder to see the seven or eight goons slowing their pace to a jog and fanning out in a line across the hill.

'Oh fudge,' said Will, as, to their left, four horsemen cantered out from the end of Ave Maria Lane. 'Down Creed Lane!' he shouted. 'I'll distract them. Just remember the plan we agreed! Don't look back!'

He shoved his siblings down the side street to their

right, and turned to run back down the hill, but immediately realised he would plough straight into the line of the Cardinal's henchmen who were now arrayed across the full breadth of the street. To his satisfaction, he saw that one particularly stupid villain had stepped in the molten lead and was rolling around on the floor in pain, clutching his leg as another rushed to his aid.

Serves you right, thought Will. He turned back to look at the horsemen who were now lined up in front of the cathedral, apparently unfazed by the fiery surroundings. Glancing to his right he caught Tilly's worried glance over her shoulder before she disappeared at the bottom of the lane.

Looking again at the horsemen, Will realised that one was the Cardinal himself. He had ditched his grand crimson robes, though retained the hat. In their place, he wore a glinting black metal breastplate over black vestments and Will was close enough to see a large episcopal ring on the Cardinal's hand, which rested on the handle of a long sword in its scabbard, hanging down to one side of the horse. The beast itself, which was almost wholly black, snorted angrily, pacing on the spot, clawing one shod hoof against the cobbles. The Cardinal's carefully sculpted facial hair was unmistakable, as were his accent, cold smile and penetrating stare. At close range, Will realised he his features were heavily sunken, almost skeletal, like the undead.

'So you are ze source of my pain,' said the Cardinal calmly through his thin mouth, seemingly oblivious to the inferno raging only a couple of hundred yards behind him, his thinning hair moving slightly in the hot wind. 'You 'ave somesing which is very important to us,' he continued, very deliberately moving his horse closer and closer to where Will stood, rooted to the spot. The other riders, similarly bedecked in glossy black armour, gathered around him, trying to cut off other escape routes. 'We would like eet back, if you pleeeze, and zooner razer zan later,' he added in his gentle French-Italian drawl. 'Time eez short,' and he gestured to the flaming cathedral behind him.

The burning wind was extremely hot against Will's face. He felt he might combust at any moment and hoped Tom and Tilly had made it into the Deanery by now, and might even be back in the present, hatching a plan to bail him out of this distinctly sticky situation.

'I . . . I don't know what you're talking about,' Will said, playing for time. 'I'm just here to save something from the fire.'

'Come, amico,' said the Cardinal, walking the horse closer still, 'do not play me for a fool. We both know neither of us should be here. I am already a dead man, and you – well, you haven't even been born yet, 'ave you?' he added, with a grimace.

'We are not so very different, you and I,' he mused. 'We are both here at someone else's bidding after all, both pawns in ze greater game.'

'All the world's a stage, and all the men and women merely players. They have their exits and their entrances and one man in his time plays many parts,' Will shot back, quoting Shakespeare to buy further precious moments.

'But time eez short,' reiterated Mazarin, ignoring him, his thin smile now disappeared. 'My whole life 'az been leading up to zis moment. You will not take this away from me. And I want what I came for!'

'I'll have to show you where we've hidden it,' said Will, defiantly, suddenly feeling very alone.

'Oh, we know where it eez now hidden, amico,' said the Cardinal, silkily. 'Where it would have been all along had I not been here to make sure that one of the great treasures of the world does not lie hidden in some ghastly little English. . .,' he paused.

'But you will steal it back for me,' said Mazarin, finally.

'Or else what?' said Will, puffing himself up and tearing off his wig dramatically, feeling that some kind of defiant gesture was required.

'Oh I don't need to kill you,' said the Cardinal. 'I'll just trap you here for all time.'

42 FIREWORKS

Two of the horsemen reached down and roughly grabbed Will under the arms, turning him back down the hill and making to distance themselves from the fire as the noise of yet another house collapsing at the eastern end of St Paul's reached their ears. The Cardinal watched, impassively.

Suddenly, all hell broke loose.

Blocks of Chinese firecrackers landed on the cobbles around Will, exploding ferociously and startling his captors, who released their grip on him in their struggle to control their mounts, which reared violently, trying to buck off their armoured riders.

'Non!' cried the Cardinal as his own horse reared, and thick green and red smoke enveloped the party. A second later, Will heard the hard splat of exploding paintball shells slapping against the exposed skin of the Cardinal's men, who, unmounted, rushed to shield themselves from the onslaught, groping around in the smoke to find a doorway to hide in or a wall to cower behind. The horses' hysteria was complete when loud barking erupted amongst them: the familiar sound of Mufasa snapping at their hooves.

'Run, Will! Run!' shouted an unseen yet familiar voice. He didn't need telling twice, and pelted up the final stretch of the hill, pursued speedily by the loyal family terrier who looked as if he was thoroughly enjoying himself.

Emerging, coughing, through the cloud of smoke, Will saw tongues of fire wrapping themselves around St Paul's portico and roofs. He slowed for a moment, absorbing the extraordinary sight. Around him the smell of burning was overwhelming. An enormous crash from somewhere in the interior of the cathedral announced that the roof wasn't simply melting but was starting to collapse in the places where the fire had already been burning for some time. Smoke poured out of the Great West Door, as though the cathedral were some giant dragon, exhaling its last fiery breaths.

Will reached down to pick up Mufasa, who was evidently waiting for a treat as a reward for helping him out of a tight spot. As he crouched down, amidst the smoke and flame, just for a moment Will could have sworn he saw a familiar silhouette gazing back at him from the entrance of the cathedral. 'Dad?' he said aloud to himself, stopping dead in his tracks. But the figure, if it was a figure, disappeared into the blazing stomach of the building, as the smoke enveloped the space where the apparition had been a moment earlier.

'I'm going completely mad,' said Will to himself, wheeling right through the arch into Deanery Yard, Mufasa under one arm, flames merely ten or so yards to his left, and ran across the courtyard to the front door of the old medieval house, which stood ajar. He could hear running footsteps and heavy breathing behind him but he didn't look back. He just needed to make it to Hades and the Beehive with its elevator and get the hell out of seventeenth century London.

The Deanery was evidently abandoned and he darted inside, making his way through the dark and dilapidated interior, down to the undercroft and the entrance to the hidden world beneath.

'Wait!' shouted that familiar voice once again. Around

the corner ran Katherine and Angus, each dressed in dark overalls and carrying one of Will's paintball guns. They looked for all the world like a SWAT team. Both were grinning manically.

'What on earth are you doing here!?' asked Will, dumbfounded.

'Not often you don't have much to say, is it, Will!?' said Katherine, panting. 'No time to explain – we've got to get back to the future,' and she led the boys down the familiar spiral staircase and through the chambers to the elevator. The doors to the lift were open, with Boffin standing ready by the controls.

'Good to see you,' he said with a wink as Will yanked the metal gate shut behind them, and the lift doors closed. They were heading home.

43 BACK TO THE FUTURE

'I think you're quite literally the smelliest person alive,' said Katherine, holding her nose and looking up at Will as the elevator rumbled its way back to the present. 'It's like a mouldy wheelie-bin in here – and you're the rubbish bags!'
'I've been in what's essentially an open sewer, thank you very much,' said Will, defensively. Angus chuckled.

'You're welcome, by the way,' added Katherine.
'Oh yeah, sorry – right, thanks very much, team,' said Will, still slightly lost for words as even Mufasa appeared repulsed by his smell. (This was probably fair enough given that his olfactory senses were around four hundred times better than a human's.)

The elevator stopped, the familiar surge of oily air filling his nostrils again. The doors opened. Tilly and Tom were waiting for them in the Beehive.

'What's the year?' Will asked, nervously.

'It's 2016, it's a Saturday night, we're in the middle of a family party, and Cousin Shaunagh's just arrived with Rosie' Tilly reassured him, helping them all out of the lift and into Hades.

'So, no secret map then?' said Angus, looking deeply disappointed, and carefully choosing to sit several pong-free seats away from Will at the round central table in Hades.

'No map,' said Will after a reflective pause, recovering himself somewhat. 'Things are as they were meant to be. I think, anyway.'

The six of them sat around, no one quite knowing what to say.

'Don't you think you should have a bath, Will?' Tilly suggested after a while. 'Might be a bit of a giveaway if we go back upstairs and you smell like a bag of fertiliser.'

'*Ha, haaa*,' he said sarcastically. 'I will, but first can someone explain how you two and Mufasa,' he pointed at Angus and Katherine, 'sprang that little ambush?'

'Well,' said Boffin proudly, scraping his hair off his face, and leaning back and cracking his knuckles, 'when Tilly and Tom returned without you, we knew that we'd have to have an escape plan ready for you already, if you see what I mean.'

'So,' continued Katherine, 'Boffin came back to us and explained what was going on, and took us back to the point in time when you were getting off Stokeld's ferry after escaping from Lambeth Palace. We then set up the ambush in the knowledge that you three,' she pointed to Will, Tom and Tilly, 'would come running up the hill and straight into the Cardinal's ambush. And we simply waited for Tilly and Tom to go and tell Boffin, so he could send us back, and we then sprang the ambush with Mufasa. Simples!'

'I see,' said Will, trying to get his head around the complexities of the time-hopping involved. 'Well it obviously worked, whatever you did.
'What's the time, by the way?'

'Oh, only about four minutes after we set off,' said Tilly, looking at her watch.

'Well, we'd probably better go and re-join the party,' Will said, getting up. 'After a long shower, of course.' Everyone laughed.

None of the adults knew exactly why the children all suddenly looked so exhausted – they simply put it down to the early onset of the family's narcolepsy.

46 REVELATION

After his shower, Will went to find his father who, having excused himself from yet another round of Articulate, was reading in one of the oversized armchairs in the library.

'Good evening, William,' said the Bishop, closing his book and putting it carefully on the side table. 'And what have you been up to?' he asked.

Will thought the question unusually pointed. 'Oh not much,' he answered, wondering if that faint smell of smoke was him or. . . 'The party's still in full swing. I'm just feeling a bit tired really.'

'I'm sure you are,' said the Bishop, allowing himself a seraphic smile.

Will tried to read his father, which was a near-impossible task at the best of times. 'You weren't –,' he began, before stopping himself.

'I wasn't what?' his father asked.

'Never mind,' said Will, 'just a silly thought really.'

'Unlikely to be silly, William,' said his father. 'Usually, one's instincts are to be trusted,' he added. 'Nature has honed them for that purpose over many hundreds of thousands of years, after all.'

'I've been thinking a lot about our conversation a week ago – you know, about time, and history, and everything,' Will continued.

'You mean our conversation a couple of days ago,' corrected the bishop.

'Oh, er, yes, I suppose it was,' said Will, forgetting he was factoring in several additional days spent in Great Fire London, days which counted for nothing in the present.

'Look, supposing history was corrupted, but then it was straightened out. That wouldn't have disadvantageous consequences in the present, would it?'

'It probably wouldn't be as simple as that,' said his father. 'As in any book, there are plots and sub-plots. It might very well be possible to make drastic changes to sub-plots with very little change to the course of the book. It is, of course, a different matter if anyone were to tamper with more fundamental things. And there will always be those who will try, and those whose work must be to stop them.'

He paused to let the message sink in.

'We'd probably better go and join the others,' said Will after a while, feeling he probably wasn't in a fit state to have a deep philosophical conversation and getting up to leave. As he turned round, he looked again at the familiar print of Old St Paul's being engulfed by flames, and the three small figures running towards it. Then the penny dropped. Will spun around again to stare at his father.

'The picture,' he said pointing at the print, 'it's in the *picture*!'

'What's in the picture?' enquired the Bishop, innocently, also standing now.

Will looked from one to the other and back again. *He knew all along*, he thought to himself. *From the very beginning.*

'Never mind,' he said, understanding all he needed to. 'Just, well, you know.'

'Usually,' said his father with a smile, leading the way out of the library.

47 JUST THE BEGINNING

The following morning saw Will, Tilly, Tom, Katherine and their cousins Boffin and Angus sitting at the mighty round table in Hades, digesting their recent adventure.

'So I'm sure he knows,' said Will, recounting to the others his conversation with the bishop the previous evening. 'I'm certain of it actually. And get this. You know that print of Old St Paul's on the library wall – the one which depicts it going up in flames?'

There was a general murmur of agreement.

'Who do you think the three characters running *towards* the fire are?' Will asked. No one offered an answer, so Will spelled it out. 'It was *us*, wasn't it? Me, Katherine and Angus. But here's the really spooky thing. Those characters have been in that print as long as we've had it, for sure. I mean, for one thing, I looked at it again before this whole episode began.'

'Which means that we were always meant to go back and, well, set things straight,' mused Tilly aloud.' And that would also explain how we can return to the present and everything is unchanged. If we were always meant to go back and do what we've done, then we are fulfilling history as it was intended, I suppose. Doing our duty.

'The other strange thing,' she continued, 'is who or what is Adrasteia? The Cardinal mentioned Adrasteia at least twice in the Palace of Whitehall. He seemed to imply he was working for him.'

'Or her,' interjected Katherine, indignantly.

'Or her,' Tilly agreed with an approving smile, running her fingers along the finely carved table edge and noticing for the first time that a narrow slit was cut into the table in front of every seat.

'When Mazarin spoke to me on Ludgate Hill,' said Will, 'he said that neither of us was there at our own behest, and that we were just pawns in a bigger game. He also said he was already a dead man.'

'What do you think he meant?' Boffin asked, looking thoroughly mystified.

'Well, if Mazarin did die in 1661,' said Will, 'then it's not impossible that whoever he was working for could have gone back to get him – if he had access to a portal himself, of course. Maybe Adrasteia is the person who took Mazarin forward in time?'

'But why would anyone have done that?' asked Tom. 'Why not just go and get the secret map yourself? You wouldn't need Mazarin to do that.'

'Perhaps you would,' mused Will. 'Or at least, perhaps his master did. Because Mazarin had spent his life tracking down clues to the whereabouts of this map – he said that to me himself – and knew its likely location. Perhaps he refused to reveal it unless he was taken to see it personally. Or perhaps this other shadowy character cannot move through time himself.'

'And I guess Mazarin would have understood the map,' said Tilly, speculatively.

'Perhaps,' replied Will. 'He'd certainly been studying the legend for years before he died.'

Tom looked somewhat perplexed. 'What are you saying, Will? That Cardinal Mazarin was working for someone else? And that we're not the only ones with a portal?'

'That's exactly what I'm saying, Tom. And I don't think Adrasteia is the King of France, either. In fact, whoever the Cardinal was working for is presumably well aware of the possibility that people like us – other time-travellers – exist. The Cardinal himself hinted at it.'

'The Cardinal did say that Adrasteia wasn't the King of France when he was talking in the Palace,' Tilly concurred. 'I heard him myself. He's something – or someone – else. Or possibly *she* is,' she added hastily, catching Katherine's intent correctional stare. 'Either way, we should probably be on our guard. My bet is that whoever used this place before us was somehow involved in this war across time, for good or ill.'

'Must be good,' said Tom, confidently. 'It's got a good atmosphere.'

'Mazarin's presence in 1666, five years after his death, tells us at the very least that someone else is able to use a portal to meddle in history,' continued Will. 'As Dad said yesterday, sub-plots of a book can change, but the overall direction of the narrative can still stay the same. But if you change something really fundamental, then you write a very different story indeed.'

'Come again?' said Angus.

'It means,' said Will, 'that there are certain fundamental turning points in history which, if you were minded to change them, would have a profound effect on everything that happens afterwards. And, if exploited, that's clearly incredibly dangerous. Mazarin implied during his conversation with that henchman of his in the Palace of Whitehall that this was his one shot. That suggests that one cannot go back indefinitely to keep trying things over again – in other words there's no Groundhog Day scenario.'

'And just imagine if you were on the losing side of history, and discovered you had access to a portal. The temptation to try and re-engineer events would be, well, overwhelming,' Tilly speculated.

'Whoever was the driving force behind the attempted theft of the Grail, this won't be the last time they try something,' Will said, darkly.

'Who do you think it might be?' asked Katherine nervously, clasping her hands tightly together.

'I don't know,' said Will, a steely glint in his eye, 'but I'm certain that we're going to find out.'

TO BE CONTINUED

Will's sketch map of Hades and the so-far discovered surrounding tunnels and chambers

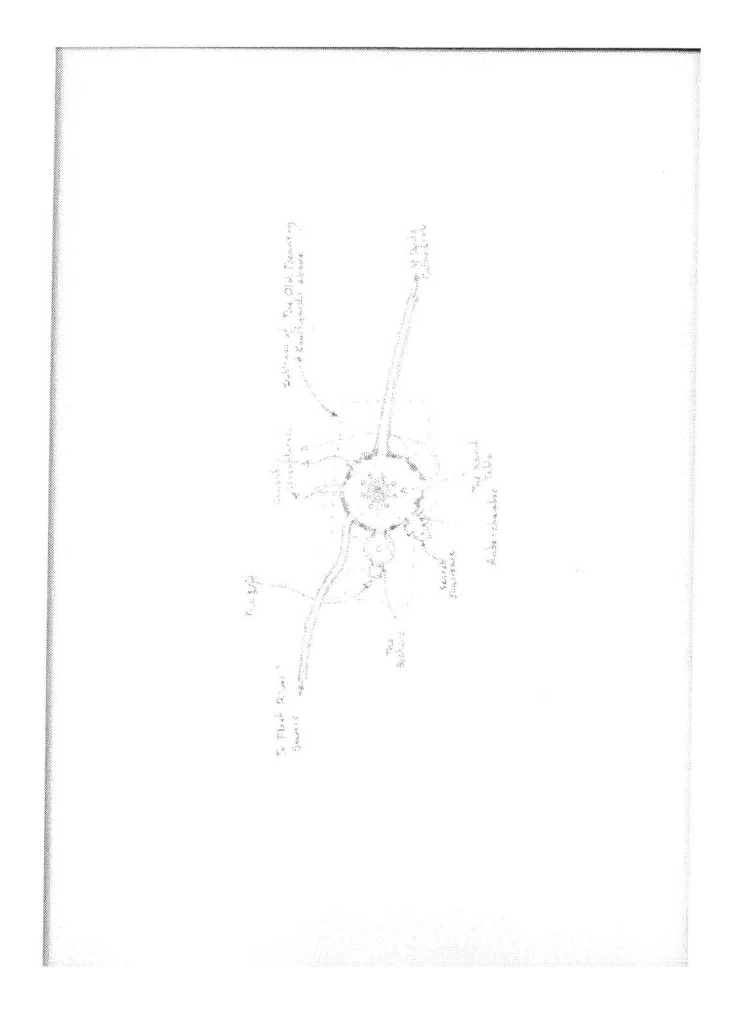

ABOUT THE AUTHOR

The author is the elder son of the 132nd Bishop of London, and *Phoenix Tales* was inspired by his childhood growing up next to St Paul's Cathedral in the heart of the City of London. The story was originally written for his younger siblings and cousins. In real life he is a fund manager.

Printed in Germany
by Amazon Distribution
GmbH, Leipzig